THE BREWER'S JUSTICE

A NOVEL

LESLIE PATIÑO

PATIÑO PUBLISHING
MONTEREY, CA, USA
MONTERREY, NUEVO LEÓN, MÉXICO

The Brewer's Justice
Leslie Patiño

ISBN-13: 978-0-9965634-0-6

First Edition February 2016

Cover design Steve Zmak
Interior design Patricia Hamilton

Published by
Patiño Publishing
Monterey, CA, USA • Monterrey, Nuevo León, México
www.LesliePatinoAuthor.com

For Hugo, a true master brewer
Para Hugo, un verdadero maestro cervecero

THE BREWER'S JUSTICE

CHAPTER ONE

July 2012

GLEAMING CORPORATE towers and trendy boutiques, a little bit Manhattan, a little bit Beverly Hills, Avenida Lázaro Cárdenas pulsated with power and possibility. The most heavily trafficked thoroughfare in San Pedro showcased the successes of Mexico's affluent classes and represented all the reasons Brad Peters had come to Mexico. He had given up a good job in Denver, moved to suburban Monterrey and committed all of his money and every ounce of his talent for the next three years for one reason: to brew the best damn beer in northern Mexico at the hottest new brewpub south of the U. S. border.

With vehicles darting around him, Brad tightened his grip on the wheel of the older, black Dodge Neon he had paid for in U.S. dollars his third day in Monterrey. Still uncomfortable with aggressive Mexican-style driving, he accelerated into a momentary gap between the cars to his right just in time to segue onto the exit ramp. At the first stop light on Avenida Gómez Morín, he exhaled a long breath. Here, among the densely packed one- and two-story buildings, traffic moved at a pace he could negotiate. The older commercial neighborhood had the comfortable, well-maintained appearance of a matronly *señora*. From lunchtime until late evening, corporate types in loosened ties unwound at the trendy restaurants. Families flocked to the nearby park and casual eateries. University students frequented the night spots. The only thing missing was an upscale brewpub, something Brad and Carlos Echeverría intended to remedy.

How Brad, a guy who had never lived outside Colorado, had ended up as the brewmaster of a future upscale Mexican brewpub was a story that not even he would have believed two years ago. Of course, none of it would have happened if he hadn't become friends with Carlos, now the senior partner and primary financial investor in MBC, Monterrey Brewing Company.

The light changed and he made it a half block before the diesel-belching bus ahead of him came to a stop. He watched a knot of passengers get off and new ones climb on to take their place. These were the maids, gardeners and employees who worked for the residents of San Pedro.

Technically, Brad was one more employee. One who wasn't looking forward to the conversation he was about to have with his boss. Carlos was a good friend, a wealthy one, who had given Brad an opportunity lots of brewers could only dream of. Brad would have preferred to forget the mess at the bank just now and simply get down to work, but he had stayed quiet more than once in the six weeks since he'd stepped off the plane. It was time to speak up.

He turned into the parking lot of the once elegant Quinta Saldaña Steakhouse, bumping over the patch of buckled asphalt and the pothole, on his way to the back lot. From the detritus piled outside the back door, he could see that the carpenters had started on the kitchen. The decades-old stainless steel cabinets looked worn and sad in the sunlight. Ditto for the commercial refrigerator.

Even with the car windows rolled up and the AC blasting, he could hear the carpenters' radio blaring *cumbias*. He parked in the shade of the sprawling oak tree, one of the few reminders of the *quinta's* early days, and killed the engine. As if on cue, a large tabby, minus the tip of one ear, padded towards the car. Brad pulled a handful of treats from the glove compartment. "Hey, Vagabundo, how's it going?"

The animal circled, rubbing against Brad's jeans and purring, delicately lifting one paw, then the other, as though dancing to the *cumbias*. He had more or less come with the property. Officially, nobody claimed him, but several nearby restaurants all fed him. In return, the homeless feline kept the neighborhood rodent population in check. The two of them had hit it off from the start, maybe because neither fully belonged here. Brad had considered taking the cat to his sardine-can apartment—he would have welcomed the company. But Vagabundo was used to the outdoor life, and all the people who depended on his mousing abilities would have protested.

Carlos appeared at the kitchen door holding out his cell phone. "Osorio," he shouted over the *cumbias* and hammering. "He wants to talk with both of us."

Given Brad's mediocre command of Spanish, he should have liked the customs broker who spoke clipped East Coast English and dressed like a New York business mogul, but he'd never cared much for arrogant assholes. Besides, his plate this morning was already full. He nodded a hurried greeting to the carpenters and chased behind Carlos into the gutted dining room. The cinderblock walls underneath the plaster, and the concrete floors exposed last week when the carpenters ripped up the old tile, kept the summertime heat in the large room bearable each day until noon or so.

Carlos focused the hazel green eyes inherited from his Basque grandfather on Brad and motioned for him to shut the door. He tapped the cell in his hand, turning on the speakerphone. "*Aquí está Brath.*" Here, everyone lisped the end of Brad's name.

"Good morning, Juan Pablo," he said in the direction of the phone.

"*Buenos días, Brath. Miren, aquí tengo una persona conmigo.*" There was someone with Osorio who apparently didn't speak English. The customs broker launched into a long monologue, speeding up as he spoke, and slowly losing Brad. MBC's brewing equipment had arrived from Milwaukee early, great news, but there was some complication. Osorio spoke like a father talking to small children. Brad's limited Spanish frustrated him on a daily basis, but what threw him now was the scowl on his partner's face. "How can that be?" Carlos snapped, interrupting Osorio.

"A *something* fee," Osorio kept repeating, "a *something* fee." Carlos's eyebrows knitted together as the conversation spun further out of Brad's orbit. Carlos ran his fingers through his tousseled hair, a habit when he wasn't totally comfortable. Brad wiped beads of perspiration from his forehead.

"He's putting somebody else on the line," Carlos mouthed.

"*Buenos días.*" The man spoke in a low, raspy voice and proceeded to use more words Brad didn't know. The ones he did understand—*delinquents, criminals, insecurity, protection*—he didn't like. If this one of Carlos's friends pranking them, the joke was backfiring.

Carlos frowned but didn't interrupt. When the man finally paused, Carlos only asked, "How much and by when?"

"One hundred thousand pesos. Call Osorio when you've got it."

This was for real. The guy was shaking him down.

"It may take us some time," Carlos said so softly that Brad strained to hear his words.

"Then it may take some time before you see your equipment." Arrogance and control oozed around the stranger's words. "And no cops. It'd be a shame to lose two hundred thousand dollars-worth of equipment." Brad watched Carlos clench his teeth.

How the hell could this be happening?

Brad wasn't naïve. He'd known about Mexico's dangers—the drug cartels, the corruption, the violence—long before he ever met Carlos. It was real. He didn't deny it. But that stuff happened in sleazy parts of border towns or in the mountains of Sinaloa where semi-literate villagers claimed to know nothing of the drug lords reputedly hiding in their midst.

"Understood, Echeverría?" the man demanded in an impatient tone.

"Understood."

Silence.

Carlos dropped the phone into his shirt pocket and blew out a breath that puffed up his cheeks. In the kitchen, the carpenters and *cumbias* continued as if nothing had happened.

Brad rubbed his throbbing temples. "Okay, Big Guy, here's what I got. Even though we're paying Osorio a small fortune to get our equipment through customs, suddenly we owe him and the guy with the Godfather voice nearly seventy-five hundred dollars, cash only, money we don't have."

Carlos threw his head back. "'That guy' is from El Cártel and he claims we owe them a safe-passage fee."

The words repeated themselves in Brad's head until he finally found his voice. "That's extortion."

"And either we pay or we lose our equipment and, possibly, our lives."

"We can't go to the police?"

"Are you whacked?"

"What about your father and uncles and all your connections?"

"They'd all tell us to pay."

"The Chamber of Commerce or the U.S. Consulate?"

"The Monterrey Chamber of Commerce can't do anything, and there's no way your Consulate's going to take on the most violent drug cartel in Mexico."

"I can't believe that you—*we*—are just going to hand our money over to criminals."

"I can't either, but we are."

"There's got to be somebody who can help us."

"*Ah, Güero.*" Here, he was either *Brath* or *Blond Guy*. Never mind that his wavy hair was light auburn. Somehow, in Mexico, his blue eyes—unremarkable in the States—and his fair skin entitled even strangers to call him *Güero*.

"Carlos, just say whatever the hell you're thinking."

"You Americans still have a wild west mentality. Just have the sheriff gallop into town and run off the bad guys. It doesn't work that way with drug cartels."

"But it's wrong."

"Hello! People who say no to these guys turn up in plazas minus their heads or hanging from overpasses."

"All that time in Denver when you were talking up a Mexican brewpub, you failed to mention that we'd have to deal with drug cartels demanding safe passage fees."

"Because, honest to God, these things almost never happen here in San Pedro." Carlos ran his fingers through his hair one more time.

"*Almost* never. Terrific."

"Are you coming?"

Brad didn't like the impatient tone. "Where?"

"The bank."

"We're really going to do this? Pay off a Mexican drug cartel?" Brad said, hurrying behind Carlos who was already in the kitchen.

"Yes, we are," Carlos shouted over the *cumbias*.

BRAD DROPPED into one of the two folding chairs at the shaky card table, the only furnishings in the otherwise cavernous dining room. His headache had evolved into a dull, nonstop throb like the tapping of a small gong inside his head. Back home in Denver, he would have gone straight to the police. By now, they'd be hot on the trail of the scratchy-voiced creep. Helplessness wasn't a feeling he was accustomed to, and he wasn't liking it.

He watched Carlos, slightly taller and leaner than himself, pace a meandering path around the large room as he talked softly into his cell phone. Inside the fat envelope bulging from his back pocket, one hundred purple one-thousand pesos bills waited, seven thousand five hundred twenty dollars. Carlos roared through life with boundless confidence, taking everybody around him along for the ride. Christ, in a tuxedo, he looked like the latest James Bond. He made things happen, from a good party to getting a Mexican work visa for his American brewer. But the tremble in Carlos's hand had been unmistakable when he punched in Osorio's number.

"They're on their way," Carlos announced, slipping the cell into his pocket and perching on the edge of the chair across the table.

"There's more than one of them?"

"Apparently."

"Great." Brad winced at a spate of loud hammering that sent Vagabundo flying from the kitchen into the dining room and his lap. He tickled what remained of the cat's right ear and reminded himself to relax his shoulders.

"What is it with you and that *gato callejero*?" Carlos asked.

"He's not just any alley cat. He's a survivor, as macho as they come. You've got to admire that," Brad said, defending the animal, as they stared at each other. Carlos bounced his leg the way a nervous drummer absentmindedly tapped any surface his fingers came into contact with. "How much longer you think?"

"No idea."

Brad studied the cat in his lap and the plaid pattern on his shirt he'd bought on sale at a big box store shortly before leaving Denver.

"Look, I'm sorry about this morning," Carlos began.

Brad waved a hand, as though swatting at an imaginary fly. He wanted to bat away the bad vibes that hovered in the room like a fog. "We've got other things to deal with right now, Big Guy." He stared through the dust-coated windows at the empty front parking lot.

"We need to discuss it sooner or later. I admit it was foolish of me to play poker until three in the morning when we had a nine o'clock appointment."

"Asinine."

"Asinine?"

"Nobody under thirty uses the word foolish."

"Asinine as in ass," Carlos said, repeating the word.

Brad's irritation rose like hackles on an angry cat. "As in how I felt lying to the loan officer this morning after he sat there and watched me call you. 'Tell him I'm caught in traffic,' you said. Oh, please."

"I won't oversleep again. I swear."

Brad exhaled and forced his shoulders down. "It's not just the appointment this morning. Carlos, either you commit to MBC one-hundred percent, or both of us might as well walk away now before we lose all our money and our reputations. And this," he made circles in the air with his hands, "this thing with Osorio adds a whole new dimension."

Outside, a small white car pulled into the front lot, somehow avoiding the pothole, and came to a stop at the front door. Brad jumped up and sent Vagabundo scampering to the ground. The car's occupants took their time getting out. In spite of the heat, the driver wore a light-weight runner's jacket. He entered the front door and pulled off his sunglasses. Brad tried not to stare at the second man.

While the large man blocked the door, the driver advanced toward Brad and Carlos with slow, deliberate steps. Each one ratcheted up Brad's tension. When the man was within three feet, he planted himself, legs apart and crossed his arms. He stared at Brad and Carlos for a beat before rasping, *"Bienvenidos al barrio."* The voice left no doubt this was the man on the phone. What did he mean, "Welcome to the neighborhood?"

"Carlos Echeverría." The narco said, pronouncing the name slowly as if enjoying the taste of each sound. A question, not a statement. He lifted his chin in a tough-guy gesture to which Carlos nodded.

"*Y Brahth Peters*, gringo brewer of Monterrey Brewing Company."

"*Sí*," Brad responded, sounding confident but surlier than he had intended.

"They call me *El Míster.*" The thug waited as though giving them extra time to mentally register the information. What kind of name was that? And who, exactly, were the "they" who called him that?

"You've got the money?"

With none of his usual confidence, Carlos pulled the envelope from his back pocket and held it out. The thug yanked it away and counted the bills in the same purposeful way he had walked in. He returned them to the envelope and tapped the top with his index finger so the bills nestled down inside. He locked his eyes on Brad and Carlos as he stashed their money inside his jacket. It was then that Brad noticed the man's intense cobalt blue eyes—and the large, black pistol holstered to his belt. He watched numbly as Carlos asked, "When do we get our equipment?"

"Ask Osorio," the narco said in a bored tone, already walking toward the door with his back to them. "*Allí nos vemos.*"

As soon as the small car had disappeared into the heavy traffic, Brad shoved his way past Carlos, past the carpenters and their *cumbias*. Running out the back door, he nearly tripped over Vagabundo. Hidden by the pile of ripped-out equipment and the overflowing Dumpster, he collapsed against the back wall, panting while the cat rubbed against his legs. His damp shirt clung to his body. Rivulets of sweat rolled down his face. The intense sunlight made his eyes ache. He coughed and gagged, stumbling over the cat to heave the remains of his breakfast into the Dumpster. The traffic out front roared by in a deafening mix with the *cumbias* and the blood pounding in his ears.

He had come to Monterrey to brew beer. How the hell had the most violent drug cartel in Mexico discovered Brad Peters?

Chapter Two

BRAD PETERS lived to make beer. Sure he enjoyed drinking it, but grappling with the complexities of brewing was what fascinated him. Just using a different yeast could change the flavor, the aroma, the appearance of a beer so much that drinkers would swear it was a whole different recipe. What bored Brad was having to follow somebody else's recipes, rules and dictates, day after day, year after year, always producing the exact same beer. His losing the in-house promotion at Coors last year had been for the best. Otherwise, he would have stayed in Golden, bored out of his mind on the graveyard shift with a manager who made sure his brewers followed corporate directives to the last letter. And Maddy leaving, well, that one was still too raw. But the Sunday poker game with the guys in the MBA program at the University of Denver, that had been incredible luck.

They'd knocked back all the homebrew he'd brought and Carlos was beating the pants off everybody when somebody joked that Brad and Carlos should open a brewery in Mexico. Brad had laughed until Carlos said he had some serious money he'd be willing to put into an upscale brewpub, if Brad would make the beer. "I'd be completely in charge of the brewing? Every aspect?"

"I don't know anything about it," Carlos had replied. Suddenly, a Mexican brewpub had looked a lot sexier to Brad than his soon-to-be ex-wife, and for the first time in months, he'd felt a spark of excitement. In Monterrey, he would be his own man, his own brewer. His knowledge, experience and work ethic were his equity. With Carlos's money and connections, the success of Monterrey Brewing Company was all but guaranteed.

And now, one of those connections sat at the card table in the gutted dining room in a third chair that Carlos had rounded up from only God knew where. Brad stifled a yawn and studied Felipe Moss's full head of silver-gray hair, combed straight back, which contributed to the imposing appearance of the man of modest height. This millionaire's visit seemed almost as unreal as El Míster's yesterday. The restless night filled with dreams of drug thugs wasn't helping Brad concentrate.

Clearly accustomed to quick answers, Moss, the owner of one of the largest architectural firms in Monterrey, narrowed his eyes. "So what does it all come down to? What makes a brewer rise above his competitors?"

Neither the man nor the question intimidated Brad. "Passion for his craft, striving for consistency, and believing he has yet to brew his best beer."

Moss nodded and continued in English almost as lightly accented as Carlos's. "I like your attitude."

The man had already told Brad more than he cared to hear about Alfredo, his son who had graduated in food science from the University of Ohio in May and gone straight to the Siebel Institute of Technology for a twelve-week brewing class. That took the kind of money not even Carlos had and Brad would never have.

"When Alfredo gets back," Moss said, "perhaps we can all sit down and chat."

Brad must have met whatever standard Moss was holding him to because the attitude he had projected coming in had softened. "Maybe," Brad said, not certain he wanted to talk with the designated brewmaster of the future Cerverceria Huasteca. Even though Huasteca would be a craft brewery and MBC was a brewpub with no bottling facilities, they were inevitably going to end up competing. Brad had agreed to the meeting only because Moss was Carlos's baptismal godfather.

Moss extended his hand. "Brad, thanks for the advice. *Carlos, gusto de verte. Salúdame mucho a mi compadre.*" Brad understood the "glad to see you and say hi to my good friend," Carlos's father. Moss threw his arms around Carlos in a hearty back-slapping *abrazo* hug before giving Brad a handshake.

As Moss's chauffeured BMW disappeared into the traffic on Gómez Morín Avenue, Carlos said, "There goes one of the biggest movers and shakers in Monterrey."

"He may have tons of money—but he's got a lot to learn about brewing. I hope Alfredo's taking good notes at Seibel. I can't imagine somebody with no hand-on experience starting up and running a brewery that aims to produce double or triple what MBC plans for."

"Felipe's shrewd—and scared," Carlos said. "He's always given Alfredo everything he asked for, and now he's realizing the extent of what they've gotten into. He got a lot of information from us today, but that's it. No more."

"Hang on, Big Guy. Here's my thinking. I've been helping fellow brewers as long as I've been in the game. I came to Mexico because craft brewing is set to take off here. If everybody and his son suddenly thinks they're brewers, they're going to turn out a lot of high-priced, crappy beer and give all of us a bad rap. A little free advice to the competition could benefit us in the long run."

"Güero, you can sing *Kumbaya* with the Mosses all you want, but I don't trust them."

BRAD STOOD in the MBC parking lot, Carlos at his side, and peered north as far as he could see down the four-lane jumble of cars, buses and commercial vehicles on Gómez Morín. "See you in five minutes," Osorio had said when he called ten minutes ago. To the south, the Sierra Madre Mountains soared into an unusually azure sky, courtesy of a warm breeze that had whipped up at dawn and cleared the smog haze. The pine trees dotting the mountains here were fewer and stubbier than in Colorado. No vast valleys of aspen shimmering in the breeze, but for a guy born and bred in the Rockies, towering mountains meant comfort.

"You must be pickled pink."

"*Pickled* pink, Big Guy?"

"Excited, pumped."

"Been watching more classic American movies?"

"What? Guys don't say 'pickled pink' anymore?"

"T-t-tickled with a 't.' No, not so much."

"Tickled?" Carlos repeated, wiggling his fingers as if tickling an imaginary person, female, no doubt.

"Correct, and yeah, I'm pretty pumped right now."

A block away the traffic light changed, sending a fresh stream of vehicles and exhaust their way. "There they are," Brad said, feeling a rush of adrenaline.

Carlos visored his eyes with a hand. "They're huge."

"Wait till you see them up close."

As the driver rolled his flatbed truck into the parking lot, he cut the wheel hard, elbowing the man sandwiched between him and Juan Pablo Osorio. He shifted into reverse, sending a steady, high-decibel whine above the morning traffic. Passing drivers gawked at the two ten-foot stainless steel fermentation tanks, lashed lengthwise on pallets, and the four smaller maturation tanks lined up behind them. The sight nearly took Brad's breath away.

The driver jumped out to direct the hoist truck behind him. Osorio, in short sleeves and tieless, hopped from the passenger door of the cab. Ordinarily a sharp dresser, he had gone casual for the day of physical labor. "So sorry about what happened. Can't tell you how bad I feel. Don't know what's becoming of Mexico," he said in English, shaking Brad's hand and pulling his lips into a tiny knot presumably meant to convey his disapproval of El Cártel and their extortion. His English was excellent, his excuses lame.

"I have great memories of Sunday dinners here at Quinta Saldaña as a kid," Osorio said to Carlos in Spanish. "You know, of course, that the place was originally built as an actual *quinta*, a country home, back in the 1930s? I never met Don Luis, but I remember his son, Pedro, well. Such a shame, Pedro's sudden passing."

"With what the property's worth today, his widow can live the rest of her life very comfortably from the rent," Carlos replied.

"My, my." Osorio clicked his tongue. "What would Don Luis say about the peaceful little valley of farms like his today filled with malls and thousands of homes?" Without waiting for an answer, he turned to Brad. "How's the remodel coming along?"

"With a few minor complications, but we still plan to open on time. We've got ten and a half weeks until September twenty-seventh." *The main complication involving you and a certain drug cartel,* he added mentally.

"Glad to hear that. You integrated the brewery into the existing restaurant really well. Those huge windows will attract plenty of attention."

Brad was relieved when the giant hoist started up and drowned out Osorio. He threw open the doors to the delivery entrance and raised the metal roll-up curtains covering the windows on the outside. Light flooded into the airy space that smelled of fresh paint and new wood. This was the reason he had come to Monterrey, and he was damn proud of it right now.

By late afternoon, Brad and Osorio's men, with intermittent help from Carlos and Osorio, had laid out what, to most people, would have appeared to be a functioning brewery. Brad could barely take his eyes off the gleaming stainless steel tanks, the brewhouse, the mill, the filter, all begging to be used. Carlos came from the dining room and clapped Brad on the shoulder. "Just got off the phone with Jack at Modern Brewing Systems in Milwaukee. We've been bumped for a rush job. Instead of

Monday, the installers will be here Saturday, a week and a half out."

"No way," Brad cried, his throat tightening. "That would put us nearly a week behind schedule. I'm calling Jack right now."

"Contractually, they can do it."

"They're going to work over the weekend and not charge us extra?"

"Get this: they'll already be in Monterrey and don't want to sit around for two days doing nothing."

"Modern Brewing is installing equipment for someone else in Monterrey?"

Carlos nodded with a smart-ass look. "The Mosses."

Blindsided, Brad stared at his partner. "But Huasteca's not opening until the end of October."

"Now they're saying September 21."

"A week before us? Damn, they'll kill our opening!"

"I told you not to trust Felipe."

Moss—the bastard!—had come across as a damn nice guy. Brad had planned in four extra days for unexpected problems, but Moss's move was going to cost them five. Osorio came through the door of the loading dock where he had spent the last hour on the phone. *Miracle the guy could straighten out his arm.* "Well, gentlemen, all we have left is the paperwork."

"That and a discussion about the future," Carlos said, clearly in a bad mood.

"Again, I apologize," Osorio replied in a cloying tone. "Osorio e Hijos is an old, respected business. I feel very bad about what happened." The papers he offered hung in his outstretched hand.

"As far as our other importation needs," Carlos continued, "assuming we continue to do business with you, will El Míster, or someone else, demand more money?"

Osorio set down the papers and spread out his hands. "Carlos, if you're asking for a guarantee, I can't give it to you. When a cartel decides they want a cut, they have me and every customs broker in Monterrey over a barrel. I dislike it as much as you do. I've worked for your uncles and their friends for years. Your father's my lawyer. You know my reputation in Monterrey. I'll find a way to make it up to you, I promise."

Carlos flashed the broker a hard look while Brad wondered when he had become invisible. "Your reputation is changing, and neither of us can stay in business if we have to pay these impossible sums," Carlos said, yanking up papers out of Osorio's hand.

CARLOS HAD a way of understating things—like having a little money to invest in a brewpub or friends who played a little tennis at the sports club. Two of those friends had just beat the heck out of Brad and Carlos. The Saturday afternoon competition and the heat had intensified as the blazing sun rose higher in the cloudless sky. Drenched in sweat, Brad followed the men past a half dozen tennis courts. On the opposite side of the main building, swimmers splashed and shouted in an Olympic-sized pool. Behind it all, golfers dotted an emerald green course backdropped by the Sierra Madres. The exertion, the camaraderie and the mountains had all relaxed Brad.

At the patio bar, they joined a loose group that met weekly for tennis and guy time, their common bond being their alma mater, Monterrey Institute of Technology, Mexico's MIT. Most of these men held graduate degrees from American universities or the Tec's graduate business school. They formed part of the educated class that, in spite of narco insecurity, fueled Mexico's robust economy and the country's future. San Pedro teemed with college-educated people schooled in English since kindergarten who peppered their conversations with words like *un website* and *el GPS*.

Brad and his group took a seat at a table under the thatched-palm roof where ceiling fans circulated a refreshing breeze. He downed a bottle of water and started on a *limonada*. His new fondness for the key lime drink was threatening to break his Coca-Cola habit, something

Maddy had attempted for years. He listened carefully, taking in new words and phrases, getting more of the gist of conversations each week. He understood when Roberto, the tall, muscled athlete who played almost every sport well, talked about his trip to Pennsylvania last week for corporate training. He was still following when Eugenio, in a maroon University of Chicago t-shirt, said he had gone to Buenos Aires where, "It was freezing cold, but the beef—" He pinched his fingers together and kissed the tips.

And then, Carlos was telling the extortion story. Roberto's brow wrinkled. Eugenio's head shook. Ex-A-Tecs at tables around them listened in. "You talk so openly about it here, but you won't go to the police?" Brad asked.

"We're careful," Roberto said. "Here at the club, in the office, private homes, sure, but we don't talk like that walking down the street."

"They even go after large companies like yours?"

"They're not extorting our CEOs, but we feel it in other ways, like when one of our delivery drivers was approached about working as a *halcón*, a hawk or a lookout."

"What happened?"

Roberto shrugged. "The company gave him a new route."

"Can't the police at least crack down on the *halcones*?"

Roberto and Eugenio both answered in rapid-fire Spanish. Brad sighed. "Can you explain that in English?"

"We have traffic cops, municipal, state and federal police, plus the military," Roberto said. "Except for the *federales*, the rest don't earn much. The cartels outgun and outspend all of them except the military. When they offer big money for a cop to look the other way. . ."

Eugenio picked up. "Especially when they see fellow officers killed for resisting. As much as we hate to admit it, the Mexican government has too much inefficiency and corruption. We're *regiomontanos*. We come from generations of businessmen who developed a certain distrust of Mexico

City and government in general. Our fathers and grandfathers couldn't rely on them, so they developed private solutions. We've had that drilled into us since childhood."

Roberto continued, "It wasn't a great system, but after the Revolution ended in 1918, it worked. Like our fathers, we believe that economic systems based on capitalism, education and transparent, democratic governments will pull Latin America out of the Third World. Nowadays, the cartels are undermining our whole system. They've changed how we do business and how we live. They're bleeding Mexico at every level."

"Enough with the lecture, professor," Eugenio said. "How about some poker tonight?"

"Can't," Carlos answered. "Brad and I have a barbecue with Americans. Have to get the word out about the new brewmaster in town."

Did everybody here read from the same script? Brad wondered. Give El Cártel what they demanded? Don't trust the government? Grease a few palms? Thank God he'd only promised Carlos three years. By then, he hoped to at least double the forty-eight thousand dollars he'd scrounged up and committed to MBC. He'd know every in and out of the business for when he opened his own brewpub in Denver where he'd tell the crazy tale of his run-in with a Mexican drug cartel, and nobody would believe him.

CHAPTER THREE

NACHO DIDN'T know Labrador's real name. Didn't care to know it. In the drug world, men went by the names they earned. Only one person currently in his own life knew him when he was just plain Nacho. As for Ignacio, the name on his baptismal certificate, nobody had called him that for years. Nacho was El Míster to every narco who knew him. El Míster to Osorio, the sappy customs broker, and to the rich boy, Echeverría, and his gringo partner. Those two were his next step up. No way Nacho/El Míster was going to let Labrador fuck things up. He knocked on the closed door. From the other side, Bala summoned him.

Nacho opened the door, his suspicious mind taking in every detail of the stuffy room, including Bala's and Labrador's presence. Not much to the room. A couple of chairs that didn't match, an old, beat-up table. Light bulb hanging on a wire from the ceiling. A grayish piece of cracked and warped plywood rested on the window sill and covered the only window. The trashy neighborhood outside wasn't worth looking at anyway. Nacho stuck his hand in his pocket, fingering the brass knuckles. He positioned himself beside Labrador who stood a good foot taller. The guy sensed something was up, but he was too dumb to figure it out.

Nacho was actually starting to like the giant covered in multi-colored tattoos of big-tit women, Day of the Dead skeletons and who the hell knew what else. Two months ago, Bala, the *patrón*, had assigned Labrador to Nacho for collecting *piso* payments. They'd gotten along okay until Labrador started the stupid shit. Now, Nacho had to rat him out before Bala heard it from somebody else and came for both of them. As far as bosses went, Nacho wasn't wild about Bala, but at least he was fair most of the time.

The sun today was way too fucking bright. Inside this tiny, dim room, Nacho was a lot more comfortable. The plywood over the window did a good job of keeping out the light—and keeping in what happened inside the room. Bala shut the door. He gave a single nod and a soft, "¡*Orale!*"

Nacho spun hard on his heels, sinking his fist and the brass knuckles into the center of Labrador's gut. The big man grunted and doubled over. Nacho laced his hands together and smashed them into Labrador's head, toppling the giant. Nacho stood ready to strike again, if necessary.

Curled on the floor, Labrador held a tattooed arm over his head. "What the fuck, Míster?"

"Gimme the money."

"I don't know what you're talking about."

"The money you skimmed off collections."

Labrador stared up at his partner, eyes wide. "Me? No way." When the pointed toe of Nacho's boot connected with Labrador's fleshy cheek, Goliath let out a groan.

"You gonna gimme the money or am I gonna take it off you?"

"Míster, *hombre*, I had some problems this month. I wasn't going to keep doing it. I swear."

Nacho strained like a pit bull ready to go into full attack the second Bala unleashed him. The sight and smell of the blood made him want more. He made eye contact with Bala. "Get up, asshole," the boss said. "And hand over every last peso you got on you."

Damn Bala! Nacho was just getting warmed up. Labrador struggled to his feet. He smeared his fingers through the blood oozing down his cheek and rubbed his hand on his jeans. He fished in his pockets and slowly pulled out crumpled wads of cash. When Labrador finished, Bala's pockets bulged. "You ever pull any shit like that again," Bala said, "El Míster finishes you off. Understood?"

"*Sí, patrón,*" Labrador mumbled, chin bowed to chest.

"Learn from El Míster. He knows how to follow orders. That mess is gonna need stitches. Go see Patel, the doctor who doesn't ask questions."

THREE WEEKS after Brad turned sixteen and got his driver's license, he grabbed a bottle of apple juice and a banana as he raced out of the house one morning. Running from the school parking lot into the science hall, he tossed the banana peel into a trash can. He dropped into his desk, drained the last drops of juice and stuffed the bottle into his backpack just as the bell rang, signaling the beginning of another Advanced Placement Chemistry class. With his ninety-seven percent average, Brad got bored during the pre-lab lecture on dry ice and solubility of gasses. He started speculating as to how much the pressure of a little dry ice and some water would increase inside the glass bottle he had stuffed in his backpack.

By the time Mr. Ebenholt finished his lecture the way he did every lecture—"We do labs because we learn best by doing,"—Brad had a hypothesis and his own experiment.

Unfortunately, his calculations were off. He hadn't expected the bottle to explode or a chunk of glass to lodge itself in the white ceiling panel. The facts that the chunk narrowly missed Mary Beth Larsen's head and that her parents were both lawyers figured into his week-long suspension.

At home, his parents grounded him for the duration plus the weekends before and after and confiscated the car keys. By the second weekend, he was so desperate that he accepted his father's offer to tag along to some meeting. In the car, he learned he'd be spending the afternoon with homebrewers. If his mother hadn't gone to her Zumba class, she wouldn't have allowed it, which made Brad all the more enthusiastic. The men, all but one older than his dad, were glad to pontificate to a new face. Brad slumped in a chair where his hand, with a mind of its own, kept dipping into the pocket of his jeans in search of the cell phone that had also been confiscated.

Before long, he was sniffing, swishing and sipping with the men, actually getting pulled in this so-called tasting. When one guy asked why his brews were frequently too flat, Ted the host suggested, "Maybe you're not using enough sugar."

"Make sure you're capping the bottles tight enough," another guy said.

Why wasn't anybody suggesting the obvious? Brad wondered. "Can't you just inject a little more CO_2 when you carbonate the beer?" he said, mindful of his newfound respect for carbon dioxide and Mr. Ebenholt.

Two men laughed. "Son, we're homebrewers."

"But your kegs are pressurized, right?"

After every man laughed, the host handed Brad his first brewing book.

From that day on, he was hooked. His mother fumed for the next year about her teenage son making beer, but Brad and his dad bonded in ways they never had before as they learned together. With a few brews, they poured more beer down the drain than down their throats. Together they learned from experience, from the homebrewing group, magazines, the internet. On some gloriously wild occasions, they winged it like blind bats.

By the time Brad went off to CU Boulder, he could take three sips of a beer and suggest that the excessive sweetness might be due to insufficient fermentation. While some freshmen changed their majors more often than their jeans, all Brad ever wanted was to get his chemical engineering degree so he could make better beer. That, and helping others do the same, was still his goal. The only exception was the Mosses. He'd learned that lesson the hard way.

A LIGHT evening breeze carried the smoky aroma of beef from the grill. From the street, it was impossible to see the patio hidden behind the two-story home. The well-manicured backyard, enclosed in high walls, was nearly covered by a canopy of trees. With the English conversations swirling around him, Brad could almost imagine he was back home in Denver instead of Monterrey.

MariCarmen and Teresa, the dates that Carlos had arranged, were gorgeous in the way of so many San Pedro women. Both wore their dark hair long and loose, their dresses short and their heels high. Coworkers at the American Consulate, their English was far superior to Brad's Spanish. While Carlos entertained the group around them, Brad swigged beer from a moisture-beaded bottle of Bohemia, Cuauhtémoc's premium beer. He'd soon be producing better beer than the hundred thirty-year-old brewing giant.

"So, it was at least thirty-five degrees—what's that in Fahrenheit, Brad, like a hundred?"

"Close."

"And the pre-historic Quinta Saldaña air-conditioning system had died. The electrical engineer had the power shut off so we couldn't even use the floor fan. I had papers spread all over the card table in the otherwise empty dining room. Without warning, the engineer flips on the electricity and the fan starts blowing like a hurricane. Papers are flying everywhere and I'm running around grabbing them—until I trip over the fan cord and crash into the floor along with the fan."

Teresa squeezed Carlos's arm and the group burst into laughter. A gorgeous female at his side, a group hanging onto his words. Carlos was in his element.

MariCarmen's laugh sounded to Brad like the tinkling of wind chimes. She was an attractive woman, especially when she smiled in a flirty way and said, "I think your brewpub's going to be a great success."

"We'll see you and Teresa at the opening?"

Her smile grew a little larger, a little sexier, as she leaned closer. "I wouldn't dream of missing it." He was a healthy, straight male. The divorce had been final for three months. Why the hell wasn't he reacting like he was supposed to with an attractive woman coming on to him?

At dinner, they shared a table with two other couples. Brad had met the Wilkes before. African-American East Coasters, they worked at the Consulate. Marc was tall and thin, with a bearing that indicated a military background. Their friends, the Millers, were from Atlanta. Susan, blonde and hot even at forty plus, had won second place in the Miss Georgia contest during her college days. Husband Nick, gray-streaked temples, an accountant with Sony, confessed he had tried his hand at homebrewing. "A lot more to it than I expected," he said, taking a deep pull on the Sam Adams in front of him. "You and Carlos concerned about competition from Huasteca?"

"Not too much," Brad replied. *Not exactly the truth.* "They'll be bottling and selling through distributors. We'll just keg and sell only in our pub."

"I had lunch with Felipe Moss yesterday," Nick continued. "He told me he'd visited MBC and was impressed. The man thrives on competition. You should see him in a *friendly* game of golf. Said that after talking with y'all, he got inspired to push up Huasteca's opening."

"So we heard," Brad said.

Serene as a Buddha statue, Carlos put an arm around Teresa. "We hear he's going all out on his promo campaign."

Nick wagged his head. "Their plans to flood stores with Huasteca girls and fifty-percent-off six packs on opening weekend? Felipe's a big believer in spending money to make money."

Brad nearly choked on his beer. Obviously he had been mistaken thinking he and Carlos had cleared up things after the extortion and the bank appointment. He decided to quietly make a point of not addressing Carlos the rest of the evening.

They had barely started eating when a small boy ran up to the table. "Our son, Tanner the Tiger," Marc Wilkes said.

The boy broke into a dimpled, innocent smile that lit up his brown face and distracted Brad from his thoughts. "Hi, everybody!"

The boy whispered something into his mother's ear and ran back to a group of kids on the lawn just as a drop-dead gorgeous blonde approached the table. Brad had seen her as soon as she'd walked into the party. *Hard not to.* He made an effort not to stare at her Playboy figure snuggly sheathed in a black dress. *The older guy she'd come in with had to make a bundle to catch a trophy like that.*

"Is it true, Marc"—her loud voice carried a southern or Texas accent—"that the U.S. government might issue a warning, advising Americans not to travel to Monterrey?" Brad pushed aside his simmering anger at Carlos, curious to hear Wilkes's answer.

"You're referring to the incident in downtown Monterrey last night, Kendra? It would take more than a three a.m. shooting between warring narcos for that." Marc Wilkes appeared unperturbed by the tone of her question.

"Hearing that from a Consulate employee doesn't make me feel very safe."

"The American government advises all U.S. citizens to take reasonable precautions and stay in safe areas in Mexico." Wilkes sounded like he was reading from a press release.

"There are all kinds of police and military patrolling the whole country. You can't go to the grocery store without seeing a truck full of soldiers standing behind a mounted gun. Is there *any* place in Mexico that's safe anymore?" *Texas accent, definitely.*

"Look at us here," Marc answered, still calm. "So much comes down to common sense."

"Like practically barricading yourself inside after dark. I don't know how people do it who have to live here forever."

"It's complicated," Carlos said in a frosty voice.

"In the three years we've lived here, Kendra," Susan Miller said, "we've never had a problem. We *are* cautious, like Marc says. We've come to love

Monterrey. We've made lots of friends. The job market is great. There are excellent schools. The fact that it's so Americanized, especially in San Pedro, makes it almost like living in the States."

"*¡Eh, Playboy!*" a man near the grill called to Carlos. "We're placing bets on the Rayados's game. Come over here."

Gradually, the others drifted away until only Marc and Brad were left at the table. "Marc, can I get your take on something?" Brad asked. Before he knew it, he was getting a crash course on everything from *piso*, a monthly protection fee the cartels sometimes demanded of businesses, to financial statistics on DTOs, drug trafficking organizations.

"Estimates are that El Cártel, which controls the Monterrey *plaza*—the turf and trafficking routes—spent over six-hundred thousand U.S. dollars every month last year on payoffs to police alone. They generate about fifty percent of their revenue from cocaine and another five to ten percent from meth, heroin and other drugs. The rest comes from extortion, kidnapping, smuggling, prostitution and other activities."

Marc paused and smiled at MariCarmen, who approached with coffee mugs just as two guitarists started to tune up. Several songs in, a dance line formed to the beat of a Juanes song Brad recognized. Tanner and several other children ran to dance around the adults. This was the Mexico Brad had envisioned when he stepped off the plane.

"Come on," Carlos shouted, pulling Teresa into the conga line as it weaved in their direction. MariCarmen followed, placing her hands daintily on Carlos's waist. Brad fell in behind, not completely comfortable with putting his hands on MariCarmen's bare shoulders—or with the information he had just heard.

Two hours later, as soon as they'd taken the women home, Brad exploded. "Why the hell didn't you tell me about Moss and his Huasteca girls? You realize they're going to pre-empt us? It's going to kill our opening night. What else are you not telling me?"

Carlos laughed and threw the car into gear. "Back off, Güero. I didn't have a clue about their promotion campaign until Nick Miller started talking."

"I'm supposed to believe that?"

"Yes, you are."

"You were bluffing your way through that conversation?"

"Hey, if Moss plays naïve, I'll play like I know more than I do. It didn't take much to figure out that he'd launch with some flashy promotion, but it still pisses me up."

"Pisses you off."

"Pisses you, me up, off, down, out. I say that from now on, we share zero information with the Mosses."

"Agreed," Brad said, holding out a fist to meet Carlos's knuckle bump.

"I'm more concerned about you, Güero."

"What do you mean?"

"I set you up with one of the most beautiful girls in San Pedro and you acted like a *monje*."

"A monkey? What the hell do you mean by that?"

"Not a monkey, although that's what you're acting like now. A *monje*, a kind of priest."

"A monk, you mean?"

"What I mean is she was falling all over you, and you acted like you were scared of her."

Brad blew out a breath. "Sorry, Big Guy. I don't know if I'm ready to get back in the dating game yet."

"That's your problem, Güero. You're not supposed to *think*. Just loosen up and do what feels good."

CHAPTER FOUR

JULY MORPHED into August with no word from El Míster and Osorio acting as if the shakedown had never happened. Brad was daring to think it might be a one-time occurrence. They hadn't heard from the Mosses either. Brad found himself falling into routines, looking forward to Saturday afternoons at the sports club and lazy Sundays. Monday mornings he woke early, eager to get back to MBC and check on his first brews. He told himself that Monterrey was like a new TV season on *The Brad Show* with Maddy's role written out.

One Sunday he had slipped into Santa Cecilia Brewery, which would be MBC's biggest competitor. The food was surprisingly good at Monterrey's oldest brewpub. Of the four beers he sampled, though, three weren't anything special and one was an embarrassment. Life was looking better than it had in a long time.

He swung the Dodge Neon into the MBC lot and around back. A large rock pinned the kitchen's screen door against the outside wall. A worn rubber doorstop held the inner door open. Vagabundo materialized and meowed. "Hey, buddy, I'm out of treats today." He paused to scratch the cat and nudge him outside. "Sorry, off limits to you now." Vagabundo might as well start getting used to the fact that he was no longer allowed inside.

"*¡No seas güey!*" Don't be an ass! The words floated above the *banda* music and hammering that filtered from the dining room where the carpenters were noisily installing the cherrywood bar. Brad grinned at their easy talk. He'd miss these guys when the remodel was done.

"*¡Buenos días!*" he shouted above the noise.

"*¡Buenos días, Brath!*" four voices chorused.

Inside his brewery, Brad closed the door to the dining room, dulling the racket to a more or less tolerable level. He pulled his laptop from the backpack and booted up.

The Friday between finals and graduation, he'd spent two hours sorting, deleting and organizing two years of part-time class notes, projects and documents into the single "DU" folder. Carlos had admired Brad's work and immediately created his own "Univ of Denver" folder where, in under ten minutes, he dumped every file related to his one, full-time year of grad school. With his memory and brains, he'd probably never have to go back to them anyway. If he did need to locate anything, he'd go to Brad.

Carlos had taped the latest countdown-to-opening sheet from his yellow legal pad to the plate glass windows between the dining room and brewery. At the end of each day, he sketched some funny version of the next day's numbers drawn with the green felt marker he always carried. Today the three in "31" wore a fedora tipped to the left. Below the hat, he had drawn in a face with a thin handlebar mustache. The "1" wore a pair of over-sized shoes.

The dwindling numbers simultaneously excited and stressed Brad. The week-long delay caused by the Mosses had eaten up all the extra days he had planned in. He'd been pushing things along ever since. If today's interviews went smoothly and nothing else unexpected happened, they'd be okay.

He focused on the laptop screen and the color-coded chart of the six beers with which MBC would open. Carlos had decided they'd name the stout Santa Catarina, after the river that trickled through the heart of Monterrey and bisected the city. It had once been a real river, before the water was diverted and used up. The broad flood plains had been carved into soccer fields and a flea market until one afternoon in 2010 when Hurricane Alex had sent a half-kilometer-wide wall of water and devastation raging through the heart of Monterrey. The flood obliterated everything in its path.

The regional names for MBC's beers had been Carlos's creation—Santa Catarina Stout, Cadereyta Pale Ale, Chipinque Wheat, Allende IPA. The two exceptions were the Morenita Porter and Colorado Red Ale, references to their respective dark and red colors. Carlos had put more time and thought into the names than he had into any assignment at DU, which had pleased Brad immensely.

These days, the brews were Brad's biggest concern. Yesterday, he had finally pinned down why he wasn't happy with the Santa Catarina. The strong burnt flavor some American brewers preferred for stouts wasn't going to fly here with drinkers who hadn't been exposed to it. His dilemma lay in the ratio of malts and their kiln roasting time and temperatures.

He looked out the window and caught a glimpse of Carlos's RAV4 disappearing toward the back lot. He tracked Carlos's path by the shouts from the kitchen and then the dining room. The construction crew ate up Carlos's rowdy greetings.

"Hey, Güero!" Carlos said as he threw open the brewery door.

"Hey, Big Guy. You growing a beard?"

"Got up late, but if the ladies like it, who knows?" Carlos said, stroking his stubbled jaw. He swung his briefcase onto the card table and popped the locks. "Check out the latest logo design. I think Julio and his PR team finally have the look we're going for. They took your mountain idea and went from there." The one aspect of marketing that Brad wanted a say in was associating his brewery with mountains. He whistled softly at the jagged rendering of Cerro de la Silla, Monterrey's iconic Saddle Mountain.

"Edgy, hipster. I like it," Carlos said. His interest and talent for marketing and sales had surprised them both.

One of the carpenters knocked on the brewery door and announced a gentleman was looking for them. He stepped aside for the visitor with impeccably trimmed and moussed hair and perfectly-ironed creases in his slacks and shirt sleeves. "*Buenos días, soy Noé Padilla.*" The third candidate for MBC restaurant manager had arrived.

Brad had rehearsed his interview questions during the weekend and practiced them at the two interviews yesterday. Now they rolled off his tongue. Understanding the answers was another matter. He was happily surprised to find that he could comprehend almost everything Padilla said in his calm manner.

"Give us your thoughts on beer and food pairings," Brad said.

Padilla currently worked as restaurant manager at the same Santa Cecilia where the food had been good and the beer underwhelming. "In Monterrey, plenty of beef and strong beers to match. I'm guessing you've got something attractive to women, a wheat maybe, and salads?"

By the end of the interview, Brad was sold. "Any recommendations of good brewers we should contact?" he asked.

"Alejandra Howard." Padilla replied immediately.

"A woman?" Carlos asked, one eyebrow arched.

"And young, but she's good and she's going to go far. At Santa Cecilia they have her tending bar most of the time. She'd jump at the chance to brew."

Brad had nothing against knowledgeable women brewers, but in the Mexican brewing world, a female bartender with brewing aspirations sounded like a bet with the same odds as Carlos arriving early for an appointment.

"Final question," Carlos said. "Why would you leave an established brewpub for an untested startup?"

"The challenge. Something new and different. Getting to help handpick my staff."

After the interview, Brad and Carlos headed next door to El Pollo Loco for lunch. On Gómez Morín, drivers sat backed-up in traffic, stopping and moving according to the dictates of the corner traffic light. "The repaved parking lot looks great," Brad said. "Although I still haven't gotten used to not hitting the pothole."

Carlos dodged a woman carrying shopping bags. "I swerve out of habit every time I turn in. Listen, you want me to give this Alejandra chick a call?"

"Know anything about her?"

"A well-recommended, good-looking female behind the bar, what's not to like?"

"Padilla said 'good brewer,' not 'good-looking.' Hold off until we see how the other brewer interviews go."

A WEEK later, the carpenters had finished installing the cherrywood bar and the tables and chairs had been delivered. The dining room, which had echoed like an empty dance hall, now had a more intimate feel. If only the brewer search were progressing so well. Three interviews in, and no luck. With his chin propped in one hand, Brad jotted a note while he and Carlos listened to Santiago Rodríguez, who sat across from them at one of the new tables. Brad would have carded the guy first thing as a customer, but his answers were spot on. Everything in his résumé supported his words and his earnest attitude. He looked open to being trained in the ways Brad expected things to be done.

"Cervecería Cuauhtémoc is a huge brewery. You understand that if you came to MBC, you'd be taking a pay cut and you'd have to tend bar during lunch?" Carlos asked.

"But I wouldn't be working the night shift." Santiago shrugged his bony shoulders. "I have a girlfriend. You know how that is."

"I do," Brad said. The kid's remark made him feel old. "Anything more you'd like to tell us?"

Santiago's bright eyes lit up another notch. "Just that I really want to work at Monterrey Brewing Company. I learn fast and I'm not afraid of hard work. I'll be the best brewer you have—except for you, Brad. You won't regret hiring me. By the way, I go by Chago."

"Thanks, Chago. We hope to make a decision by next Monday," Brad said, shaking the kid's hand as a lop-sided grin spread across his face. *And you'll be the first brewer I offer a job to.*

Chinga la espera. Fuck the wait.

For at least the twentieth time, Nacho paced over to the tiny window. Exterior metal bars sliced up the view of the outside world. Labrador leaned away, allowing Nacho to squeeze by. The dark heat pressed in relentlessly. Whenever they were waiting for a ransom payoff, time moved slower than an old lady. Ever since Nacho beat the honesty lesson into Labrador, the guy had shown proper respect. Nacho was still a long way from trusting either Labrador or Bala. Neto, leaning against a tall pile of *sarapes*, was the only one who truly had his back. Neto would give up his life for Nacho, and vice versa.

During the day, the road outside was like a goddamned highway, but from eleven at night till daybreak, the warehouse district was a ghost town. Nacho was sick of looking at the idiot boys and at Bala, who was lording his *patrón* status. "S'up?" he murmured to Neto, barely moving his lips.

Neto shrugged one shoulder. Dude never had been a talker. Here they only knew Neto as Matagatos, the Killer of Cats. The other day, screwing around, Labrador had called him Míster Junior. Neto was short, but he more than made up for it in strength and meanness. He lunged so fast Labrador didn't know what hit him. Neto smacked his shoulder straight into Labrador's gut and growled, "There's only one Míster." Neto's comment came across as respectful, but Nacho heard the jealousy, too.

Now, Nacho sighed. The waiting always bored him. He turned and, in the weak light, took in the stacks of *sarapes*. He liked the dim light, the agreeable smell of the wool, the silence. Outside, sparse lights along the road and around the warehouses formed isolated pools of brightness in the ocean of darkness. Inside, the light was faint but more evenly distributed. Nacho pulled out his phone and checked the time. Not much longer.

"Míster," Labrador's low voice rumbled. Bala jostled past Nacho as if Labrador had called him. "They're turning in," Labrador said without moving to accommodate Bala.

Nacho never felt so alert as in these moments. Agile as a feline, he glided past the *sarapes* and the boys. The American was going to need a doctor, but it was his own damned fault. Saying *chinga-a-tu-madre* to any Mexican was asking for trouble. Whispering fuck-your-mother as soon as your kidnapper turned his back, shit, might as well kick a pit bull in the face. Neto and Labrador were the reasons the kid was still alive.

"Neto, Labrador!" Nacho commanded. The men scrambled to his side. Fuck the ransom and fuck Bala leaving the dirty work to them. When it came time to claim the money, Bala was all over it.

"*¡Chíngale, mano!*" Fuck buddy, Nacho snapped when Labrador's AR-15 crashed against Nacho's leg. He pulled the mask over his face and cracked the back door. The van rolled to a stop ten feet away. The driver killed the engine like Bala had instructed him to do.

"*¡O-o-o-renle!*" Bala's drawn-out shout shredded the silence. Neto and Labrador burst through the door, weapons trained on the van. Nacho flicked on the halogen spotlight and leapt between them. The slap of his shoes hitting the asphalt echoed in his ears. His breathing was so loud it sounded like somebody had stuffed a mic up his nose. Each accelerated beat of his heart thumped in his chest.

"Everybody out. Hands up!" Bala screamed from inside the warehouse.

The passenger door opened slowly, revealing a tall, skinny man. He lifted his outstretched hands until his fingers touched the van's ceiling. Dressed in black, he slid out and squinted against the bright light, keeping his hands high. Nacho would have had to close his eyes against so much light. A bag sat on the floor of the passenger side. The older, balding driver came around slowly, hands barely above his head, eyes down, skin a pasty white in the harsh halogen beam. He made Nacho think of those old cowboy movies, good guys in white, bad guys in black. Except this guy was a joke with his sickly skin and paunchy stomach.

"Open the side door!" Bala barked. The tall dark one jerked the handle and shoved the door panel back. Nacho edged forward, beamed the light inside, then moved on. He wasn't about to touch the bag in front. Not yet. On the other side of the van, a scrap of paper stuck out from underneath the driver's seat. Probably not important, but right now, Nacho held more power than any of the assholes here, and he planned to make the most of it. He took his sweet time walking around the van. He retrieved the paper. Even though he was perfectly capable of pronouncing the name in English, he barked, "*¡Yon R-r-ryerson!*"

"*¡Soy yo!*" The old man's head jerked around, fear spilling from the words.

"Dropped your boarding pass from last week." Nacho drilled into the man with his eyes. After a long beat, he pocketed the stub. He'd throw it out later, but John Ryerson would be freaked for days. He eased back between Neto and Labrador and their weapons. "All clear!"

"You, the tall one, unzip the bag!" Bala ordered from the safety of the warehouse. Did the gringos detect the nervousness in Bala's voice, Nacho wondered. It was pathetically obvious. The tall one edged toward the gym bag, the cheap kind that wouldn't attract attention, and pulled the zipper. Nacho shined the light inside. His heart was already pumping. At the sight of so much cash, it started pounding. He jerked the bag out of the

American's hand, zipped it closed and tossed it inside the warehouse.

One last wait while Bala counted the money. A truck rumbled by on the road out front. Nacho wasn't worried. The driver couldn't see them behind the warehouse. Without taking his eyes off the Americans, he listened as the truck, probably a semi, faded from earshot. The damned mask was hot and itchy. He hated wearing it, especially in the heat. Crickets chirped under the parking lot light. Everyone waited. So close, so much at stake. What the hell was taking Bala so long?

Finally, Bala's cry pierced the humid night air. *"¡Libérenlos!"*

Shoved out the door, the boys stumbled and fell. Hurtado, the Mexican, righted himself in spite of the zipcuffs. The American hit the asphalt and yelped like a baby then lay in a fetal position. Nacho didn't give a shit whether they lived or died.

"Jeff, Rodrigo! American Consulate," the tall gringo shouted. "Inside the van! *¡Consulado americano, métanse a la camioneta!"* He helped the boys in as the old American jogged around to the driver's seat, belly bouncing up and down. The old guy gunned the engine, and the van shot out just as a pickup rounded the side of the warehouse in a blaze of lights and screech of wheels.

"¡Vámono-o-o-s!" Bala screamed. Nacho sprinted toward the truck, yanked the double doors and scrambled into the back seat. Neto and Labrador crammed in after him. Bala jumped into the front. The driver hit the accelerator so hard that Nacho's head smacked the back window.

Damn, if they all died, it wouldn't matter one *pinche* bit to the *patrones*. Every one of them—Bala included—was worth less to the *capos* at the top than the goddamned thirty-thousand dollar pickup. What really mattered was the hundred thousand dollars inside the bag that Bala clutched in a steel grip. Who the hell knew those asshole kids were so valuable?

Whoever ordered the kidnapping had obviously known. During the wait, Bala had spilled that Jeff Miller's father was some goddamned

American millionaire. This was the biggest, most *chingón* kidnapping Nacho had ever been in on. The day was coming when he—El Míster— would be calling the shots. He had no intention of collecting measly *pisos* forever.

CHAPTER FIVE

A WOMAN, dressed in a black top and pants, emerged from the red car in the MBC parking lot. She retrieved a black briefcase from the back seat and, with a minimal gesture, flipped back the black ponytail that had spilled over her shoulder.

"Your lady brewer has arrived," Carlos whispered to Brad as the woman entered MBC.

She dropped her black sunglasses into the briefcase, smiled and extended her hand. "*Buenas tardes.* Alejandra Howard." She continued in Spanish. "Thanks for the compliment. I do hope to become MBC's 'lady brewer'."

"Excuse me?" Carlos said, sounding as surprised as Brad felt.

"I'm blessed, or cursed, with very good hearing."

Trying to cover his own surprise, Brad said, "A hop necklace. I don't think I've seen one of those before."

Alejandra Howard fingered the charm with a green cone. "I found it on eBay." Her voice was confident, almost husky. Not overly attractive, she was a nice change after the Teresas and MariCarmens. Her slender figure and pale coloring suggested a fragileness that contrasted with the firmness of her handshake. The palm of her hand, when Brad shook it, wasn't particularly soft, a good sign if she was a serious brewer.

At the interview table, Carlos began. "Howard, not a common surname in Mexico."

"My father's from Alabama. At twenty-two, he came to work on a ranch near Saltillo."

"And stayed," Carlos guessed.

"Married the rancher's daughter and the ranch."

"And the rancher's granddaughter decided to brew beer."

"She did," Alejandra confirmed.

"How's your English?" Brad asked.

"Except for the Alabama accent, probably a lot like yours," she answered in English with a noticeable drawl.

The rest of the interview bounced between languages. Alejandra had graduated Tec valedictorian in chemistry two years earlier. At Santa Cecilia, owner Patricio Bustamante hired her half-time in the brewery, half-time nights behind the bar, which meant long, lousy hours.

"If I asked you to create an unusual beer," Brad asked, "what would it be?"

Alejandra tapped a finger on the table. "A mango lambic."

Brad smiled. "Why a lambic and why mango?"

"I tried it once. A spectacular failure. More like a foul-tasting alcoholic kombucha. I read about fruit lambics on the Beer Advocate website and liked the complexity of working with different yeasts and bacteria all in one beer. Someday when I'm a better brewer, I'll get it right."

The woman and her answers were one surprise after another.

"You understand," Carlos said, "that the position wouldn't be one-hundred percent brewing initially? You'd work the bar during lunch."

"I understand, but I imagine that as MBC grows, there would be the possibility of moving into the brewery full-time." She hesitated, fingering the hop necklace. "The brewing community in Mexico is overwhelming male, tightly-knit and, often, *machista*. Some refuse to engage in serious dialogue with a woman brewer. I figure an American has a different mindset." She flashed Brad an unflinching look. "I'm hoping he'll give me the opportunity to prove myself."

As they watched Alejandra Howard nose her car into the Gómez Morín traffic, Carlos said, "I'd never ask her out, but she appears to know what she's talking about, and you seem to have made up your mind."

"You heard her talk about studying brewing magazines and websites," Brad replied. "Noé Padilla was right. She's going places."

"You want to call and offer her the job?"

"That's your role. Just don't leave here before you've hired her."

THE THICK cloud layer shrouding the Sierra Madres increased the mugginess in the valley below. Brad wiped the sweat from his forehead and yawned. With less than a month before the grand opening, he was staying late more evenings than he cared to count. Last night, he hadn't gotten himself out the door until nine. He had taken a long, hot shower to scrub away the brewery smells and stuffed his dirty work clothes in a plastic garbage bag until he could wash them. After that, he scarfed a ham sandwich, drank a beer, watched TV, downed another beer and went to bed. Just before he fell asleep, he realized that he hadn't thought or dreamed about Maddy all week. Working twelve plus hours a day had its advantages.

He and Chago, now in his second day on the job, were tweaking the mill rollers. "If we set the aperture too tight, the grain shatters. Too loose and it falls through without getting crushed," Brad explained. He was happily tinkering when the hail started, first a single crash on the roof above them, then another and another. In the time it took Brad to drop his tools and scramble to the brewery's front window, walnut-sized hail pounded everything in sight. Carlos raced into the brewery, hand raking his hair, mouth moving, words unheard until he stood between Brad and Chago, shouting, "This is going to wreck my new car!"

After the repaving, they'd started parking in the front lot where their cars were completely unprotected. Brad watched helplessly as the hail slammed the cars and bounced off. Suddenly, he made out the hunkered form of Vagabundo underneath Carlos's RAV4. "Grab a bar towel!" he yelled, bolting from the brewery. The noise of the pounding hail drowned out any other sounds. Balls hit and skidded around him. There was nothing to do but dive into the storm. Jumpy and nervous, Vagabundo edged toward Brad until he was able to scoop up the cat and wrap his arms tightly around the animal.

Back inside the brewpub, Brad wiped the dripping cat with the towel that Chago threw him. Hail crashed and bounced in the open door which Carlos hurried to shut. Brad held the shivering animal against him, rubbing Vagabundo's wet ears. The cat's trembling slowed, and he let out one long, desperate howl, followed by another. Carlos stared at him with a disconcerted look. "Easy, buddy," Brad said. A deafening crack exploded above the noise. Vagabundo screeched and leapt to the ground, raking Brad's arm with his claws. Above the hail, Brad heard fizzing and popping. The lights blinked several times and went dark.

Still clutching the wet towel, Brad ran to the brewery, telling himself that somehow, the control panel on the mash tun—where ground malt and water first mixed—would still be lit, that he'd hear the machine's comforting hum. He stared at the darkened panel. *Not a power outage, not now!*

Five minutes later, the hail ceased as quickly as it had come. Icy mounds clogged the storm sewers along the curb. Rivulets of dirty water puddled in the street and parking lot under a steady, gentle rain. Until the electricity came back on, Brad wouldn't be able to assess the damage. The maturation tank test, though, was a wash. Not convinced that the tank was cooling properly, he had filled it with water yesterday to monitor the progress. The lack of power invalidated the test, but now he had other bigger concerns.

"My car's totally trashed," Carlos moaned.

"Mine, too," Chago echoed.

"For now, we need to concentrate on the beer," Brad said. "Ninety minutes without power will start to compromise the brews in progress. The most vulnerable, the pale ale will start to sour that quickly."

"What are we going to do?" Chago asked.

"Not much we can do," Brad said. "Worst case, we dump the brew.

"That's a lot of beer and money down the drain," Chago said in a nervous voice.

"Enough that we could have cops knocking on our door if we pour it into the public water source," Brad added.

"I think the city has more to worry about right now than beer in the sewers," Carlos said.

"Then there's the stout in the second maturation tank that will heat up."

"And the porter in the fermentation tank?" Chago asked.

"It's heating up a lot faster, but both should be okay up to twenty-four hours."

"There's no way of knowing that until they're finished though, right?" Chago said.

"Exactly."

"So we could conceivably end up throwing out thousands of dollars of beer?" Carlos's voice rose in disbelief.

"Conceivably. More importantly, all three yeasts could heat up and die. If we have to propagate more, it'll push back the opening by at least two weeks."

"No way. We can't afford it!"

"You don't have to remind me, Big Guy," Brad said, thinking of his dwindling checking account. "What do you call an old-fashioned yard sprinkler in Spanish?"

"*Un regador.*"

"Come on, Chago. We're going to buy *un regador.*"

Outside, the low, heavy clouds gave the appearance of dusk. They tried a small hardware store, but without electricity, it was closed. The Walmart parking lot was a jumble of cars fighting to exit with no traffic signals working.

"There's got to be someplace we can get a sprinkler and a hose," Brad said in desperation.

"My parents' backyard?"

"Holy crap, Chago, why didn't you say so before?"

"Because I still don't get what you're doing."

A half hour later, they were back at MBC, toting the Rodríguez's garden hose and a green, three-armed sprinkler. Rigged like an upside down piñata, the sprinkler rotated in jerky circles, dripping icy water from the maturation tank onto the five-gallon carboys of yeast that Brad and Chago had positioned near the floor drains.

"I have a whole new appreciation of the term 'American ingenuity'," Carlos said.

With Chago's help, Brad spent the next hours scrapping the pale ale brew and cleaning out the mash tun. He worked to focus on the task at hand and not think about the future. The electricity finally kicked on near seven p.m., brightly illuminating the disaster. "Let's get the yeast back in the walk-in cooler and clean up this mess," Brad sighed. "We're a day and a half behind on the brew schedule and we've tossed five hundred dollars of ingredients this afternoon, not to mention the cost of our labor."

"But we'll still be able to open on time, right?" Carlos sounded like a kid whining for parental assurance.

"Hopefully," Brad replied. "Chago, why don't you take off?"

"Let me help you finish cleaning up."

When they were finally done, and Brad had pushed Chago out the door, Carlos said, "The guy looks like he's going to be worth his weight in gold."

"All ninety pounds of him," Brad added.

"Güero, I'm meeting some guys at a sports bar for dinner. Come with me."

Brad yawned and thought about his bank account. Then he considered the crackerbox apartment. "I could use a good meal and a little distraction."

TWO NIGHTS after the storm, Brad sat in his apartment, watching television and fretting about his financial future. The move to Monterrey had blown through what little money he hadn't sunk into MBC. His own money and MBC's were flowing out faster than draught beer from an open tap. September rent was due in six days. He could still push production along enough that MBC would probably make the September twenty-seventh opening date, but his bank account was another matter. He and Maddy had never missed a mortgage or credit card payment. He hadn't asked his parents for money since his undergrad days. They hadn't been wild about him going off to Mexico. As much as he hated the thought, he was going to have to ask Carlos to float him a loan.

That was the state of things when his phone rang. "Good evening, Brad," Felipe Moss said in a pleasant tone. "Alfredo and I would like to sit down with you and get your thoughts on some things."

The guy was incredible. He had called Carlos shortly after Alfredo had gotten back to Monterrey, to invite Carlos and Brad for a visit to their brewery. "Not a snowflake's chance in hell that we'd go," Carlos told Brad. "I didn't say it like that to Felipe, but I let him know we're not playing ball with him anymore."

"I think it's a snow*ball's* chance in hell, but, yeah, I hear you. I'm not real inclined to talk with the Mosses anymore, either."

And now, Felipe was calling him at home, at ten o'clock at night, three weeks before Huasteca's opening.

"Brad, we need some help," Moss confessed.

"Sorry, I'm not your man."

"I'll pay you fifteen hundred dollars for an initial four-hour meeting."

Fifteen hundred would cover rent and groceries for a month. And totally piss off Carlos. "I'm awfully busy these days."

"Okay, two thousand. We can meet on Sunday so you don't miss any time at MBC."

Brad took a deep breath. "It would be a confidential consultation?"

"If you want it to be, absolutely."

"What time on Sunday?"

CHAPTER SIX

CARLOS WHIPPED the hail-pinged RAV4 into what appeared to be the only empty parking space amid the ocean of vehicles in the Soriana lot. The Mosses had saturated the radio, TV and newspapers with publicity for a week before their debut. With their connections, they had managed to get Huasteca's brews into more locations than Brad had expected, including all the Soriana grocery stores in Monterrey.

Brad's covert Sunday consultation three weeks earlier at Huasteca had uncovered burnt deposits in a kettle, grain residue in the mash tun, yeast residues in supposedly clean hoses. A five-gallon carboy of yeast in the refrigerator which should have been creamy and clear had turned murky brown. The dark deposit at the bottom indicated wort—essentially unfermented beer— and unhealthy bacteria due to poor cleaning. And those were just the quality control issues.

Felipe had wanted Brad to study the recipes, but Alfredo balked. No sharing his secrets with a competitor. At the end of four quick hours, Felipe handed over two-thousand U.S. dollars in cash. The sudden cushion in his bank account had eased Brad's financial situation but not his conscience.

Brad and Carlos entered the mega supermarket on a mission. They worked their way past lines of carts at a dozen registers and threaded through aisles packed with canned goods, crackers and shoppers. On the far end of the wine and beer section, they found the two Huasteca girls. In their minimal tops, short skirts, white cowboy hats and boots, they looked like NFL cheerleaders. Two adolescent boys stood gawking until a mother rounded the corner and yanked them away. The men gathered around clearly didn't care about the mother shaking her head and scowling. Brad reached for a coupon from the glossy-haired brunette wearing too much makeup.

Back at MBC, Brad and Carlos called a taste test at the bar. With one week before their own opening, Chago and Alejandra were working full-time. Noé began his days at noon and wrapped up wait staff training around nine. "Not awful, but nothing special about it," Alejandra said of the first Huasteca sample.

"I've tasted better imports that cost less," Chago added.

"Alejandra," Noé said, "that beer you brewed last Christmas at Santa Cecilia was better than this."

"You created a seasonal brew?" Brad asked.

Noé answered. "Bustamante shot it down, but Alejandra's was better than this by a lot."

"Thanks," Alejandra replied with a noticeable blush.

"By the way, guys," Carlos said, "the Mosses have tried to get all sorts of information from Brad and me. They're old family friends. I tried to play nice, but they hit us below the belt. From here on out, we're close-lipped with the Mosses. Right, Brad?"

"From here on out," Brad said, pouring the remains of the Huasteca beer down the sink.

OPENING NIGHT! They had made it.

In spite of narcos, Mosses and Mother Nature, MBC opened for business precisely at five o'clock on Friday, September twenty-seventh. On Monday, the bank would deposit the second installment of their loan into MBC's account and Brad would breathe a little easier. When he gave up a secure job and headed off to Mexico against his parents' advice, this was the dream that had motivated him: Monterrey Brewing Company with customers enjoying themselves and drinking beers that he had created.

No corporate dictates, no management oversight. This night was worth every risk and hassle he had dealt with.

Adam Levine and Maroon 5 were pumping out "Moves Like Jagger" when tennis buddies Eugenio and Roberto came in the door. Eugenio, curly mop semi-tamed with a generous dose of gel, held his hands high, pulsing to the music. He danced over to Paty, the hostess on duty, and waggled a beckoning finger. Roberto, moving with the ease of Jagger and the grace of a natural athlete, shouted into his phone, "We just walked in. Where are you guys?"

Paty expertly deposited her dancing partner in front of Brad, and Eugenio threw his arms around him like they were childhood friends. "*¡Felicidades, Güero!* This is awesome."

Carlos's acquaintances streamed in all evening sharing stories: classmate with a near-photographic memory, partying his way through college while everybody else poured over books and pulled all-nighters. Unpretentious guy always ready to help a friend in need. Good-looking guy who constantly had a different girl on his arm but never settled down with any one for long. Eligible bachelor from a wealthy family whom most potential mothers-in-law would be overjoyed to spoil for the rest of their lives. And who, according to one storyteller, a few potential fathers-in-law would have fought a tiger to keep *away* from their daughters.

Eugenio and Roberto moved toward the bar where the Ex-A-Tecs had gathered. The door opened and a burly man called out in English, "Son of a gun, Brad Peters. This is something else!" Bob Lockwood grabbed Brad in a bear hug even though they'd only met at the American barbecue weeks ago. Lockwood was the quintessential Texas good old boy businessman right down to his trophy wife Kendra, the blond who had freaked out on Marc Wilkes. The only thing missing was Lockwood's Stetson.

"Congratulations," Kendra said in a breathy Marilyn Monroe voice. A cherry red dress clung to her curves. When she kissed Brad's cheek, he breathed in her perfume and her sexiness.

"Let me take you two over to the bar and get you something to drink," he said.

"Damn shame about the Millers, isn't it?" Bob said as they worked their way between people and tables.

"They've sure kept it quiet," Brad replied. "What do you know?"

"They're back in Atlanta. Paid some god-awful amount. Kidnappers beat the boy up pretty bad. No permanent damage from what I heard, thank God."

"Alejandra," Brad called, "the first drinks are on the house." Both brewers had quickly agreed to tend bar on opening night. Alejandra's experience at Santa Cecilia showed as she easily kept pace with Paco, the full-time bartender. Brad turned to see Carlos laugh and raise a frothy glass at a large table. His connections and personality might prove to be his strongest capital.

Minutes later, Alfredo Moss came through with a drop-dead blonde on his arm in a dress almost as tight as Kendra's. "Carlos!" the woman squealed. Carlos hugged her lightly, brushing his lips against her cheek.

"*Buenas noches, Alfredo*," Brad said, holding out his hand.

"Congratulations," Alfredo replied in English, his eyes scanning the crowd beyond. Unlike at their clandestine meeting, tonight Alfredo was freshly shaved and wore a pressed dress shirt. A recent haircut made him look more businessman than college student.

Behind Alfredo, Felipe Moss walked in the door. He beamed at Brad like a proud father before bestowing a strong hug. "Brad, great to see you. Congratulations."

"¡*Felipe, compadre!*" a voice boomed from the door.

"Hey, Tony, I didn't know you were in town."

"Flew in this afternoon," said the man whose thinning hair made the deep wrinkles in his forehead more pronounced. The two men exchanged a long *abrazo* before Tony pumped Brad's hand. He said in a Texas accent as thick as Kendra's, "You've got to be Brad Peters, the brewer people are talking about. Tony Vargas."

"Tony's a *regiomontano* who defected to Houston years ago," Felipe said. "Owns distributorships in five Texas cities."

"But I still come home to Monterrey every few months," Tony added.

Fresh customers were queuing up behind the men. "We won't monopolize your time," Tony said, taking out his wallet. "Here's my card. Let's stay in touch."

Brad pocketed the card, doubting he'd call a friend of the Mosses. Paty took three couples to their table. Two men moved to the head of the line. "Dinner or drinks?" Brad asked.

"Drinks at the bar," responded the burly one with biceps that looked ready to split the sleeves on his polo shirt.

"Right this way," Brad said, not liking the vibe.

At the bar, he watched Alejandra's face break into a smile directed at the bodybuilder who deigned a faint smile and soft, "*¿Qué onda, Alejandra?*" Obviously, they were more than casual friends. He lifted his chin in a way that reminded Brad of El Míster, and leaned over the bar for Alejandra's puckered lips to meet his.

"Luis, this is Brad who I've been telling you about," she said. The guy raised his chin again, this time like a boxer sizing up his opponent. "Brad, my boyfriend, Luis."

"Nice to meet you, Luis."

"Same here," Luis replied with a shake that said otherwise.

In her two weeks at MBC, Alejandra had worked as hard as Noé and Chago, sometimes more. She was sharp and a quick thinker. How could she fall for a guy who looked like his I.Q. didn't reach the triple digits? Chago had mentioned his girlfriend Graciela, but Alejandra had never said a word about her personal life beyond her Alabama father.

At midnight, Brad was studying the sheet where Paty had been keeping the customer tally. "How you holding up?" he asked her.

"Doing great!"

Brad glanced up as the front door opened again. The paper slid from his fingers. The evening had been fantastic, and now, his worst nightmare was moving toward him. In the dress shirt and trousers, El Míster could pass for an Ex-A-Tec. Two men followed.

Brad watched the narco's eyes sweep over Paty's full figure. El Míster nodded. "Table for five," he rasped.

Paty looked over at the waiting party of four. "It shouldn't be more than a few minutes."

El Míster stared at her, his eyes as hard and blue as Brad remembered them. "It's late. Don't make us wait."

"Have the check delivered to the group in the back corner," Brad instructed. "I'll take them to the bar first." He turned to El Míster. "*Five in your party?*"

"My associates, you, me, Carlos."

Brad recognized one of the "associates." The large man's thick neck spilled out of his dress shirt in spite of the open buttons. A jagged, partially healed scar marked his cheek. The too-short sleeves on his jacket revealed a band of tattoos on each wrist. The other man stood erect, shoulders back, chest out in a cocky, athlete stance—a shorter, darker version of his boss.

"Meeting starts in three minutes," El Míster stated.

"I'll get Carlos," Brad said, flexing his neck.

He found Carlos in the kitchen. "The tamales are sold out and we're … what's wrong?"

"El Míster. He brought *two* goons this time."

The narcos sat with their backs to the wall, studying the crowd. "Have a seat," El Míster ordered. He raised the half-empty glass in front of him, "Beer's good." He drained the contents. His associates did the same. "We're here to inform you that Monterrey Brewing Company's *piso* is ten thousand pesos a month."

Over seven hundred and fifty dollars! *Was this asshole out of his mind?* Brad had no idea how to respond. What had Marc Wilkes said? That the cartels generally didn't bother businesses the size of MBC, not in San

Pedro? But if they did demand *piso*, you didn't have many choices? No doubt the Ex-A-Tecs and Carlos's relatives would agree.

"We don't have that kind of money," Carlos said in a voice as low and calm as the narco's.

The short man rose from his chair. *"¡Cálmate!"* El Míster snapped. The man fell back. "Matagatos doesn't like it when people don't let me finish." He leaned forward and locked Brad and Carlos in his gaze. "Since you've just opened, we're gonna cut you a break, two, in fact. No payment for October. Only half for November. Come December first, the full amount kicks in."

No way! This guy was beyond crazy. "We'll go to the police," Brad blurted.

"Güey"—idiot—"what country do you think you're in?" El Míster barked a harsh laugh and the associates smirked. "Matagatos makes great Molotov cocktails. He could put your nice little brewery out of commission in minutes." The criminal stood. His companions followed. "See you November first."

They headed for the door, the tattooed hulk leading the way through a group of women. El Míster paused in front of a petite brunette and leered down at the exposed cleavage. The woman's mouth dropped. She and her friends turned and began pushing their way toward the bar. Brad watched until the narcos were out the door. Was Matagatos—the Killer of Cats—who never said a word, really capable of destroying MBC with a single homemade bomb?

He turned to Carlos. "We're fucked."

CHAPTER SEVEN

IN THE FOUR weeks since MBC's opening, El Míster's threats had lurked in the background of every interaction between Brad and Carlos.

"This is insane. There's no way we'll survive. I'll call the police myself. You don't have to get involved," Brad had told Carlos.

"Do that and we're history."

"MBC or our friendship?"

"Both."

Brad didn't get the whole *inseguridad* business—the extortions, protection payments, kidnappings, petty crime to million-dollar drug deals. Everybody claimed to hate "the insecurity." Nobody had a clue how to stop it. Kendra Lockwood had been blunt and loud with Marc Wilkes, but most Mexicans quietly agreed that the military patrols were mostly window dressing. But if they were pulled off the streets?

Brad hadn't slept well all week, dreaming about Maddy one night and El Míster the next. In one dream, Alfredo Moss and Carlos joined forces with Felipe Moss and Tony Vargas as their bodyguards. Everybody was mad at Brad for his deceitfulness and would never trust him again. The dreams morphed between Monterrey and Denver and some non-existent place.

After the last of the staff left on opening night, Brad had wondered aloud to Carlos how they were going to handle the blackmail. "Pay whatever they demand," Carlos snapped.

"But—"

"But nothing. We don't have a choice."

In two days, they'd make the November first payment. Maybe then Brad could sleep. He unlocked the door to his brewery and stepped into the early morning silence. He was an engineer, trained to be analytical, methodical, organized. In his four months at MBC, he had developed solid recipes, protocols and routines. Each morning when he walked through the door into this brewery with its fifteen-foot high ceiling, he closed his eyes and inhaled the rich aromas of hops and fermenting wort, the smells he loved. At MBC, the scents of recent construction, fresh paint and new lumber, tinged the mix. This was the smell of *his* brewery. He wasn't religious, but those first minutes each morning felt as close to holy as anything he'd ever experienced.

At eight o'clock, he was reviewing the wheat recipe. If everything went well, they'd have the brew in the fermenter by six. The door opened to a cheerful, "*¡Buenos días, Ingeniero!*"

"Good morning, yourself," Brad said, returning Chago's handshake and smile. He'd given up trying to get his assistant to drop the Engineer title. The skinny guy reminded him of a gangly puppy loping gleefully into adulthood.

Alejandra reported in next and, after a trip to her locker, returned wearing an MBC shirt and hairnet. Safety glasses hung from her neck. "Roll up your sleeves, guys," Brad said, "and start milling the malt. I'll be over in a few minutes."

"You got it," Chago said, making a show of turning up the sleeves on his t-shirt.

With a few notations, Brad wrapped up his review and went to help his brewers. He found Chago making his way to the mill with a fifty-pound malt bag thrown on his shoulder. Alejandra shrugged. "I told him to use the dolly."

"Guys'll be guys. Let him have fun," Brad said.

"Are you two free on Sunday?" Alejandra asked. "My roommates are having a party."

"Any special reason?" Chago grunted.

"My birthday. Bring Graciela."

Chago reached the mill and slid the bag to the floor. "Sure thing."

A party in the company of Luis sounded about as fun to Brad as standing in a hail storm. "I can't make it, but take a couple of mini kegs with you on Friday."

In the sunlight and the daily reality of his brewery, Brad felt foolish—asinine—for letting a few ridiculous dreams steal his sleep.

JUST AFTER ten p.m. on November first, the door swung open and Brad's stomach clenched. El Míster, thumbs hooked in the pockets of his jeans, sauntered in trailed by his "associates." A chin lift and, "*Feliz Día de los Muertos.*" Happy Day of the Dead.

Brad hurried over to Paty. "Get Carlos."

With luck, they'd simply hand over the five thousand pesos and be rid of the thugs for a month. El Míster scanned the room. His head moved to the rhythm as Beyoncé warned all men over the speakers that if they liked it, they should put a ring on it.

"We'll be in the bar," El Míster said, leading the way. Brad fell in behind the associates, his stomach churning. The narcos looked side to side, inspecting the crowd. The thick-necked one had dowsed himself in cheap cologne. "*Tres estouts,*" El Míster demanded.

"*Buenas noches,*" Carlos said, coming from the kitchen, no trace of a smile. El Míster lifted his chin again. The associates' eyes took in the room. El Míster's darker clone—Matagatos?—pulled his lips into something that didn't quite reach the level of a smile. Brad rubbed his sweaty palms on his pants.

El Míster lifted the stout that Paco had poured him. He shot Brad and Carlos a hard, blue stare. "*¡Salud!*" Cheers. He downed half the beer then nodded to his men. Each chugged his drink. El Míster had positioned himself against a wall with the associates flanking him, all the while scouting the crowd. He finished off the beer and growled, "The money?"

Brad watched Carlos pull out his wallet and the cash. El Míster thumbed the five one-thousand peso bills with the cool ease of a banker, nodded and stuffed them in his own wallet. "See you December first. Don't forget, ten thousand."

"DAMN, YOU'RE smooth, Míster," Labrador crowed. Every time Nacho looked in the rearview mirror, the giant fool was there taking up half the back seat. He must have bathed in cologne. It was a wonder he didn't choke on the smell. "He was good, huh, Matagatos?"

Nacho cut his eyes from the road to Neto in the front passenger seat. "El Míster's always good," Neto mumbled to the window.

Nacho knew Labrador's brown-nosing shit for what it was, but he wasn't going to let Neto's hard feelings drag him down.

"I just follow instructions." Those five thousand-peso bills felt real comfortable in his wallet. Gave him a feeling of power. God-damn shame he was going to have to hand them over to Bala.

BRAD PULLED up at the gated entrance to the twelve-story apartment building and announced that he was invited to the Wilkes's Sunday afternoon party. He probably would have enjoyed Alejandra's party if Luis weren't there, but he had accepted the Wilkes's invitation first. A serious-looking guard buzzed the residence. After struggling with the pronunciation of the guest's name, he confirmed that this American, like the others, was indeed expected. Brad waited as the gate lifted. In the newer areas of San Pedro, high-security, skyscraper apartment complexes were going up faster than Lego cities, another trend brought on by *la inseguridad*.

The elevator opened at the eighth-floor landing where a bright painting of red, yellow and green birds covered half the wall. Below it, a large vase filled with artificial flowers repeated the color scheme. Two months had passed since Jeff Miller's kidnapping. A week later Brad had seen Marc Wilkes, who responded to his inquiries about the Millers the way he had to Kendra's questions at the barbecue. Brad hadn't pressed the issue.

He rang the bell at apartment 8C, and Jessica Wilkes opened the door wearing a colorful sundress that made Brad wonder if she was trying to blend in with the landing décor. He held out a mini keg. "Sorry, I'm not much of a cook."

"Ah, one thing Marc and I can't make." She led him into the living room where the air-conditioning hummed. Through the sliding glass door, Marc waved from the balcony. He stood between a smoking grill and a heavyset, older American in a Hawaiian shirt and shorts. The man smiled and nodded at Brad. The Sierra Madre Mountains towered in the background.

"Have you met Beth and Emily from the International School?" Jessica asked.

"Beth Richards," said the older woman. Her short hairstyle and handshake indicated a woman who meant business. She nodded toward the man beside Marc. "My husband, Fred." The man beckoned her outside. "Excuse me," she said.

"We haven't had the pleasure yet," said the other woman extending her hand. "Emily Whitcomb." Masses of tight brown curls fell over her shoulders. Brad pegged her age at twenty-five.

"Brad Peters," he replied. Her soft, warm hand seemed to invite his to get comfortable and stay a while.

"Mom!" wailed a tiny voice from a hallway.

"Coming, Tiger," Jessica called.

"So what do you do at Internacional?" Brad asked, using the Spanish name he had heard for the pricey private school.

"I'm here for one year teaching math." She brushed back a strand of curls. Her sleeveless white top highlighted the tanned and well-defined muscles of her arms.

She seated herself on the sofa, and Brad settled into an armchair. "We must have come about the same time."

"I got here July 24. I've actually been to MBC a couple of times. Jessica tells me you're from Denver."

"The Mile High City."

She lifted her margarita glass from the coffee table. "Go Broncos!"

"You're a fan?"

"Semi-hard core."

"How did that happen?"

"Growing up in Wyoming, I loved everything about the outdoors and sports. The Broncos are my dad's team."

"And your favorite team is?"

"I'm more into doing sports than watching. During the winter, I'm on the slopes every chance I get."

"Skier?"

"Boarder, dude."

"So you shred those black diamonds."

"The ones with fresh powder and bumps are my favorite. How about you?" she asked before taking a sip of the margarita.

"On a board, I can rip almost any bunny hill in Colorado."

She snorted and grabbed a napkin. "Sorry. I don't do dainty very well."

"I don't know about that," Brad said, realizing it had been a long time since he'd flirted with a woman.

Emily's laugh revealed perfect teeth as white as her top. "How are you on skis?"

"I can make it down a blue slope intact most of the time."

She leaned toward him. Her perfume was subtle, one he could still like at the end of a date. "Gosh, you're making me homesick," she said.

He grinned, taking in her hazel eyes. The doorbell rang followed by Tanner shouting, "I'll get it!" When the six-year-old bounced into the living room with the Lockwoods and another couple, the group on the balcony moved inside.

Conversations about potlucks, the weather and Sunday football in the States swirled around Brad the rest of the afternoon. He was fairly certain that in another year he would only remember one thing about this party. By the end of the evening, he had learned that Emily was twenty-six, had been a swimmer all through college, had a weakness for Oreos and swore that doing calculus had to be easier than making beer. He also had her phone number and a date for Thursday night.

"I NEVER thought of Applebee's as a romantic place until now," Emily said, tucking brown curls behind her ear. With a mouthful of cheese burger, Brad nodded. "I miss the States so much," she added. "You couldn't have picked a better place." She kept her eyes on his as she bit into her burger.

She made eating look sexy, made him want to kiss those puffy lips. He wasn't ready for a relationship, didn't want or have time for one. But, crap, he was twenty-seven and missed sex. "You want to hear some really romantic talk?"

Emily chewed and nodded.

"McDonald's, Burger King, Wendy's, Walmart, Costco."

"You're driving me crazy!"

"I tend to have that effect on women."

"I didn't have you pegged as a player."

"Excluding blind dates arranged by my business partner, this is my second date post-divorce."

"So, you'd probably rather discuss the Broncos or how great these burgers taste."

"You're a very perceptive woman."

The girl-next-door smile she flashed from a face that bore hardly any makeup made him want to kiss her even more. They talked about life as ex-pats, their upcoming trips home at Christmas, family, friends, sports and American politics. Dinner and drinks stretched into three hours and an invitation to come up to Emily's apartment for coffee. The evening ended only when Emily's roommate barged in and caught them making out like middle schoolers on the living room sofa. Jenn, the roommate, dashed by muttering, "Sorry, Em." It had been a good thing, her interrupting. He shouldn't have let things go as far as they had.

The next morning, Brad was in the brewery reviewing inventory when he heard the door open and a bright, "Good morning!"

"Morning, Alejandra."

Her straight black hair, usually pulled back, hung loose and still damp. Suddenly the memory of Maddy with wet hair hit Brad so intensely he could practically feel his fingers running through the silky strands. The feel of his hands in Emily's hair last night, even though the curls were something new, had stirred all sorts of emotions he had suppressed for months. From the night Maddy walked out, he hadn't thought seriously about any woman in a romantic way. He had focused on his work and his MBA classes. Last night, he experienced emotions and desires he hadn't felt in a long, long time.

Alejandra was back, tugging a hairnet over her head. A sleeve on her t-shirt shifted, revealing a discolored bruise on the underside of her arm.

"Jeez, what ran into you?"

"What do you mean?" She hurriedly pulled a long-sleeved MBC shirt from her bag.

"Your arm."

Her eyes changed, windows slamming shut. She tucked her arm against her ribs. "I fell on the stairs at home."

"From the looks of those bruises, it must have been pretty serious."

"It's nothing. What do you want me to start with?" she asked, slipping on the long-sleeved shirt.

"Want to inventory the malt?"

"Sure."

He stared at the clipboard. Half the time, he didn't know what he'd worn the day before, let alone what anyone else had on. Yet, he had noticed Alejandra wearing long sleeves a lot lately. Last Friday, when Chago rolled up his t-shirt sleeves, she'd kept her arms covered all day. Several times that afternoon she had mopped perspiration from her forehead but she never took off the shirt or exposed her arms.

Falling on the stairs was bullshit.

CHAPTER EIGHT

THE WHITE of Roberto's shorts and shirt was intense even through Brad's sunglasses. "The secret to tennis," Roberto said, dropping his voice in a conspiratorial tone, "is your mental game. One: stay totally focused. Two: be in the right place at the right time. Three: be prepared."

Brad hadn't had any coaching since high school, but if he was going to keep playing with Carlos and his friends, he had to get his game to the next level. Lessons with the star player seemed like the way to get there. Roberto crouched, leaned onto the balls of his feet and bounced on his toes. "So, overhead shots at the net?"

"That's one of my weaknesses, for sure."

"Okay, you know where to be and the type of shot to expect. All you have to do is stay focused. Legs apart—not too far out. Racket in front of your body. Blow out a breath. Relax your arms. That's it. You comfortable?"

"Yeah."

"Bounce a little," Roberto said, demonstrating. "Too many players see a clean shot and think 'no-brainer'. They get over-confident, and then blow it. Good players stay calm and relaxed. They're confident but realistic, aware of every step they make. They've thought through and practiced everything until it's all automatic. They're focused at every second.

"I'm going to serve balls that just clear the net. You're back in ready position. Run forward, raise your racket, lob it back. Can you see that in your head?" Brad nodded. "You going to get the ball back over the net?"

"Yeah."

"Say it *con ganas*, with confidence!"

"YES!"

"*¡Eso!*" Roberto continued, raising his voice and speaking faster. "You twist your body, rotate your hips. You don't just hit that ball. You *control* it. You *attack* it!"

"Yes, I do!"

"Let me hear you say it: ¡A*taque!*"

"*¡Ataque!*"

"Louder!"

"*¡ATAQUE!*"

Roberto's first serve was a freebie that Brad slammed back. He'd barely stepped away when the next ball came at him, inches above the net. He swung and nipped it with the edge of the racket, sending it into the net.

"Stay focused. Be prepared," Roberto said, pulling another ball from his pocket and bouncing it on his racket.

The gesture and Roberto's tone goaded Brad. He crouched, focused and ready. The ball whizzed over the net to his right. He pounced and returned it, flying left. Roberto easily hit it back. "What's the key word?"

"*¡ATAQUE!*"

Adrenaline was kicking in. Brad pounced and slammed the next ball back. Roberto shot forward and sent it flying. Brad hit it with an easy backhand shot that Roberto lobbed far out of Brad's reach. "Way to go, Güero," he said with a quick grin.

An hour later, with balls littering the court, Eugenio's voice broke Brad's concentration. "General, no fair coaching the opposition." Brad turned to see Carlos in a Rocky's cap and Eugenio, a sweatband pushed back to keep the curls out of his face. "So, Roberto's got you doing the *¡ataque!* drill," Eugenio continued.

Brad nodded. "You recognize it?"

"Boring as hell after a couple of hours, but it really improved my game."

"Ready to play an actual match?" Roberto asked.

Brad twirled his racket with the cocky confidence of Rafael Nadal. "Game on!"

"HEY, GÜERO, how's it going?" Carlos asked from a corner booth in the back of MBC's dining room.

"*¡Ataque!*" Brad said, plunking a plate of steak tacos on the table.

"Very funny." A partially eaten sandwich and a pile of yellow papers from Carlos's ever-present notepad lay on the table. "You hear that your cat left a rat outside the kitchen door this morning, a present for you, apparently?"

"He's not *my* cat."

"He thinks he is."

Brad rolled his eyes and slid into the seat opposite Carlos. "You give Vagabundo too much credit. The way I heard the story, it was just a field mouse. So how did the meeting with the accountant go?"

"Terrific. That malt order you wanted to double, we can swing it."

Brad held up a hand to high five. "Any chance we can do that with other orders?"

Carlos shook his head. "Not for a couple of months, at least. Our cash flow is razor skinny."

"Razor *thin?*"

"That, too. Bottom line, sales are twenty percent above our highest initial projections, we can double your order and still make December *piso.*"

"I've been thinking. Do you know if they're hitting up Santa Cecilia or Huasteca?"

Carlos rubbed his stubbled chin. "Can't say. Whether they are or aren't isn't going to change anything for us."

"I don't like living in ignorance and fear. We can at least take some control over our ignorance."

"*Sicosis.* That's the name they give to what you're talking about. The psychological crap that *la inseguridad* causes, the way it starts to mess with your head over time."

"It really sucks," Brad said, once more recalling his conversation with Marc Wilkes at the barbecue. He motioned Noé Padilla over from the bar. "Were you ever aware of the cartels charging Patricio Bustamante *piso*?

Noé scratched his head. "Not as far as I know. Is that what those three creepy guys were doing here a few weeks ago?"

"It's probably better for you to know," Brad said, "in case they come when Carlos and I are both out."

"You're right, Güero," Carlos said. "In the future, we'll leave the ten thousand pesos in the safe a day in advance."

Noé eyes widened. "Ten thousand?"

"Every month," Brad said.

"Jesus," Noé said under his breath.

Brad managed two bites of his taco before Alejandra interrupted with her purse on one shoulder. Her hair, free of the net, was still pulled back. She had taken off her MBC shirt and wore a short-sleeved t-shirt. Brad could still see a faint bruise on her arm.

"I'm sorry, Brad, but Luis needs a ride to pick up his truck from the shop."

"Now?"

"Patience isn't one of his strong points. I'll work late and make up the time."

"Tell Luis I said hi, and don't worry about the time."

As soon as she was out the door, Paco came over. "Last Thursday, when she got off work, Luis came in and said they were staying for a drink. She looked tired as hell and didn't say much. Twenty minutes later, after he'd downed three beers, I cut him off. He was a real snot about it. I don't get what she sees in him."

"That makes two of us," Brad replied.

WITH PACO off for the evening, Brad stuck around under the pretense of helping Alejandra behind the bar if things got too busy. Emily had algebra tests to grade, and he didn't want to face going home to the tiny apartment or a solitary supper. When nobody was in earshot, he casually asked, "That bruise all cleared up?"

Alejandra's hand flew to her thigh. "How did you know?"

"The one on your arm. You know, from falling on the stairs."

She jerked her hand to her forearm. "Oh, um, it's fine."

As a liar, she was hopeless. Her large, naïve eyes were as readable as a neon sign. "It's not my business," Brad said, "but the biggest mistake I've made in my life, was ignoring the red flags before I married my ex-wife. I could have saved both of us a lot of grief and money."

"One wheat and two stouts," a waiter called out, slapping his serving tray on the bar. Alejandra jumped to fill the order.

Brad looked out in the dining room and spotted Alfredo Moss come in the front door. He sucked in a breath. He had to keep Alfredo and Carlos apart. Without his father or his usually cocky walk, Alfredo looked like any other young professional in San Pedro.

Alfredo offered a handshake. "Can we talk? In private?"

Brad tilted his head toward the brewery. Even with the low light in the long shadow of the kettle, Alfredo's face looked haggard and drawn. "What's up?" Brad asked. He wouldn't mind seeing Alfredo Moss squirm a little.

Alfredo shrugged and his eyes drifted toward the ceiling. He jammed his hands into the pockets of his jeans. "I need your help."

"Sorry."

"Soriana called this afternoon. If sales don't improve in the next two weeks, they're dropping Huasteca."

Brad had no intention of getting any more tangled in the Mosses' problems.

"I admit I'm in over my head," Alfredo pleaded.

"Carlos would go ballistic."

"But my father." The look in Alfredo's twenty-three-year-old eyes was pure desperation. "I'll get him to pay whatever you ask."

Brad blew out a long sigh and ran a hand along his chin. Neither Alfredo's panic, nor the money the Mosses stood to lose, mattered to him. But how Monterrey's discriminating beer consumers viewed craft beer could make or break his own future. "A hundred dollars an hour and we only meet on Sundays."

"A hundred and twenty, and no one will ever know," Alfredo offered.

Brad should have felt some pity, but he didn't. "And one more condition neither of us can control: Carlos Echeverría's permission. Without that, no deal."

Stress crept back into Alfredo's face. "He'll never agree."

"I'll take care of that," Brad said. "We'll need to start from scratch. No holding back information. Email me your recipes tonight—not tomorrow. I'll need to oversee several brews at every step to understand what's happening. Talk to Felipe about dumping the excess inventory."

"Can't we just sell it off cheap and take the loss?"

"No way. A first-time bad beer, no matter how cheap, practically guarantees no second chance."

The minute Alfredo was out the door, Brad headed for the office. He knocked on the open door and took a deep breath. "Got a minute, Big Guy?"

Before Brad could finish, Carlos raked a hand through his hair and exploded. "Hell, you might as well go to work for Huasteca!"

"Chill for a minute. Part of my advice will be for them to find themselves a full-time brewer who knows what he's doing."

Carlos studied Brad. "The Mosses have done a one-eighty toward you. You've been helping them all along, haven't you?"

"Only one time."

"Jesus H. Christ!"

"They came begging a month before Huasteca opened. They were a mess. Obviously, I didn't turn them around."

Carlos narrowed his eyes and locked his arms tightly across his chest as Brad continued. "It was the end of August. I couldn't cover my September rent."

"Why didn't you come to me? I would have loaned you the money. Hell, I would have *given* you the money."

"Look, I screwed up. I should have been honest. For what it's worth, I've felt like shit about it."

"Which is exactly how you should feel. While you're on a roll, what else don't I know?"

"Nothing. That's it."

"Why should I believe you?" Carlos's cheeks had turned a mottled red.

"Crap, Carlos. I didn't have to tell you. I'm being up front." Carlos blinked rapidly but didn't say anything. "You want me to call and tell him no deal? I will."

"If I say 'no' and you get mad and leave, that'll be the end of MBC. I don't really have a choice, do I?"

"Big Guy, if they fail, it's going to give craft brewing a major black eye in Monterrey. All I'm going to do is help him tweak his recipes and walk him through brewing procedures. Think of it as pulling a drowning man—your father's *compadre*—into a life boat. He's going to have to row himself to shore and figure out what to do from there. Someday, we may be the ones needing their help."

"Do whatever you think you have to do," Carlos said, storming out the door.

"They're paying a hundred twenty an hour. I'll put half into MBC's cash flow."

Carlos pivoted, his mouth hanging open. "I'm still not convinced." He took a deep breath and said in a resigned voice. "But after we pay the ten thousand we owe in *piso* in a few days, December's going to be a hell of a tight month."

"We don't *owe* anything. It's pure extortion."

"I'M NOT able to answer the phone now but leave a message, and I'll return your call," the voice recording said in the pissy cadence of rich Mexicans.

Echeverría and Peters probably spent almost as much as the *patrones* on a night out with their women. Don't think it hadn't occurred to Nacho to tack a little extra on their *piso*. Hell, he knew a government health inspector who issued certificates to restaurants where he wouldn't dare eat. The guy was always pulling out wads of cash—fifty-, one-hundred-peso bills. The government let employees get away with all sorts of crap. But El Cártel didn't. Just ask Labrador.

Nacho looked at the paper in front of him and punched the numbers into his phone. He couldn't waste time, not today. It was his first full collection from MBC and his first visit during the day. The gringo picked up on the third ring. "*Eh, Peters.*" He made his voice extra hoarse. "I'll be there in fifteen minutes. Have the money waiting."

Echeverría and Peters were the easiest marks Nacho had ever dealt with. San Pedro collections were a piece of cake. Of course, he'd worked his butt off to get there. When he started with the mom and pop businesses in Guadalupe, his biggest collection was five hundred pesos. He had to work most of a goddamned day to bring in what he did with a single visit to MBC. The worst part back then was dealing with the assholes who didn't pay on time.

In the beginning, he and Neto would go in, wait around until there weren't any customers. That didn't take more than a few minutes with Neto standing at the door like a bodyguard. On the first offense, Nacho would tell the idiots he wasn't running a fucking charity and that he'd be back in an hour. He and Neto, or later Labrador, would return in exactly an hour. If the suckers still didn't have the money, or if they messed up a second time, Nacho would ball his right hand into a tight fist and drive the message home. That was when he'd started carrying the brass knuckles. The violence had never bothered him. What he hated was dealing with losers and working his ass off for lousy pay. Kill a motherfucker, rough him up too much and the police got involved—not that he cared, but it brought unwanted attention and got him in trouble with the *patrones*.

He had worked his *culo* off to make it this far. And he had every intention of moving on to much bigger things. He stuffed the phone in his pocket. "*¡Vámonos!*" he yelled to Neto as he stalked out to the car.

CHAPTER NINE

"BRAD PETERS! What up, dawg?"

Mike Rutledge had bulked up considerably in the decade since his high school linebacker days. He came at Brad like a bear.

"Good to see you, man," Brad said once he had his breath back. Dance music blared over the sound system. The community room in the Denver condo complex was filled with Christmas decorations and partiers, almost all of them his friends or acquaintances. "There must be sixty people here."

"Yeah," Mike grinned. "I don't know what happened. When I checked Facebook this afternoon, there were only forty-two coming."

"We slackers are hopeless." Brad wasn't about to get into the real reason he hadn't RSVPed.

Behind them, a familiar foghorn intoned, "Brad the Brewer!" He swung around and met Eric Villarreal's high five just as Scott punched his arm.

"How's it going down 'Me-hee-co' way? Do they even have internet down there?" Scott said from behind a goatee he hadn't had the last time Brad saw him.

"Hey, dude!" Brad said, hugging his old friend. Two minutes at the party and it was like old times.

"Beer's at the bar, men," Mike said, herding them toward the kitchen counter where he filled flimsy plastic cups from a keg.

"So, Brad," Eric said, moving closer and lowering his voice, "have you talked to Maddy yet?"

"And if you haven't, are you going to?" Scott asked.

"I'm not going out of my way to find her," Brad said. *Damn Maddy!*

Two hours ago, when he'd scrolled through the Facebook list of people going, her name hadn't been on it.

"You should check her out at least," Scott said. "We hardly see her anymore. Ever since the *5280* magazine article and the divor—I mean, since you left, she's kind of dropped us." Brad's stomach cramped. The article about her law firm and the photo with her front and center among the partners was his wake-up call the marriage was disintegrating. She looked like she belonged with those people. He didn't fit into the picture.

"Dude," Mike said to Scott, "we're not good enough for her anymore."

"She looks damn good, I'll say that for her," Scott answered.

"She looks out of our league," Eric added. "Have you seen the BMW she drives now?"

"Sweet," Mike said.

None of it surprised Brad. The night she walked out, she had declared the marriage a mistake. "We're just too different. You don't get my level of ambition and how far I intend to go." She made it sound like an accusation and indictment all in one, as though he couldn't understand ambition.

He had no intention of finding her. In fact, he was going to do his damned best to avoid her. Acquaintances paraded by, asking about his brewery and life in far-flung, exotic Monterrey and how were the beaches there? By the end of the second plastic cup, he didn't care that the beer was bland or that Maddy was somewhere nearby. He was having a damn good time. Less than two and a half years and he'd be back in Denver with his own brewpub. No wonder Carlos had so much fun as the center of attention every night. Brew by day, party by night.

Then he saw her. It felt like a lame beer commercial—guy partying with macho friends, gorgeous blond emerges from the crowd, moving toward him in long, leggy strides, never taking her eyes off his. He gritted his teeth and flashed back to all the negative crap and drama she had caused in his life. A new song started, louder than the last.

"Hi, Brad."

She hadn't used her sensuous voice on him in ages and definitely not during the last year of their marriage. It sounded deeper, more mature, than when he had first heard it in their sophomore year at CU. He was aware of the guys waiting to see how the encounter would play out.

"Hey," he said. She had let her hair grow since the last time he'd seen her with the short, severe cut. Nothing like the old Maddy, which was the whole point, he assumed. She was thinner, or maybe it was the black dress and the leather jacket. She'd always thought her legs were her strongest asset, and he had agreed. The short dress and the high heels showed them off to maximum effect.

"You have a minute?" she asked.

"I guess." He wasn't sure why he said it. Maybe the volume on the music would keep the conversation short.

"Let's go outside where it's quieter," she said, tilting her head toward the patio on the other side of the glass doors. And like a well-trained dog, he followed.

The clubhouse surrounded the patio on three sides, effectively blocking the winter wind. The snow had been shoveled. "How's Abby?" he asked. He'd never paid attention to cats before Maddy brought home the playful kitten. Within a week, Abby ruled the house from the cat condo that Brad had gone out and bought to keep her from shredding the sofa. He thought of Vagabundo and wondered if he was finding enough to eat.

"Abigail has grown into a lazy cat whose greatest pleasure is lying on top of the heating vent in winter."

"You can't blame her."

"How are you doing in Monterrey?" Maddy wore a new perfume, her post-marriage scent. Scott was right about the outward trappings being more impressive than ever.

"Can't brew beer fast enough. What about you?"

"I wish I had five more hours in every day. I got a promotion a couple months ago, did you know? I'm dealing almost exclusively in family law."

"That's a change."

"Yes. You could say the divorce got me started. One of the most frequent comments I hear now is how I really *get* what my clients are going through."

Still the smart, insecure girl she'd been at twenty, the impressionable first generation of her family to go to college. Seven years later, she was the newest member in a large law firm where the spouses of her peers were jetting across the world on business trips or completing medical residencies. She'd never cared about brewing, didn't even drink beer. A husband who couldn't attend evening social functions because he was working the graveyard shift at Coors wasn't exactly a career asset.

She'd always had a knack for making the most of the opportunities that came her way. Was it really surprising that she had used their divorce as her next step up? He was tempted to ask how her deadbeat dad and dysfunctional family were doing.

He was relieved when her cell rang. She wrinkled her brow the way she used to when he said something that ticked her off. She reached inside the expensive jacket. "Sorry, it's a client who's going through a really tough time. I've got to answer. See you inside." She turned and paced to the end of the patio just as a gust of wind kicked up some dead leaves. He had never understood how the so-called delicate sex could tolerate bare legs in sub-freezing temperatures.

"Christ, Jessica, you are *so* needy," she muttered. "But you're the one paying after-hours rates." She tapped the phone on and put it to her ear. "Hi, Jess. Everything okay?"

Brad moved into the shadows, listening to the take-charge voice that he knew so well. Early on, it had impressed him. By the end, it had become shrill and irritating. She stood on the edge of the patio, her back to him. "Calm down, Jessica. People can get weird during the holidays. Remember what I told you. If you want to keep the house in Denver, use the Aspen cabin as leverage."

For a minute, she said nothing, then spoke like a mother to a stubborn child. "Jess, listen to me. I want you to understand this. It's going to be important when we go to court. Are you listening?" Inside, a catchy song started up. "You know Colorado is a no-fault state. It doesn't matter that you cheated on him. He cheated on you, too. He's been a bastard and we're going to get every cent we can from him."

Brad turned toward the lights and the music. Mike stood beside a bearded ski-bum type, waving him back inside. "I know you don't want to hear this, but you may just have to let Geoff take the dogs." Another silence. "Okay, Jessica, I get that they're like family, but Chloe is five years old. You have to decide which is more important to you: the dogs or full custody." Brad slid the heavy glass door open and music poured out into the cold night.

"Brad!" Mike shouted over the music. "Come meet Kris. He's a homebrewer with a question about dry hopping."

Eric intercepted Brad on his way through the crowd. "How'd it go out there?"

"She says the cat's fat and spoiled," Brad said with a shrug before sticking out his hand. "Hi, Kris, what can I do for you?"

She left without saying goodbye, which was fine with Brad. The Maddy he fell in love with and married had disappeared long ago. He'd had enough of the party. He said his goodbyes and crunched through the snowy parking lot. The frigid air smelled of wood smoke and tickled his nostrils. It was all so familiar—the smells, the bracing cold. The friends and the conversations were the same as ever, but he had changed, moved beyond his old life. He was ready to get back to Monterrey.

As he reached to open the car door, his phone pinged. He pulled it out and glanced at the screen. His hand began to shake so much he nearly dropped the phone in the dirty snow. He stared at the fresh text from Carlos. "Felipe Moss killed in car crash."

CHAPTER TEN

February 2013

BRAD ROUTINELY hefted fifty-pound bags of malt. Thanks to Roberto's weekly lessons, he was holding his own in the Saturday tennis matches. A two-hour hike on the mountain trails in Chipinque Nature Park should have been easy, but Emily Whitcomb made hiking an extreme sport. His heart was thumping at cardio levels it hadn't reached in a long time.

Covered in dust and sweat on a warm winter afternoon, they drove down the mountain with the AC cranked up, laughing like teenagers. "This makes me so miss the mountains around Jackson," Emily said. "The Sierra Madres are definitely not the Rockies."

"They're beautiful in their own way," Brad replied. "If Monterrey didn't have mountains, then I'd have a hard time."

At his place they fell through the door wrapped around each other. Unlike Maddy, Emily didn't care if the bed wasn't made. She dropped into the mess of sheets and nuzzled beside him. She nibbled his ear and planted kisses, working her way around his neck and face. By the time she crawled on top of him and thrust her tongue into his mouth, there was only one thing on his mind, and it wasn't the unmade bed.

When he woke, Emily slept beside him, naked and beautiful. He studied her toned body. She viewed any physical activity as a competitive sport. Sex with her was unlike anything he'd ever experienced with Maddy. Of course, at nineteen, sex, even when it wasn't great, still had a forbidden appeal. Together he and Maddy had explored and grown. Emily was twenty-six and a veteran of two relationships. Comparisons weren't fair, Brad told himself. And yet, except for Emily's two weeks in

Jackson at Christmas, they'd been having sex for twelve weeks, and it just kept getting better. He hadn't realized how much he missed sex until Emily reminded him. Both were looking for some good times and a little company, neither for commitment. He rested his hand lightly against her thigh. With her eyes closed, she smiled faintly and put a hand on his chest. This kind of a relationship he could handle.

AFTER MADDY Left and the headaches started, Brad finally broke down and went to a doctor who advised stress management classes and counseling. He ignored the doctor and the advice. Peters men didn't do get-in-touch-with-your-body breathing exercises or talk to strangers about their feelings.

A month later, Brad was in the passenger seat when Grandpa Peters, driving twenty miles an hour, crashed his car into a fire hydrant. The autopsy determined that the heart attack hit so fast, Grandpa probably never realized it. He hadn't made a sound or shown any reaction. The EMTs had to pry his hands from the steering wheel. After the funeral, there were mornings when Brad walked out of Coors with his shoulders as tight as a twist-off bottle cap. One night, his supervisor, asked, "Neck hurting you?"

"How'd you know?"

"Lately you've been turning your body instead of your head, the way old men do. You might want to get that checked out."

The first counselor swore Brad could solve ninety-eight percent of his problems with a combination of Chinese cupping, acupuncture and kundalini yoga and, by the way, he taught kundalini classes three nights a week. Brad left the appointment with his shoulders tighter than when he went in. His second counseling attempt a month later went better. Tom encouraged regular exercise, whatever Brad enjoyed. If and when Brad wanted breathing exercises, he could give some suggestions. It took several months of weekly massage to unknot Brad's neck and shoulders. Meanwhile, at sessions with Tom, he unknotted his feelings about Maddy, the divorce, Grandpa Peters' death and what he himself wanted out of life.

Now he stood in his brewery beside the malt bags, filling his lungs with air, letting it settle in his stomach before exhaling. He had needed the down time at Christmas. What he hadn't anticipated was missing Monterrey. He returned even more seriously committed. This was his reality now.

He opened his eyes, ready for the day and the meeting with Tony Vargas. The distributor hadn't said much when he called on Friday, only that he had a business proposal. Brad couldn't help thinking it had something to do with Alfredo Moss and Huasteca. Tony, who dropped into town every couple months, had stopped by MBC twice since opening night. Brad had come to respect the man who knew so much and so many people.

With Carlos's reluctant permission, Brad had provided some consulting for the Mosses. He emailed Alfredo from Denver as soon as he heard the news. Felipe and Alfredo's mother had been driving back to Monterrey after a Christmas shopping trip in Laredo, Texas. The driver of an oncoming car fell asleep, crossed the center stripe and hit their SUV head on. Mrs. Moss walked away from the accident. Like Grandpa, Felipe died instantly. Brad hadn't had any contact with Alfredo since. From what he'd heard, Alfredo wasn't handling his father's death or Huasteca well.

A familiar voice wishing him a good morning jolted Brad back to the present. When had Alejandra started to sound so sad?

"Hey, you're in awfully early."

"Stout brew today?" Her tone was all business.

"You got it."

"Okay if I get started?"

"Sure. I'll help you get the malt in the mill."

"I can get it," she said, reaching for the bag on the shelf. Brad hurried over and grabbed the other side. "I said I could do it!" she snapped.

"Okay, all yours." He backed off, hands in the air.

"I'll just need your help dumping it in the mill," she said, shoving her hands underneath the bag. Her shoulders hunched and her face tightened as she maneuvered a bag nearly half her weight onto the dolly. Her expression changed to something that might have been anger or determination as she wheeled it to the mill.

He raised his hands in a T. "Hey, time out. What's going on?"

She bit her lower lip and threw her head back, eyes toward the ceiling. For a moment she said nothing. "I broke up with Luis last night."

"Oh, man, I'm sorry," he lied.

She waved a hand in front of her face and took a deep, ragged breath. "He said he was glad, that he didn't want a *marimacha* tomboy who's more interested in playing at brewing than becoming a good wife and mother to his children."

"You want to talk about it? Or about those marks around your wrist?"

She stiffened and bit her lip again. Her eyes filled with tears. "Or this?" she asked, yanking at her shirt collar to expose a yellowed bruise on her collarbone.

"Jesus, Alejandra. Did Luis do that?" She stared at the floor. How could his tough-as-nails brewer look so vulnerable and defenseless? "In the U.S., a woman could press charges for that."

"In the U.S., women do all sorts of things we can't, or won't, do here."

"Alejandra, you're a smart, educated woman. I never understood what you saw in him."

She trapped the hem of her shirt cuff with her fingertips and wiped the tears. "His family owns a ranch near ours. Our parents are *compadres*. The first time my mother explicitly told me that her dream was to see us married, I was fifteen.

"Luis was two years older. Imagine what it was like to have one of the richest, most handsome boys in Saltillo romancing me. All the girls at school were jealous. Do you know how many other boys I've dated?" Brad shook his head, not sure he wanted to hear.

"Two. They lived in Mobile and never knew that Luis existed. In Saltillo, every boy knew I was off limits. Back then, things were okay. I mean, he didn't hit me. He wasn't an angel, but people told me it was normal for guys to party and stray. And I believed them.

"After high school, Luis came to Monterrey and the Tec. I followed two years later. He graduated and went home to work on the ranch. I'd go to Saltillo every weekend. Everybody assumed that as soon as I graduated, we'd marry. When I stayed to work at Santa Cecilia, my mother practically had a heart attack."

"You never told your parents about the abuse?"

Alejandra shook her head and looked away. She continued so softly he could barely hear her. "It's only been in the last months since Luis took a job here in Monterrey. He's been frustrated with me. I didn't turn out to be the woman he expected or that my parents thought they had raised." She paused and looked up. "The ranch is the center of my world. But I don't want to live the rest of my life there, and I don't want to be Luis's wife."

"You've got to be honest with your family."

She shook her head. "My parents are going to be so disappointed. I'm the only daughter. I was supposed to live nearby and give them lots of grandchildren."

"Even if your husband eventually beat you to death?"

"They'd say Luis would never hurt me."

"Would they believe it if you showed them those bruises?" Brad asked, pointing to her wrist and shoulder. "Call your parents right now and tell them you're being sent to Saltillo for the day. Then get in your car and go! Show them. I'm guessing there's a whole lot more to the story." Her tears welled again. "Show them the evidence. Tell them the truth, and don't hold back."

"But we've got to brew the stout."

"Chago and I can handle the stout. You've got more important things to do."

"Brad, you remember what you told me that night when we were working the bar together? How the biggest mistake you ever made was ignoring what you didn't like about your ex-wife before you married her?"

"And I meant it."

"I finally got the nerve to break up with Luis because of what you said."

"I'm glad to hear something good came of my mistakes."

"PACO!" BRAD curled his hand around an imaginary glass and flicked his wrist. Behind the bar, Paco nodded and pulled out a tray. The lunch crowd had begun to trickle in as Brad and Carlos walked Tony Vargas from the brewery to a table.

"Brad, you keep your brewery so well-organized and clean," Tony said. "I've seen some that don't come near MBC's."

Brad thought about the unwashed breakfast dishes piled in the sink at his apartment as they sat down, but his brewery was a different matter. The Texas distributor continued, "So many years in the U.S. have turned me into an American when it comes to doing business. I'm going to dive right in. Tell me about your plans for the future."

"A second brewpub, possibly sometime next year," Carlos said.

Paco arrived with a tray of samples. There was the customary *brindis*, the clinking of raised glasses and repetitions of *salud*. In his last discussion of the topic with Carlos, Brad had reiterated that he came to Mexico to brew beer, not to tend bar on a daily basis or get side-tracked developing new menu items. And how did Carlos plan to handle everything when Brad went back to Denver in a couple more years? Besides, with their current cash flow and El Míster's demands, they had no business thinking about a second pub now.

Tony directed the conversation back to Brad. "What competitions have you entered?"

"None yet. I haven't had time," Brad answered, knowing neither one of them believed that.

"You should get your products into some Mexican festivals. Tijuana just had theirs in January. Y'all definitely need to get into the Festival Internacional de la Cerveza in the *D.F.*," he said, pronouncing it, "*day efay*" the way Mexicans referred to Mexico City.

"Hell, go for some international competitions. Bottom line, get your beers out there. Start winning awards. Good marketing is just as important as good product. Y'all are doing great things. You're off to a helluva start."

Entering competitions was the stuff Brad had dreamed of at eighteen. During his early days at Coors, he had imagined developing award-winning beers. In Monterrey, he had drifted from what mattered most, bogged down in narco harassment, emergency subbing in the pub and endless things that had little to do with brewing. And, if he was totally honest, he had been afraid his beer wouldn't measure up. He could tolerate lots of things, but not winning wasn't one of them.

"The most important advice I have," Tony continued, "is that y'all need to think big."

Carlos laughed. "You're joking, right?"

Tony smiled and leaned back in his chair. "I'm as serious as a priest in confession. When I was young, I made some stupid mistakes. I deserved to crash and burn, and I would have if my *compadre* Felipe Moss hadn't stepped in. He made a career of quietly helping people, including Alfredo. He invested heavily in building Huasteca. Let's just say Alfredo is young and has made some mistakes of his own. He's the eldest of four sons, and Felipe's death has hit him extremely hard.

"He told me how you'd helped them, Brad—with Carlos's approval. He and Felipe were very grateful to both of y'all." Tony paused. "Alfredo has decided that, in the interest of the family, Huasteca should be put up for sale."

Brad inhaled sharply. Alfredo had made a lot of mistakes, but how could he possibly walk away from a fabulous brewery and all his work? "Buyers don't exactly line up for gently-used breweries," Tony continued. "Because of your generous commitment and help, the Moss family would very much like to see Huasteca end up in your hands. They're open to negotiating a price in MBC's favor."

Brad's mind raced through the implications. "The facility and the offer are terrific, but from the start, I committed to three years in Monterrey. What you're talking about would involve a lot more time. My Temporary Resident Visa is only good for four years."

"Oh come on," Tony said. "After the four years, you convert to a Permanent Resident Visa. It's practically automatic."

"I'm not sure we could swing it financially," Carlos said.

"Echeverría, with your name, any bank in Monterrey will loan you the money. You wouldn't have trouble finding investors or shareholders. Within a year, y'all could turn a profit at Huasteca."

"We appreciate your confidence in us," Brad said.

"Don't thank me yet. The sooner Alfredo sells Huasteca, the better for the family. I've come to y'all first, but Bustamante over at Santa Cecilia would jump at the chance, although he can be—"Tony cleared his throat, "—a little hard to do business with. There are two of you, one of him. I don't have to tell y'all that running a pub and a brewery is a lot of work. Talk it over. Just think; y'all could have your beers bottled and on store shelves in months. This could be fate dropping y'all's dream in your lap a lot sooner than you expected."

Brad's head spun. It was a wild, crazy idea. One for which he'd be willing to stay in Mexico a few more years.

CHAPTER ELEVEN

"ABSOLUTELY NOT. No. Way."

"But you heard what Tony said, this is like fate dropping our dream in our lap."

"*Your* dream, Brad. Not ours. Not mine," Carlos said.

Standing in the cramped office, Brad wanted to shout that he had spent the last eight months sacrificing for the greater good of MBC and Carlos Echeverría's dream. Maybe it was time to think about Brad Peters's dream. Instead, he took a deep breath. "Look at the success of MBC and other Mexican brewpubs with good product and strong management. We both know that the craft beer movement here is five to twenty years behind the U.S."

Carlos, with his arms crossed, looked firmly unconvinced.

"Nowadays in the U.S., craft breweries can't open fast enough. That's Mexico's future, and we can be in on it early. We've got the know-how and the experience that Alfredo Moss didn't have. We'd be insane to say no. You really want to let Bustamante beat us on this?"

"I don't doubt you could run it and make some of the best beer in Mexico—for a lot less than Alfredo. But this isn't the United States, Güero. Half of Mexico can't afford craft beer. And a lot of those who can are used to buying imports."

"Because there aren't enough high-quality national alternatives."

"If we grow too much, we'll attract the attention of the big breweries. They could start throwing up roadblocks. We've already got narco thugs to deal with. We'd be insane to take on Cuauhtémoc or Modelo."

"Exactly. We can't compete. We do what craft brewers in the U.S. have done: we carve our niche. Look at Minerva in Guadalajara. Five years from now, we could be swimming in money."

"Or have drowned in an ocean of debt. Or had heart attacks because we worked eighty hours a week. And since when are you talking about five years from now?"

"Since twenty minutes ago when Tony made us the offer of a lifetime."

"What about Emily? You're not going to follow her back to the U.S. when the school year ends and leave me without a brewmaster?"

"What the fuck?"

"Hello, Brad? It's pretty obvious."

Instead of punching Carlos in the face, Brad slammed his fist into the office desk. "That's the stupidest thing I've ever heard you say."

"That's not the way it looks."

Brad sucked in a sharp breath. He wanted to break Carlos's perfect nose, but his right hand was throbbing from the impact with the desk. Instead, he smacked his left fist into the leather chair. "To answer your question, hell no, I'm not following Emily anywhere. But the topic under discussion is whether or not we're going to buy Huasteca—at a bargain price. What happened to the intrepid Carlos in Denver who refused to accept all my reasons about why he shouldn't open a brewpub in Mexico?"

Carlos rolled his eyes like a teenage drama diva on the verge of a meltdown.

"Remember the Carlos who was willing to risk so much to forge his own destiny instead of becoming a lawyer like other Echeverría men?"

Carlos blew out a noisy breath and flopped in the chair Brad had just hit. "Enough. Give me some time to think and to talk with my dad—but don't expect me to work eighty hours a week."

BRAD'S HEAD was stuck in overdrive. He'd have to make adjustments in his recipes for the increase in production. Of course, he'd take Chago and Alejandra along and keep on the best of the Mosses' employees. Eventually he'd have to hire others. He'd have to plan for handling bottles in addition to kegs. The more he thought about it, the more he needed to get back inside Huasteca before he could seriously develop his plans.

He spent an hour on the phone with his dad who concluded, "If I were your age and in your place, I'd damn the risk and jump at this in a minute." Somewhere after midnight he finally fell asleep.

The next morning when he pulled into the pub's back lot, Vagabundo was waiting. "Morning, buddy," he said, offering a handful of dry cat food. He scratched Vagabundo's ears while the cat ate and purred. There was a lot to like about Monterrey, especially after Tony's visit. He let himself into MBC's five-barrel brewery imagining what it would be like to walk into his own craft brewery five times as large.

"Morning, Brad." Alejandra's greeting pulled him back to reality.

"What are you doing here an hour and fifteen minutes before you have to report in?"

"I figure that in five days, I will have made up for missing yesterday."

"You don't have to do that, you know." He hadn't seen her smile in weeks. "How'd things go?"

"Hard. Very upsetting for my parents. I ruined a thirty-year friendship for them."

"No. Luis ruined it the first time he abused you. You did the right thing."

Chago burst in the door. "*¡Buenos días, Ingeniero! ¡Alejandra!* How's the most beautiful brewer at MBC?"

"What's with you guys?" Brad asked. "Your starting time is eight o'clock, Chago. What are you doing here now, and why do you have that ridiculous grin across your entire face?"

"Couldn't sleep."

"Graciela said yes?" Alejandra asked with her own over-sized smile.

"Of course. That was never a question."

"Congratulations!" Brad said, extending a hand.

"So when is the wedding?" Alejandra asked, never letting her own heartbreak show.

"In five years if I'm lucky."

"Get out of here," Brad said. Mexican courtships were slow affairs, but even he knew they weren't that glacial.

"I am serious. Her father said he'll give his permission as soon as I've saved up a twenty percent down payment on a house."

"Tell him," Alejandra said, "that his daughter will be so old by then that he'll never be a grandfather."

Chago tightened an invisible belt. "We plan to eat nothing but beans and rice and watch lots of TV for the foreseeable future."

For Brad, Mexico was a land of contradictions. How could bright, educated, employed adults let parents and future in-laws rule their lives and decisions?

"Why are you two here so early?" Chago asked.

Brad took a deep breath. It was insane sitting on such crazy news, but the only thing Carlos had committed to was talking to his father. "I'm a morning guy," he shrugged.

"Lately, not so much," Chago muttered. "You didn't break up with Emily did you?"

"We're just friends."

"If it walks like a duck," Alejandra said in English.

"*¿Si camina como pato?*" Chago asked. "What does that mean?"

"That we need to brew beer," Brad said. "*¡Vámonos!*"

NACHO STAGGERED into the dark bedroom. María stirred and mumbled something. He reeked of alcohol and sweat, but he was too drunk to care.

He aimed himself in the direction of the bathroom. He should have just pissed outside. With the next step, his toe crunched against the wall.

"Shit!"

"Amor, ¿qué pasó?" María turned on the bedside lamp.

He held up a hand against the light and stumbled to the toilet. Bala had thrown one hell of a party. He had treated Nacho well, but he damn well should. Nacho had never, not once, showed up short on *piso* collections. He never whined about complications or made excuses.

He turned on the shower to warm up and pissed, not caring whether or not he hit the toilet. The shower cleared some of the fog in his head, though not much. Naked and still damp, he held onto the bed and moved around to his side where he let himself fall. It felt so goddamn good. He was going to sleep for ten hours.

María nuzzled against his chest and whispered, "You're drunk." She began tracing loopy circles with one finger on his chest, moving down to his stomach and below. Jesus, he was so drunk he probably wasn't going to be able to get it up. He hadn't had any trouble the other two times tonight, but he hadn't been so drunk then. The first *morenita* wasn't even especially good-looking, but she was practically begging, and who was he to turn down a woman who needed to get some? The second one, she was hot and in no rush, which made him more determined. She strung him along, made him work for it. Jesus, it was sweet.

María was alternating between the finger circles and playing with his dick. Before he knew it, he had flipped her over and was shoving himself inside her. Pushing his body against hers felt good.

"Ay, amor, not so hard." María squirmed underneath him.

He pinned her arms and drove his dick deep inside.

"Nacho, it hurts!"

He thrust himself harder and deeper until he finally collapsed. Her soft crying made him mad. "You wanted to get fucked. I obliged."

"Not like that, I didn't."

Even sober he hated it when she mouthed off. When he was drunk, he couldn't stand it. He raised an arm. She sprung out of the bed and cringed against the wall. "We're going to have to be more careful from now on," she said. She pulled a lock of her long, blue-black hair over one ear and straightened up. Naked, she was a goddamned goddess. Neither of those *putas* tonight came close.

"Shit, you're getting boring," he said, rolling onto his side so he faced the other wall. Women needed to hear stuff like that every now and then. He closed his eyes, already dozing off.

"Nacho, I'm pregnant."

He lurched out of bed. The room was spinning hard. He fell back, his legs hanging over the side of the bed. His heart was pounding crazy hard like when they kidnapped those teenagers. He took a deep breath and willed the spinning to slow down. "That's a joke, right?"

"No." She moved cautiously toward the bed and sat on the edge.

"I don't want any goddamned kids. You know that."

"I'm sorry. I don't know how it happened."

"Get rid of it."

María watched him, her large, amber eyes filling with tears. She shook her head.

"There's no way in hell you're keeping it."

"Nacho, the Church says it's a sin."

He flew at her and wrapped his hands around her neck. He threw her against the bed. "Goddamned *puta*!" He squeezed his hands tighter. She coughed and struggled against him.

"As soon as I turn loose," he said, pushing her down harder, "you're gonna call your sister and get the number of that doctor. Then you call him and ask what time you can come in tomorrow. I'm taking you myself."

He let go of her neck. She sat up, gagging and shaking. "You know as well as I do that he nearly killed Silvia. She'll never be a mother because of him."

Nacho leaned over his side of the bed and, on the second attempt, managed to snag his pants from the floor. Damn, he shouldn't have drunk so much. He fished in a pocket for his phone and hit Silvia's number.

"No, Nacho," María begged.

"*Qué pasa, Nacho?*" Silvia said, more asleep than awake. "Has something happened to María?"

"I need the number of that doctor, the one who took care of your problem."

"What the hell for? You got somebody you want to kill?"

"Just give me the damn number."

"I don't have it anymore. If one of your buddies has a girl in a bad way, tell him to find a real doctor who will treat her like a human being. And don't call me again at four in the morning."

"Christ," Nacho said. "Women are such idiots."

CHAPTER TWELVE

ONE BOW-TIED waiter cleared dishes from the table and another produced the dessert menu. "Just coffee for me," Emily said.

"We'll split a slice of chocolate tiramisu," Brad told the waiter.

"Only if I can have all the chocolate," Emily said in a teasing voice that aroused him even after a long day at work. "Thank you, Brad, for making this a special birthday. It's hard being so far from my family, my dad especially, you know? My best friend Sarah and I always go snowboarding on our birthdays."

The waiter returned with coffee. Brad held up a hand. "None for me. I've got to get to sleep at a decent hour tonight."

"You're pretty excited about tomorrow," Emily observed.

"It'll be incredible if we can put this deal together."

"You're serious about spending at least the next four years here?"

"If we get Huasteca, yes."

She sipped the coffee and looked over the rim of the cup into his eyes. "My principal sent an email today. Any teacher who doesn't plan to continue next year needs to inform him by March twenty-second. I've got a week to decide."

The waiter interrupted with an elegant square of cake drizzled in syrup and topped with chocolate curls. He placed two forks and an extra plate on the table. "I only want a couple bites," Emily said.

Brad transferred a third of the tiramisu to the empty plate and handed her the rest. "Happy birthday to the most beautiful woman in the restaurant."

"Said the sexiest guy in the restaurant. What happened to two bites?" she protested, putting the first one in her mouth. "Oh my God, this is incredible."

Brad tasted his and wished they'd ordered two slices. "The principal has known all along that you're here for one year, right?"

"I've been thinking," Emily continued. "And I'm torn. I mean, I've got a good job. Internacional is a fantastic school. I love my students. Jenn and I get along well as roommates. What's not to like, you know?"

Brad was suddenly finding it hard to enjoy the cake.

"You're looking at me like either you're clueless or I've scared the shit out of you," Emily said. She took another bite and chewed slowly, giving him precious seconds. He chewed and re-chewed, swallowed, took a sip of water, rubbed his chin.

Emily threw out her hands. "You're not exactly making this easy. What I'm saying is, if you and I have a future, I'll sign on for another year."

"I'm sorry, Em. You took me by surprise."

"Is it really a surprise? We've been dating for four months." She ran her fork over the empty plate and licked it, eating him with her eyes.

Dating sounded so formal. What they had done was hang out, help each other keep the homesickness at bay. Sure, it had turned into a friends-with-benefits thing, but he'd never led her on. It had been less than a year since the divorce and only three months since the Christmas party back home when he had finally realized he was ready to move on.

"I enjoy spending time with you. You're a gorgeous girl who can actually out-run me and probably out-snowboard me."

"I'd leave your gnarly butt in the powder, dude. Whatever you want to call it, I think we've progressed beyond sports buddies sharing a beer." She opened her mouth wide and slowly moved the tip of her tongue around the curve of her upper lip. She inserted the fork and closed her lips around it, sucking.

"Jesus, Em, you're going to get us thrown out of the restaurant," he said, fighting off a stupid grin.

Underneath the linen tablecloth, she planted the tip of her shoe on his chair. She nudged one of his thighs, then the other, slowly working her way up. She really was going to embarrass them when she reached his rock-hard dick, especially if she burst out laughing. He grabbed her foot and gently pushed it toward the floor.

"Do you get that red when you have dinner with all your sports buddies, Mr. Peters? What do you say we get out of here and make a quick stop at your place before you take me home? No more conversation for tonight. We'll just play one quick round of a contact sport we both enjoy."

He lifted his hand and caught the waiter's attention. "Check, please." This hook-up was going to come with a hell of a price tag, but he didn't care.

CARLOS PRESSED his key fob and, simultaneously, the lights on the RAV4 flashed, the door locks clicked and Brad yawned. The partners walked through the underground garage. "Remember last July?" Carlos said. "When you got all pissed off because I was late for the bank meeting?"

"What about it?"

"What you said was true. I appreciate that you didn't turn it into a lecture."

"Are you insinuating that I'm slacking?"

A tone sounded and the elevator door opened. "Let's just say that you've yawned your way through a lot of days lately."

"Is it affecting my work?" Brad asked as the elevator and his temper rose.

"Not seriously. By the way, you might want to check your tie in the mirror behind you."

Brad pivoted. It was too late to deal with the tie's uneven ends. He settled for yanking the knot toward the center. The elevator lighting exaggerated the bags under his eyes. In normal light, they were barely noticeable. After another tone, the door opened onto a marble-floored landing with an enormous picture window overlooking San Pedro twelve stories below. Last night's marathon romp was indeed coming with a price.

"Try not to yawn while the lawyer is talking," Carlos said as they walked into the offices of Garza Oveido y Asociados, S.C.

This could be fate dropping your dream in your lap. The amount of debt they were considering taking on was staggering, but Tony was right. They had to dream big and act on it quickly. A deep-hued painting of flowers and indigenous women in the style of Diego Rivera hung on the oak-paneled wall of the law office. Behind the reception desk, a dark-haired woman, mid-twenties, low-cut top, stood and came toward them. Her heels clicked against the floor. "Carlos, how have you been?"

"Sara, it's been ages. You look terrific." They embraced loosely, exchanging cheek kisses.

A door opened and senior partner Pablo Garza Oveido smiled widely. "*Buenos días, Carlos,*" the attorney said. He gave Carlos a formal but effusive *abrazo.* What remained of his wavy gray hair was combed back. His suit easily cost more than all the shirts Brad owned. "It's a pleasure to meet you, Brad," Garza Oveido continued in Spanish. "You and your brewing skills are making quite a splash in Monterrey. In fact, I keep hearing good things about MBC—a lot of it from your father at the country club, Carlos. He's pretty proud of you." Brad caught the sparkle in Carlos's eyes.

Inside Garza Oveido's office, a wall of windows framed another panoramic view of the city fanning out below until it bumped up against the steep mountains. "Beautiful, isn't it?" the lawyer offered. "Have you lived near mountains before, Brad?"

"Born and bred in the Colorado Rockies."

"I vacationed in Vail several times. Great skiing." Garza Oveido motioned to two chairs in front of his desk. "Please, have a seat. Would you prefer to speak English?"

Brad had started to think about his Monterrey life as before and after the Christmas trip to Denver. Since his return, Spanish had seemed easier. He'd never understood the grammar explanations back in school and still didn't, but somehow he was getting what people were saying and he could answer them. During the next minutes, though, it was going to be crucial to understand everything and he already had the start of a headache. Why hadn't he taken Emily home at a decent hour? "English would be nice."

"Fine," Garza Oveido said, changing languages. "Stop me if I'm telling you things you already know. In Mexico, a real estate attorney represents the interests of both buyer and seller in a transaction like this. That's the reason Carlos's father can't be your lawyer. Now, here's what has to happen for you to purchase Huasteca. First you two, the buyers, make a *promesa de compraventa*, a preliminary agreement that you commit to formalizing by a certain date. In it you establish the price to be paid, the conditions of the operation, penalties for either party if one doesn't follow through, and so on. The seller, Alfredo Moss, accepts the *promesa*. This is followed by the actual *contrato de compraventa*. Am I making this too simple?"

"Not at all," Brad said.

"Carlos, you're following the English okay?"

"No problem."

"The final step then," Garza Oveida continued, "is the closing where the seller hands over the property title. Before that, he will have obtained the *Certificado de Libertad de Gravamen*, a lien release, affirming that there are no outstanding taxes or other debts on the property. Each document has to be filed with a notary public—me, in this case. I then file all the paperwork with the Registro de la Propiedad, the Office of Land Records.

"It's all fairly straightforward when the buyer and seller are in agreement as you two and Alfredo Moss seem to be. If there are delays, they'll most likely come at Registro." Garza Oveido patted his palms on the desktop and exhaled. "You know how it is dealing with government agencies. Sometimes Registro can get 'backed up'."

Brad wasn't sure what the lawyer meant. What didn't take longer in Mexico? "Start to finish, how long do you anticipate it will take?" Carlos asked.

"The whole transaction could be completed within a month."

Brad took a deep breath. "What's our first step?"

Garza Oveido smiled and opened the leather folder in front of him. "*La promesa.*" He nudged a multi-page document toward them. "If you all are ready, we can go over this draft that I've written up based on the information Carlos has given me."

Brad eyed his partner who stared back, pursing his lips. Carlos turned to the lawyer and nodded.

With that, they were on their way to buying a brewery. It all sounded so easy.

CARLOS WAS out on a sales' call when American Consul Howard Fenton showed up at MBC and pumped Brad's hand in a firm, American handshake. Behind him, three men and two women smiled. "Good to see you again, Brad. How are things going here at Monterrey Brewing Company?"

"Good afternoon, Consul." *Why, of all days, had the guy chosen the first of the month for a surprise visit?*

Fenton smiled broadly. "I've brought this delegation from Los Angeles to have lunch. Nothing like hearing from the source about the great business opportunities for Americans here in Monterrey."

"Welcome to MBC," Brad said, leading them to a table by the large windows separating the dining room and the brewery. Hopefully, no one would inquire about the going rates for *piso*. He refused to think about the consequences if El Míster showed up while the Americans were there.

"Any word from Marc Wilkes?" Brad asked Fenton.

"I talked to him a few days ago. Other than a little trouble adjusting to the altitude in Mexico City, he and Jessica and Tanner are doing great. Marc's a real go-getter. We all knew he wouldn't be with us for long."

Brad went straight to the kitchen. "Bump this order to the head of the line."

While Fenton and the Californians ate, Brad's imagination churned. El Míster making a grand entrance. Matagatos barging in the door, waving his pistol. Narco kidnappers realizing the gold mine sitting in MBC. A shootout between thugs and the consulate driver and bodyguard discreetly waiting outside. MBC ruined. His and Carlos's reputations trashed.

At last summer's barbeque, Carlos had summed up the situation as, "It's complicated." Brad hadn't understood those words then like he did now. They were the simplest description of the insecurity, the drug cartels, their power, the ineffectiveness of the government and the military, the crazy reality that Mexicans and Brad Peters lived with always in the background, day in and day out.

"Don't ask if they want a second round of beers," Brad instructed Paco and the wait staff.

"We've got to get to a meeting," Fenton finally said, requesting the check.

Brad's phone vibrated as he swiped the credit card. No name appeared on the caller ID. "*¿Bueno?*" he answered in a soft voice.

"Peters," El Míster said. "We're on our way. Have the money waiting."

"Give me ten minutes."

"Since when do you give the orders?"

Brad started to say he was sorry but stopped himself. He wasn't going to apologize to his extortionist. "It's crazy busy today."

"We get there when we get there. Have the money and a couple of cold *chelas* waiting."

Pissed with the narco and his arrogance, Brad returned Fenton's credit card and the receipt just as one of the Americans made some joke and the others laughed. "It's been great," the older woman in the group said. "Congratulations on your success."

"Thanks," Brad replied. "I don't want to keep you. The traffic in Monterrey can get bad."

The woman laughed. "We're from LA. We wouldn't know what to do if the traffic weren't bad."

Brad breathed a huge sigh when their car pulled out onto Gómez Morín.

BRAD YAWNED, pushed his tired body off the sofa and shuffled to the kitchen with his empty plate and Morenita bottle. He washed and dried the plate, putting off the call he'd sworn this morning that he would make before the day ended.

While he carried an overly full trash bag to the dumpster, his mind re-ran the day's events. El Míster and Matagatos had shown up less than two minutes after the Americans left. The actors knew their roles. They almost could have been two more vendors collecting on their bills. Brad hated seeing them, hated the extortion, but he no longer wasted time or mental energy on the wrongness or the weirdness of it all. He accepted it the way he accepted that almost every female who greeted him kissed his cheek. He had looked at those Americans today and seen himself—a long time ago. In spite of the extortion, he and Carlos were making a profit and, most importantly, they were weeks away from owning a fantastic brewery.

Back in the apartment, he pulled out his phone and stared at the screen. He didn't want to do this. Wasn't looking forward to it. He drew in a deep breath and tapped Emily's number.

She answered on the second ring. "Hey."

"Hey yourself. How've you been?"

"Busy with school. And you?"

"Good." He paused. "We met with the lawyer, and we're going ahead."

"Congratulations."

"Thanks." Another silence. He deserved it. "So it looks like I'll be in Monterrey for a while."

"Yeah?" She wasn't going to meet him halfway.

He sighed. "I've been thinking a lot about what you said. I haven't been fair to you not clarifying where we were headed. The truth is, I don't know."

"I don't either, but I think it's time for this discussion." She sounded relieved and ready to talk.

"Look, I'm willing to give it a try, but I'm damaged goods, Em. I don't know if I can be the guy you deserve. I'm not good with emotions. And if you ask my ex-wife, I'm lousy husband material."

"You're a great guy whose ego was stomped on by a bitch for way too long. I know we started out with no commitments. I didn't intend to fall in love with you, and if you want, we can still both walk away from this, no hard feelings. But I think we're at a crossroads."

Jesus, he'd rehearsed this conversation for almost forty-eight hours. He'd spun it going all sorts of ways, but hearing her say out loud that she loved him made him forget every line he'd practiced.

"Em, I don't know if I'll be able to live up to your expectations."

"I might not live up to yours. What if we take it a day at a time?"

"I think I can do that."

CHAPTER THIRTEEN

NACHO SAT behind the wheel of the Range Rover idling in a stand of trees. He was thinking. Thinking about how empty his place was, about how much he missed María's cooking. Damn, the woman could cook. He missed the convenience of the sex. Now he had to go out and find it. He hadn't expected the bitch to up and leave. She and her sister weren't even answering their phones. He didn't have a clue where she'd gone. Good riddance and good luck paying for that kid all on her own. It pissed him off, though, that there'd be some *huerco* out there with no clue who or where his father was.

His own back and forth childhood hadn't exactly been so great. Los Mochis to Dallas to Los Mochis to Dallas, sometimes for three weeks, once for three years. In Mexico, they called him El Míster. In the U.S., the gringos called him damned-Mexican like it was a single dirty word and never mind his blue eyes and skin lighter than a lot of theirs, or the tour of duty he served in Iraq wearing Uncle Sam's uniform. He had rolled into Monterrey at twenty-one, following a *ruca* named Ana Elba.

Three months later, she was gone and he was working for El Cártel. It was a job, and it paid better than anything else he could get in Mexico or in the U.S. Paid off then when he was young and stupid, still paying off now when he was eight years older and a lot smarter. Now he had a future and plans for it. He had a hell of a lot more brains than some of the *patrones.*

Some of them did such dumb shit he wondered how they ever got to be the bosses. Shit like expecting him and his crew to pull off a major hijacking at two a.m. and then collect first-of-the-month *pisos* a few hours later. He pulled on the sleeves of the stolen federal police uniform Bala had thrown at him before they left. Damn thing was too small, especially with the bullet-proof vest underneath. As Nacho was driving them through the darkness into the middle of nowhere, Bala had softened some. Tomorrow was Sunday. They could hold off a day on April collections.

In the Range Rover's back seat, Matagatos's phone rang. He flipped on the speakerphone. A tense, low voice said, "We're right behind them, about to crest the hill." Nacho yanked up the face mask around his neck and pulled it over his nose.

In the passenger seat beside him, Bala shouted into his own phone, "*¡Orenle ya-a-a!*"

Instantly, blinding lights flooded the lonely stretch of country highway. From opposite sides, two dump trucks swung onto the road to block both lanes. Nacho threw on the Range Rover's flashing police lights and hit the accelerator, swerving the SUV in front of the trucks. Men poured out of vehicles, running toward the Matamoros-bound bus as it shuddered to a stop.

"*¡Policía federal!*" Bala screamed, banging the butt of his AR-15 against the bus door. "Open up!"

The driver pulled the lever and hung his head, his entire torso hunched over. "Turn on the lights!" Bala shouted. Nacho sidled in beside him. "Anybody who doesn't hand over all valuables and documents dies," Bala barked.

Nacho took in the sorry bunch of men crammed three to a seat meant for two. Even with the windows of the un-air-conditioned bus open, the smell of filthy bodies and sweat almost knocked him over. They were young and thin, the skin-and-bones look of the poor, broad noses and short, dark, compact bodies typical of Mayans and other Indians in the south. They looked tired and scared and hungry as hell. Twenty-six hours on this shitty bus that had started out from Tapachula on the Guatemalan border would do that. Most of them had probably never traveled more than ten miles from their villages or rural huts. They'd made it all the way here, less than two hours from the U.S. border and the *coyotes* waiting to herd them across like pack mules, laden with drugs.

The silence was broken only by the rustling of men pulling out what cash and few possessions they carried. Matagatos and Labrador moved down the aisle holding open burlap bags stamped in English, "Montemorelos Oranges Product of Mexico." Nacho followed, his forefinger on the trigger of the Smith & Wesson revolver. A slight breeze blew in the open window, stirring the smells of unwashed bodies.

One by one, the men dropped in U.S. dollars, Mexican pesos, Guatemalan quetzales, inexpensive trinkets, a few cell phones, a driver's license, a passport, a cheap wedding ring, a yellowed paper folded into a small rectangle with worn crease lines, a black and white photo of a woman. The hands of a kid, maybe fifteen, shook so much he missed the bag. A wet spot spread across the crotch of his pants. "Pick it up and try again," Matagatos ordered.

The eyes of a guy in the next-to-last row caught Nacho's. His head, covered in a dark hood, didn't hang as low as the others. Dude was watching Matagatos's moves too closely. Suddenly, the asshole's knife came out of nowhere, slicing with lightning speed.

"Son of a bitch!" Matagatos screamed. He dropped the bag and clutched his hand that dripped blood. The man sprung from his seat and raked the air inches from Matagatos. Nacho's shot sent the knife flying out of the motherfucker's hand as he crumpled into the floor. Matagatos started smashing his boots into the body again and again, grunting like an enraged bull.

"Enough!" Bala finally shouted. "Go to the car. Send in somebody else." Matagatos staggered up the aisle, leaving a smeared trail of blood. Nacho retrieved his bag.

"Who's the *coyote*?" Bala demanded. The men sunk lower, some visibly trembling. No one answered. Bala lifted the AR-15 so the muzzle rested against the chest of a man in the first row. "Which one's the smuggler?"

The man whimpered like a puppy.

"Speak up!"

"Six rows back."

"Walk back and put your hand on him. I don't want any mistakes."

The man stood and moved slowly. Nacho held the burlap bag in his left hand, the pistol ready in his right. Blood from the battered corpse trickled toward his shoes.

The man stopped near the middle of the bus. Nacho could see tears on his face. He reached out and pointed at a guy hunkered in his seat. "This is the fucking *coyote*?" Bala shouted to every man on the bus.

"*¡El es!*" The angry growl came from the teenager who had been seated next to the now dead man. Heads nodded.

"*¡Tarado!*" Bala said, idiot! "How many men on this bus?"

"Fifty-two," the *coyote* said in a shaky voice.

Bala slammed the back of his hand against the smuggler's head. "Fucking liar! You paid passage for fifty-two, but I'm gonna ask one more time. How many men on this bus?"

"Sixty-seven. They sent more than we expected," the *coyote* pleaded.

Bala grabbed the man's hair and jerked his head back. He stared into the smuggler's eyes. "You shoulda thought of that before you started the trip. Nobody—*nobody*," he yelled into the guy's face, "traffics in Cártel territory without paying full price." The explosion of the semi-automatic firing inside the bus caused men to drop to the floor between seats. Many covered their ears and heads. No matter how much practice Nacho had with weapons, he'd never get used to the decibel level of a firing AR-15, especially without ear protection. His own ears would ring for the next hour.

"Forget the United States," Bala shouted to the rest of the men. "Keep your mouths shut and do as you're told."

Bala looked at Nacho and jerked his head. Labrador leaned over the bloody heap in the aisle and passed Nacho his burlap bag, heavier than Matagatos's. Nacho moved toward the door. In the seat behind the dead *coyote*, a man groaned, clutching his shoulder where a blood stain was growing on his shirt. Nacho stepped over one of the *coyote's* legs splayed across the aisle. Now Bala stood with the driver on one side and Matagatos's replacement on the other.

Nacho squeezed himself and the bags between them and hopped to the ground. Half those fucking Indians weren't going to survive a week in the fields of Cártel ranch where they were headed. And if Matagatos was sitting in the back of the Range Rover bleeding all over the seat, Bala was going to be pissed. Now for sure the damn *piso* collections weren't going to happen tomorrow. There were times when this job was fucking stressful.

BRAD JUMPED the instant he heard the door open. He had developed the habit on the first of each month, a nervous little jolt every time someone came in. When it was finally El Míster and his thugs, the tension ratcheted up. This month had been the worst. Yesterday, the first, had come and gone without the narcos. Now they were here.

"I'll get Carlos," Brad told El Míster and Matagatos, whose right hand was encased in a bulky white bandage. Brad hurried into the office. "They're here."

Carlos swiveled his chair around and began twirling the lock on the safe. "*Buenas*," the narco said from the door of the tiny office. He still wore his sunglasses. Carlos jerked and fumbled the combination.

"Take your time," El Míster rasped. He looked and smelled like he'd slept in yesterday's clothes. He hadn't shaved. Carlos turned the lock with the uncertainty of a twelve-year-old, making a full stop on each number. Finally, he tugged the door open. Following his own advice, El Míster took his time counting the bills and storing the envelope in the old Dallas Cowboys jacket he wore.

Each month the narco grew more arrogant. Last month, Brad had again pushed for contacting authorities, but Carlos reminded him that they had learned of two other San Pedro bar owners also paying *piso*, and they weren't going to the authorities.

Carlos's phone rang. "Go ahead, Echeverría. Answer on speakerphone," El Míster's smile made Brad's skin crawl.

"Good afternoon, Carlos. Pablo Garza Oveido here. A bit of a problem has come up with the *gravamen*. The land on which Huasteca is built was purchased by Felipe Moss twelve years ago. It seems the previous owner was late paying the property taxes in 2006, and the payment was never properly recorded. Felipe had a photocopy of the cashed check which Alfredo now has. Unfortunately, the woman at Registro who's working on the sale won't accept it as proof."

"What about the former owner?" Carlos asked.

"Died in 2008. I contacted his heirs, but didn't get anywhere. We'll get this sorted out, but it may take a while."

"The name of the woman at Registro?" El Míster whispered.

"Sorry, Carlos, what was that?" Graza Oveido asked.

Carlos spoke into the phone slowly, watching El Míster. "What's the name of the woman at Registro?"

"Eustolia Aguilar. Why do you ask?"

Another pause. "I'll see if my father has any ideas to move things along."

"It's worth a try. Alfredo would like to have this deal completed as soon as possible. I'll let you know when I have any news."

"Thanks, Pablo."

El Míster stared at the wall. He snapped to and said, "I need some beer to go."

Brad silently swore to himself. "I'll get a mini keg."

"That sounds too small."

"It's fourteen cans."

"What's the next size?"

"I think I can find an eighth barrel—forty-one cans," Brad said, struggling to keep his voice neutral.

"Do that."

In the storage area, Brad snatched up one of the two eighth barrels he had used for his earliest test runs. Without cleaning it, he filled it three-quarters full. His hefted the barrel to waist level and followed El Míster and the silent Matagatos to the parking lot and a late model Range Rover. "On the floor," the narco said, opening the door behind the driver's seat. Brad dumped the keg and refused to think about what could have caused the large, brown blotches that stained the seat and floor under his keg.

"*Hasta mayo*," El Míster said. See you in May.

BRAD, CARLOS, Alejandra and Chago took their seats at the bar where Paco the bartender had their glasses lined up. From the first experimental brew, Brad had put Carlos and himself through daily taste tests. As soon as he had Chago and Alejandra on board, they were included. A brewer who couldn't distinguish his own beers was a brewer in trouble. Brad picked up the water glass and sloshed some in his mouth. He sipped the first beer, swished, swallowed and jotted a note on his card. The others did the same.

Just as Brad took a sip of the second beer, Carlos's phone rang. He looked at the screen and said, "The lawyer, Brad. We'd better take this call."

Brad followed his partner to the office, where Carlos tapped the speaker.

"Good news!" Garza Oveido said. "The woman at Registro issued the certificate this morning and I've got it here in my office."

"That's fantastic. How did you change her mind?"

"I didn't do a thing. Sometimes those government bureaucrats let the power go to their heads. They hold things up just to remind everybody who's in charge. Yesterday, she was adamant. Today she was pleasant as could be and said she'd decided the cancelled check worked. She even offered to expedite the paperwork on the closing. How does ten o'clock Thursday look for you and Brad?"

Brad glared at Carlos and gave an uneasy thumbs up. "Great, Pablo. See you then," Carlos said though a big grin.

He ended the call and threw up his arms. "Can you believe it?" He pinched a thumb and forefinger together. "We are this close to owning our very own brewery!"

"Look, I'm the know-nothing American, but doesn't this strike you as a little more than coincidental? On Monday, we hit a wall—set up by Registro—with no ideas to overcome it. We also happen to have two gangsters listening in. On Tuesday, the wall disappears and the head cheerleader from Team Registro is rooting for us."

"We have an amazing opportunity," Carlos said, "and I'm not going to complain. I think we're getting paranoid about El Míster and how much power he has. Even if he could influence Registro, why would he want to help us?"

Chapter Fourteen

June 2013

"*DISCULPEN, ACABO de cambiar tres azulejos rotos en esta escalera. ¿Pueden bajar por la otra allá?*" the tile layer said, gesturing with an arm.

"What did he say?" Julia Peters asked her son.

"That he just replaced three broken tiles on this staircase, so we need to use the other one," Brad answered, anxious to hurry his parents along for lunch at the pub. "Carlos just called on his way from the airport." They stood on the upper level walkway that ran along one wall of the former Huasteca Brewery, now MBC, and looked out over the construction workers below, wrapping up a month of improvements. The partial upper level housed the office, pilot brewery and storage areas.

"You talk Spanish as fast as they do," Julia said. "How did you get so good?"

"Don't tell Carlos when you see him. He'll bust a gut laughing. When you have to communicate, you learn pretty fast."

"This brewery blows me away. Amazing," Jim Peters said. Brad smiled at such high praise from his father.

"But we're still worried about your safety," Julia said.

"Mom, I'm here, all in one piece," Brad said, knowing it was what she needed to hear.

Yesterday when they had eaten at the pub, Paty and the wait staff had treated his parents like celebrities. Even Vagabundo had shown his friendly side, rubbing against Brad's father who usually scared cats away. Behind the bar, Paco had listened patiently to Dad's ideas on brewing until Brad hauled him away. His mother, whose Spanish vocabulary didn't exceed twenty words, had taken a liking to Alejandra, declaring that not only did the girl speak perfect English but she sounded like a Southern belle.

At dinner last night, Em had been subdued, his parents, polite. His mother could be funny that way. She'd always acted reserved around Maddy, intimidated, she claimed. Brad suspected that she had been secretly relieved by the divorce. When he questioned her last night after dinner, she said, "I just get a little uncomfortable around wealthy people."

"I don't think Em's family is rich."

"Just take things slow," his father cautioned.

Now, on the drive to the pub, his dad asked, "Does Carlos travel this much all the time? That leaves you with a lot to handle."

"I like making beer, and Carlos has turned out to be great at selling it. I swear the guy could sell snow boots in Monterrey. Yesterday, he nailed a contract with a Mexico City group that owns nine restaurants."

At the pub, his parents again got the A-listers' greeting from Paty, including hugs and squeals. Carlos breezed in, liberally distributing hugs, handshakes and kisses. Paco grinned and waved as Brad escorted his father directly to the table beside the large windows between the dining room and the pub brewery. "You all are smart to shift all the brewing to the new location," his dad said, looking through the tableside window. "But it's a shame you'll have to shut down such a nice little brewery." He waved at Chago and Alejandra who were filling kegs at a finishing tank. They smiled and waved back.

Brad frowned at Chago and pointed to his own eyes, mouthing, "*Lentes.*" Like a kid caught misbehaving, Chago pulled on the safety glasses that hung around his neck. Brad shot a rounded thumb and forefinger okay. His brewers had learned a lot, but in another week, they and two of Alfredo Moss's former brewers were going to be learning a whole lot more.

"It's going to be pretty intense during the transition," Carlos said. "We'll have all the production shifted by August. Brad's challenge is going to be learning to delegate."

"When it comes to beer, he's always been a perfectionist," Julia said.

"I have high standards," Brad countered. "And they're the reason MBC's beers are selling."

"Those poor brewers don't know what they're in for at his Brewing Boot Camp on Monday," Jim said. "He'll be tougher on them than a drill sergeant on new recruits."

"It's a good thing we leave tomorrow," Julia added.

"It's a shame you aren't staying longer," Emily said.

"Oh, Lord. If we did, I'd never get Jim home. He'd want to help teach the class."

Em's face brightened. "And I can't wait to get home. Jackson and Yellowstone are beautiful in the summertime. The only thing that will keep the next five weeks from being perfect is that Brad won't be there."

THE FOLLOWING morning, his mother cooked up a stack of fluffy pancakes, scrambled eggs, fried bacon and hash browns. "I'm reliving my childhood," Brad said as he helped himself to seconds of everything.

"I made extra pancakes and left them in the freezer. They thaw out well."

"Your cooking is one of the things I miss most."

"Doesn't Emily cook for you?"

"I'm a modern guy. We cook for each other." The truth was that Em had fixed him a few sandwiches and, one time, she cooked steaks that ended up charred on the outside and red inside. She lived off take-out, cereal and Brad's cooking.

"What you and Carlos have accomplished in a year is incredible," Jim said. "But your cash flow concerns me."

"We get a little concerned, too, but Carlos and I are committed now. We'll be okay."

"Your mother and I want you to know that if you and Carlos get in a bad way, we have some savings."

"Absolutely not, Dad."

"We didn't offer before because I wasn't convinced this was going to fly, but you've done everything right. All I'm saying is that if you ever get in a bind, call us. The only other advice I have is, don't get overly ambitious or committed here."

"What's that supposed to mean?"

"We're proud of what you've accomplished, but you've gotten so wrapped up in it. If things get too dangerous, leave Monterrey. Your life is more important than money or any job."

BRAD OBSERVED his crew outfitted in hats or hairnets, safety glasses and MBC shirts. "*Buenos días y bienvenidos.*" Discussing brewing in Spanish came almost as easy as in English these days. "Welcome to day one of Brewing Boot Camp. I hope you've all had time to look over our agenda for the week and today's topic, Cleaning Procedures. Right now you guys are all thinking, 'I've cleaned hoses and valves and tanks hundreds of times. I know how to do it.' Chago and Alejandra can tell you guys that I'm a pain in the butt about cleanliness."

"The absolute truth," Chago said. Alejandra nodded. Lalo and Rodrigo, the former Huasteca brewers, laughed.

"We're going to clean thoroughly at all times, and do it in exactly the same way. Let's start with hoses. Alejandra, you want to demonstrate as I explain the how and why of the MBC way?"

"Sure."

"We'll start with the brewhouse area."

Lalo, with his pencil-thin mustache, was the oldest of the group. "Let me unhook that hose for you," he said jumping between Alejandra and the kettle.

"Thanks, but I can get it," she said, moving by him.

Stony-faced, Lalo backed up. Alejandra squatted to loosen the heavy hose. Even with short, unpainted nails, her hands were unmistakably feminine. At first, her strength and dexterity had surprised Brad. Now she worked the hex nut, but it wasn't budging. She knelt on the concrete floor so she could apply more pressure. Rodrigo shot Lalo a smirk and whispered something.

"Yes, I will," Alejandra said without taking her eyes off the hex nut. She pinched her lips and yanked the wrench. From there, she spun the nut off with one finger.

"You're really good at that for a— " Rodrigo stopped short. "You're really good. Sorry about the other comment. I didn't mean for you to hear it."

"Heads up," Brad said. "She has incredible hearing, and you're right about her brewing skills."

The rest of the day, his four brewers joined in a whirlwind of disassembling valves, scrubbing gaskets, disinfecting tanks and general cleaning. By five p.m. they had a thoroughly sanitized brewery and the beginnings of a team. "You guys look a little tired," Brad grinned. "What do you say we head to the break room for a beer?"

"Oh yeah, quitting time," Rodrigo said, high-fiving Chago. Rodrigo, with his beard and fuller face, looked older than Chago, even though the two had graduated from the Tec at the same time.

"We're not done yet," Chago warned.

Brad pulled a mini-keg from the fridge and grabbed a plastic bag with MBC sampler glasses. "Alejandra, take us through the steps." She had proved to be a better taste tester than Carlos or Chago, possibly better than Brad himself. She walked the men through observing, swirling, sniffing and tasting.

"MBC produces six beers," she said. "Let's begin by eliminating what this is not."

"Not a pale ale," Rodrigo said.

"Why not?"

"The color." Lalo's whisper echoed Rodrigo's words. "Not a stout or porter for the same reason," he added. Like a coach watching his team run drills, Brad leaned back in his chair, pleased with the day's progress.

"SHUT UP your goddamned dog!"

That was what Nacho had shouted at his asshole neighbor last week after he nearly pounded down the *pendejo's* front door at ten p.m. Why the hell had the idiot ever thought it was a good idea to get a German shepherd when he couldn't even control his *huercos* that ran all over the neighborhood day and night? And why the fucking hell did he think it was okay to keep a dog that barked 24/7 in his tiny backyard, right next door to Nacho?

"Shut him up or I will!" Nacho had given fair warning.

Now, he marched next door and beat on the door. The house was dark. The only answer was the damned animal barking his head off in the backyard. Nacho stormed back to his house. He loaded his Baretta M9 and a grabbed ladder María had bought for God knows what reason. He flipped on the back porch light and set the ladder against the wall. He shimmied up and leaned over the wall, making faces at the idiot dog in the dark yard below. Even from that distance, he could smell the filth. The mutt barked and bounced itself against the wall like it was possessed. Nacho fired once. He was finally going to get a good night's sleep.

CHAPTER FIFTEEN

THERE HAD been some rough moments in the four weeks since they cleaned that first hose. At the pub, it had taken a while to get Chago into the habit of using safety glasses. At the brewery, there were days when Brad thought Rodrigo would rather put out an eye than use the glasses. Rodrigo and Lalo were still too lax about quality issues in general. Alejandra had exploded at Lalo after he tried to help her once too often. He defended himself saying that he wouldn't let his eighteen-year-old daughter lift a heavy bag of malt while he stood by not helping. Alejandra declared she was neither his daughter nor eighteen; she was his fellow brewer and she'd lift the damn fifty-pound bag by herself, thank you. Today, though, they had kegged the Sevillana Pale Ale, the first beer produced at MBC Brewery. Tasting the results of their work, the brewers had been as excited as a high school football team winning the first game of the season. They were starting to look like an experienced brewing team.

With Emily gone, Brad was putting in twelve-hour days and more. What little time he had left, he spent at the tiny apartment, vegged out in front of the TV. In three more days, he'd have her back. He was watching CNN International when his phone signaled a new email. *"Hey Brad,"* it began.

"It's SO beautiful here in Wyoming. It feels great to be back in my mountains. The time in Yellowstone was absolutely jaw-droppingly, incredibly phenomenal. That old saying about how you have to leave home to realize what you've got has been true in my case. The wide-open expanses, the towering peaks, the cool nights are the reality I grew up with and love. I jogged five miles every

morning in the woods of Yellowstone and never worried about kidnappers or smog or crazy Mexican drivers. The weirdest part was that yesterday when I was in an area with cell phone reception, I got a call from the principal of the high school where I used to teach. One of the math teachers suddenly resigned."

Brad's chest tightened as he re-read the last sentence.

"Basically, the job was mine, but I had to decide by today. I spent the entire ride home agonizing. I talked to my parents and my brother. If it weren't for you, Brad, it would have been a no-brainer. I want you to understand that the decision was very, very hard. I emailed my resignation to Internacional this afternoon."

He didn't want to read the words again, but he couldn't help himself. He re-read them until his heart was galloping.

"Machado called. He's royally pissed with me. I'm pretty sure I'll never get a letter of recommendation from him, but here in Hole where they know me, nobody really cares what the principal of some school in Mexico thinks, no matter how exclusive it is. What few things I left at the apartment, I told Jenn she could have or toss. So, the only unfinished business I have is you."

Unfinished business. Like a forgotten library book with an unpaid fine.

"Please, Brad, understand that you are so important to me that I'm taking the cowardly way out and emailing instead of calling. I just cannot go back to Monterrey. What I can offer you is a life in Hole. I know pretty much everybody. You'll make a good living with a nice brewpub once you get here."

She hadn't given a thought to whether he would actually want to live in Wyoming. He was a big city guy. A few days of vacationing in the mountain towns in Colorado had proved that. Brewpubs and bars that actually survived in those places made it on a mix of tourists and oddball locals. If he had to choose between spending the rest of his life in Monterrey or Jackson, to use Emily's cliché, it was a no-brainer.

"You just don't get my level of ambition... The only unfinished business I have is you... You just don't get... unfinished business" Maddy's and Emily's voices melted together, their words looping through his head. Was it him

or the women he fell in love with? He wouldn't sit by and let Emily walk out of his life the way he had with Maddy. He should have manned up and discussed the future from the start. He'd had vague thoughts of Em going back to Denver with him someday, but him living in Jackson? That wasn't going to happen.

If he called her tonight, it would be a shouting match. His thumbs worked the keypad. "*Call you tomorrow 9 pm Monterrey time.*"

BRAD HAD been tinkering with the bottling line for an hour, convinced it could move more smoothly than it had in yesterday's test run. He was glad to have something that took his mind off Emily.

"Hey, how's the brewer-in-chief?" Carlos asked as he swaggered in. Wearing a sky blue dress shirt, perfectly-knotted tie and sunglasses, he rocked the role of successful Monterrey businessman.

"Morning, Big Guy. You realize that this time next week, we'll be bottling MBC beers?"

"Better work on how you're going to up your production figures. I've got contracts for ninety percent of what we planned on bottling for the first month."

"Awesome! I'll be upstairs in a minute."

When Brad entered the comfortable office that Felipe Moss had designed, he found Carlos, phone to ear, sitting behind the desk. "Absolutely. We can do that. I'm looking forward to seeing you on Monday." Carlos ended the call and threw his feet on the desk.

"What's gotten into you?" Brad asked.

"That was El Depósito in Guadalajara."

"Don't tell me you got us in with them."

"In Guadalajara *and* in Vallarta."

"You go, Big Guy!" Brad said, pumping the air with his fists. "Now we can hire the new bottler I've been lobbying for."

Carlos blew out a breath. "I guess. By the way, *Milenio* is sending a reporter over."

"For?"

Carlos raised his eyebrows. "A feature on 'the best new brewery in town'."

"And I thought this was going to be just another routine meeting."

BRAD HAD hardly stopped thinking about Emily. Part of him wanted to let her go and be done with it. He couldn't live life at her pace all the time. His parents hadn't exactly been wild about her. He wasn't sure he could ever commit to marrying her. Why couldn't women—especially Emily Whitcomb—just lob *¡ataque!* tennis shots or punch bags instead of being so complicated? His long work hours were one of the reasons Maddy had said she wanted a divorce. Telling himself he was going to work any less when Emily came back was a lie.

Now, the ringing jarred him awake. The phone clattered to the floor as he pushed himself up to a sitting position on the sofa. He fumbled to retrieve it. "*¿Bueno?*"

"Brad, this is Emily. Why are you answering in Spanish?"

"Oh shit, I must have fallen asleep. What time is it?"

"Nine twenty there in Monterrey." She paused a beat. "Right now you're probably madder at me than Machado is."

"I don't know what I think or feel, Emily." Sleepiness hung like cobwebs in his mind.

"I'm sorry, Brad," she blurted. What followed sounded like a sniffle. "But I can't go back to Monterrey."

A longer pause. Then her words poured out. "I know I'm not being fair to you. But you know that I hadn't wanted to stay more than one year. There were times when I didn't think I'd make it that long. Then, with you, I thought I could do it, I really did. But I got back home and, I don't know, I feel happy and whole again, like I'd only been half alive for the last ten months. Can you understand that?"

Yes, after the Christmas trip home to Denver, he did understand in a way. But he had come back to Monterrey and his responsibilities.

"It's not about you or about us, Brad. I want us to be together, but I *can't* live in Monterrey. Did you read all my email? There's a way to work this out. I talked with my dad. He's done some venture investing, and he's open to financing a brewpub or brewery or whatever here in Jackson. He said he wasn't sure what it would involve, but would five hundred thousand be enough or would you need more?"

Her words spilled like water over a dam. "So what do you think, Brad?"

"That you just said a helluva lot."

"You don't have to make any decisions tonight. You're really going to like my dad." Hope edged around her words. "I miss you so much, Brad. If I had you here with me, I'd be all over your body with little kisses everywhere. Can't you just feel them?" Her voice had turned sexy and teasing.

"Enough already, Em," he said, grinning, in spite of his resolve.

"Go to sleep and dream about me and a cute little brewery in Jackson. Love you."

THE NEXT NIGHT, Emily answered on the first ring. "Hey! I just got in from a ten-mile run. I'm a hot, sweaty mess. If you were here, I'd take you to the hot tub on my parents' deck, no swimsuits."

"At the moment, it's nearly a hundred Fahrenheit here in Monterrey. A pool sounds more appealing."

"It's a pleasant sixty-four here. You're so going to love Hole."

She was the bubbly, energetic Emily at her best. Brad felt like shit for what he was going to say. "I've given your dad's offer some serious thought."

"If you need more than half a million, I'm sure we can talk him into it."

"It's a fantastic offer, Emily." He drew in a deep breath. *Just get the words out.* "But I can't accept it."

A long silence. "Why not? You just said it's fantastic."

"If I'd had this chance two years ago, I would have jumped at it in a second." *And maybe even in another year, when MBC and my brewers are further along.* "But right now, I can't do this to Carlos or to MBC."

"I don't mean this to sound negative," she said, sounding desperate and angry, "but MBC has four other brewers now. There will come a day when you're not there and MBC will survive."

"Em, have you thought about what would happen if I went to Wyoming and we broke up?"

"Then it would become a business deal between you and my father."

"And if your father decided I was a jerk who broke his daughter's heart and he was pulling out his investment? I'd be totally screwed."

"What you're being is totally stubborn."

"I'm sorry, Emily. I can't do it."

"Brad, you're an asshole." He had never heard her so angry. "And you know what? When you finally get fed up with the goddamned heat and third-world narcos and Mexicans, and you get over your huge ego about how you're the best brewer in the world and they can't live without you, don't bother to call me because I will have moved on."

He was left listening to a painful, blessed silence. The jab about his ego had pissed him off. She'd shown her real colors on that one, and she sounded way too much like Maddy. He was done with romance for the foreseeable future.

CHAPTER SIXTEEN

BRAD KILLED the engine on the van, one of several purchased from Huasteca and repainted with the MBC logo. He hopped out into the blaze of summer heat and swung open the back doors as Chago parked his car. "Okay, Superman, let's get these kegs inside," Brad said, grabbing the dolly. They lowered the first keg and wheeled it into the idled brewery of MBC brewpub.

"It feels so strange," Chago said, "and so small."

Through the windows, Paty waved from the dining room and hurried to greet them, lassoing each man in an ebullient hug. Two waiters and Noé followed. Paco greeted them saying, "The wheat's a little too foamy lately."

Behind the bar, Brad shook his head before the first glass was full. He took three sips, swishing each in his mouth. "No problems with the flavor, and we cleaned the line last week."

Back in the cooler, he checked a gauge. "Here's the problem, Paco. Carbonation's too high. The next time this happens, adjust it here."

When Brad and Chago finished changing out six kegs, the task that had brought them to the pub, Brad sent his helper back to the brewery. "If I don't make it back this afternoon, you and Alejandra know what to do." He was averaging nearly sixty hours a week at the brewery, and he resented having to hang around the pub today waiting for El Míster. He had tried to talk Carlos into letting Noé handle the *piso* payments without them. "One of us needs to be there," Carlos had contended. "I'll take responsibility."

Then the out-of-town owner of several Monterrey restaurants had insisted on meeting today, and Carlos had dumped the fun-filled *piso* meeting on Brad. Chago was taking out the last keg when he almost collided with Noé and El Míster.

"It's August first," the narco announced.

The muscles in Brad's temples tensed. "The money's in the office."

"Your manager can get it."

The look Noé gave Brad on his way out made his head tighten a little more. El Míster studied Chago and lifted his chin. "*Y tú, ¿quién eres?*" And who are you?

"*Santiago Rodríguez Almejo a sus órdenes,*" Chago replied. Brad winced. "At your orders" generally amounted to nothing more than a polite phrase, but the narco might decide otherwise.

Instead, El Míster leveled his blue eyes on Brad. "Everything okay with Registro? No more problems?"

"No problems," Brad replied, feeling a chill run through him.

El Míster crossed his arms and nodded slowly. His bizarre stare made Brad uncomfortable as hell. Finally, Noé hurried in and handed off the white envelope. The narco counted the bills, returned them to the envelope and stuffed it in his back pocket. "See you in September—at your new brewery." He was gone as quickly as he had come.

Brad saw the questions in Chago's look. "Forget you saw any of this."

"Sorry. We hear about extortions all the time, but actually seeing one go down is unnerving." Chago crossed his arms tightly against his chest. "Ingeniero, everybody at the pub knows it's going on. And my uncle, he owns a bakery. They make him pay, too. Five hundred pesos a month. It's just a little bakery, and they're killing him—figuratively, I mean, although one day, they might do it for real."

"I'm sorry, Chago. For all of us."

AS SUMMER drifted into fall, Noé and Carlos were hard at work planning a weekend of specials to celebrate the pub's first anniversary. At the brewery bottlers were filling, capping, labeling and packaging two thousand bottles an hour. Brad stood with Carlos and Tony Vargas at the glass window separating the brewery and the building entrance. "We hired both of those guys from Huasteca," Brad said, pointing to Abelardo, whose ponytail was hidden under a hairnet, and to Abraham, the barrel-chested senior bottler.

Abelardo steadily uncased bottles and positioned them on the conveyor belt. Abraham, working the labeler, shouted something. Abelardo flipped a switch and brought the line to a halt. With the speed of a race car mechanic, Abraham shucked off the empty cardboard cylinder and replaced it with a fresh foot-wide roll of Chipinque Wheat labels. Uncapped beer picked up oxygen and lost freshness by the second. Every minute the line was down cost money and quality. Abraham raised a thumb and Abelardo threw the line back into noisy motion.

"It's been quite a ride in the last six months," Brad continued. "Alfredo and his dad built a fantastic brewery, but they didn't manage it well. I spent hours on projects like fine-tuning the mill that had never been properly calibrated."

"Brad, I knew having you take over this brewery was the best decision," Tony said as they started up the stairs. "How are things going at the pub, Carlos?"

"Really well. Noé Padilla has taken over day-to-day operations so I can spend more time getting MBC's products into the market."

In the office Brad pulled bottles from the mini-fridge and glasses from the shelf above while Tony seated himself at the small conference table. "Where are your beers currently available?" the distributor asked.

"At over twenty-five restaurants and pubs," Carlos replied. "We're working on a contract with the HEB Mexico grocery store chain."

Tony sipped the beer Brad had handed him. "Great smoothness. Nice finish. By the way, Brad, congratulations on the first place award. That gives y'all some real bragging rights."

"Thanks," Brad said, "for pushing me to compete." The medal his Morenita Porter had won last month in Guadalajara was one of his proudest accomplishments.

"And the *Milenio* article" Tony said. "That was something else. 'Best new brewpub in town and Monterrey's hottest brewer,' pretty impressive stuff." The award had come on the heels of the article and had Brad pumped for days.

"Remember our conversation back in February?" Tony continued, "I said y'all weren't thinking big enough. What you have here is the result of thinking big. So far, y'all are a textbook example of how to grow a small business from the ground up."

"It wouldn't have happened without you," Brad said, raising his glass.

"When will y'all be ready to take the next step?"

Carlos raised his eyebrows. "Remembering the last time you said that, I'm curious as to what you have in mind. The textbooks have plenty of stories about companies that grew too fast."

"Hear me out," Tony said. "Brad, you said you're are currently using about fifty-five percent of your production capacity?"

"Correct."

"So you'll eventually double your production, maybe run more than one shift."

Brad massaged his jaw line and thought for a moment before answering. "I don't know if we want to grow that much. Right now, we don't threaten Cuauhtémoc-Moctezuma or Modelo. If we aim for that kind of production, and manage to sell that much beer, the big guys could decide they want a piece of the action. It happened in the U.S. when craft beers started to take off. The big breweries can almost always produce a similar product at a lower cost—think Coors's Blue Moon or Anheuser-Busch's Shock Top. Or, they buy out successful craft brewers like Redhook and Goose Island."

"Remember, be bold. Think big. Carve out new markets." The excitement in Tony's eyes told Brad that the distributor was getting to his point. "I think y'all need to export MBC products."

"To the U.S.?" It seemed to Brad that his words bounced against the office walls and echoed in the ensuing silence. He shook his head. "Too many good craft beers in the U.S. already. Part of our success here is due to the lack of competition. Plus, transportation and export costs would run up the retail price."

"Your beers are every bit as good as the ones being produced by top craft breweries in Texas. Here, your labor and production costs are lower. Y'all would be something new and different—a little Mexican brewery with damn good beer. Sales of macro U.S. brands are nearly as flat as the Texas Panhandle. Imported beers are up. Craft beers are where the growth is. Y'all came through for me and the Moss family. I owe you something, but as I've told y'all before, I'm a businessman, and I'm out to make money. I add MBC to my portfolio. Y'all break into a big new market. We all win."

Brad's mind had started to spin with the implications. "What are the chances that a drug cartel could highjack our freight truck?"

"Not very likely. The Carretera Nacional between Monterrey and Laredo is too heavily trafficked for them to pull off that sort of thing."

"I don't know if we're ready."

"Do y'all realize the opportunity I'm offering you? Craft brewers practically go through a goddamn courtship with distributors who demand they pre-sell their products to X number of outlets before they even sit down to negotiate. I'm coming to you. I'll push your products. I'll be honest and fair with you."

"If we say no," Carlos asked, "will you go to Patricio Bustamante?"

"I haven't decided. There's a substantial untapped market, but Bustamante doesn't have the capacity y'all do. And, y'all know as well as I do," he looked directly at Brad, "y'all brew better beer." Tony leaned back in his chair, hands clasped behind his head. "I believe that within a year, your biggest problem could be that you're running out of brewing capacity."

As soon as Tony left, Carlos said, "We've got to do it."

"Big Guy, we're both putting in close to sixty-hour weeks, and we've barely started up the brewery. We can't neglect the pub. Besides, higher profits are bound to mean higher *piso*."

Carlos leaned forward and ticked off arguments on his fingers. "One, Noé is handling the pub just fine. Two, we have a serious debt. A foothold in the U.S. market could be huge. Three, El Míster and El Cártel don't see our books or care about what happens in the U.S. Four, to quote your mother, don't be such a perfectionist."

"Quoting my mother is hitting below the belt."

"Where are your *¡ataque!* balls, Güero?" Carlos asked, grinning as he punched Brad's shoulder. "Hire the new bottler and a brewer, too. And learn how to delegate. Otherwise, you're going to drive both of us crazy."

Chapter Seventeen

NACHO STARED into Neto's lifeless face. The florescent lights made the white coffin lining so bright it hurt his eyes. His head ached like hell. Even with the bruises and swelling, death had softened Neto's face. Nacho tried to remember a time when Neto's face had been open and trusting. By the age of fourteen, Neto—Ernesto—had earned the nickname Matagatos and his face was already hardened. Back then, there was no El Míster, just Neto and his kid brother, Nacho.

Neto was already practicing the hard face the day Nacho started kindergarten, when Amá walked them to the school yard and said, "Neto, take care of your little brother."

"*Vente, mocoso.*" C'mon, snotty brat, his third-grade brother said, walking so fast that Nacho had to trot.

"Don't talk that way to your little brother," Amá called after them. Then they were just two more of the *mocosos* pouring into the school building.

Their father had done the same as millions of other poor Mexicans. *Se fue pa'el otro lado*, going to the other side on a bus that ran the eight hundred and twenty miles from Los Mochis to El Paso, Texas. Then he kept going. When Apá finally got his papers, he hung two images just inside the door of the small apartment in Dallas, La Virgin de Guadalupe, patron saint of Mexico, and Ronald Reagan, father of the 1988 amnesty. Then he went for his wife and sons. *His sons.* Apá knew the truth. Everybody knew it. Neto beat the crap out of two older boys for telling the truth.

The school yard judges gave Neto the win. The school gave him a suspension. Amá gave him a tongue lashing. Then, at the kitchen table, she had pulled Nacho into her lap. Even today, the smell of the beans simmering on the stove and the softness of Ama's lap infused his memories of the afternoon when he learned he was a bastard. "*¡M'ijo, my son,* I want you to hear it from me and not from those *tarados.*" He stared into her big brown eyes that looked sadder than they ever had, waiting to hear what a bunch of idiots knew that he didn't. Back then, he used to wonder what was wrong with him that he didn't have warm brown eyes and rich bronze skin like Amá, Apá and Neto. "This won't be the last time mean kids make fun of you, saying that Apá isn't your real father."

"But he is."

Ama shook her head, tears at the edges of her beautiful eyes. Nacho wanted to reach out and touch her eyes, feel their brown warmth on his finger. Amá's eyes were what love looked like. His own eyes were the color of the swimming pool in the apartment complex. Most kids liked the pool, but Nacho hated it. Even on the hottest summer afternoon, the water was freezing. He once spent a long time staring into the bathroom mirror. He knew that his eyes would feel like the pool water. Instead, it just stung when he poked one with the tip of his finger. He was disappointed that it hadn't felt as icy as the swimming pool. That hadn't changed how they looked, either.

"A true father," Amá said, "is one who raises a child. In that, Apá is your father. But the man who gets a woman pregnant, he's the father in another way."

Nacho tensed and gripped the coffin. He hadn't seen Amá in three years, but he sensed her presence, could practically feel her hands on his arms, smell the lotion she always used to keep her hands soft.

"*M'ijo,* you remember your grandmother's hens and the rooster on the *rancho*?" she asked that afternoon. "The rooster makes the hens pregnant so there are eggs and chicks. When Neto was born, Apá was the rooster. With you, there was—" She wiped her eyes with sleeve of her apron. "Another rooster."

"Where is this other rooster?" Nacho shouted.

"Far away. He's a bad man."

"Then you aren't my real Amá?" Twenty-four years later, his stomach knotted when he forced himself think about that moment—the one when he had realized that a single small truth can change everything forever. Life was one motherfucker of a teacher.

Amá had wrapped him in her arms, crying, "I am your mother. And Apá, he loves you just as much as he loves Neto." Then Nacho was crying, beating her arms. How could Apá possibly love another man's son as much as he loved his *real* son?

"*¡Son pinches mentirosos!*" They're damned liars, calling him son of a bitch," Neto had shouted from the kitchen. "I didn't have any choice. I had to beat 'em up. They say it again and I'll kill 'em. No one says that about my Amá." That was the first time Nacho had seen Neto's face truly hard and angry. It had scared him and thrilled him knowing that eight-year-old face was on his side.

Nacho breathed in deep and quick. He jabbed his hand in the coffin and clenched the cold arm of his brother, the skin a sick imitation of Neto's rich color in life. This was Matagatos, Neto, his *mano*, his big brother who had been a father almost as much as Apá, more than the rich owner of the fine hotel in Los Mochis who believed his maids' duties included sexual favors. If the woman didn't agree, he took what he wanted by force.

The funeral home director who let Nacho in the back door of this shitty D. F. *funeraria* in a crappy neighborhood was one who did work for El Cártel. The place was a dump. It smelled of death. Nacho dropped to his knees and pounded the concrete floor. "*¿Por qué, Dios santo?*" Why? he prayed to a silent God. "*Virgencita de Tepeyac, ¿por qué? Blanquita, ¿por qué? ¡Jesús Malverde, ¿por qué?!*" He silently cried out to the Virgin of Guadalupe and the narco saints that the Catholic Church didn't recognize. Why hadn't the bullet taken him instead?

The asshole *cabrón* Ramírez fucked them over. The federal agent had been in on two previous kidnappings in Mexico City that went fine. This time, though, things had fallen apart, and in this business, there was no room for mistakes. Nacho, Neto and Labrador had pulled off six other kidnappings in Monterrey and the D.F. Up until tonight, the only complicated one had been the boys last August. That only happened because the little gringo prick called Nacho a son of a bitch. The kid was lucky he hadn't beat him to a pulp. He would have if Neto hadn't been there to pull him off. It was like he was finally getting revenge on the assholes from elementary school and the fucking hotel owner.

This time should have been like the last, a simple hand off, the American businessman for the two hundred thousand dollars. There wasn't supposed to be any gunfight. The American bastard with the *federales* didn't need to shoot. And he sure as hell didn't need to fire on Neto from a few feet away. Coming from behind, Nacho had bashed the motherfucker's head with his Smith & Wesson double action revolver and dragged him into the van. He'd gotten off a couple of shots while Labrador heaved a hostage he had grabbed into the van. Grillo, who was in on the gig, hauled Neto in and they sped away. Nacho yanked the ski mask off the man who had killed Neto and held the blazing hot revolver barrel a half inch from the guy's neck. He wanted to look the fucker in the eyes before he finished him off. "I'm American, don't shoot," the man said calmly in Spanish.

They had strict instructions: bring in all Americans alive. It turned into a fucking mess. Nacho's finger twitched against the trigger. He could have shot and said he hadn't known the bastard was American. But Bala and the *patrones* had ways of finding out the truth. He might as well order his own death. He needed to shoot somebody. He ripped the mask from Labrador's prey and almost shitted in his pants.

"There's nothing lower than a traitor," he rasped. He pressed the gun barrel against Ramírez's temple. "Why'd you get Americans involved?"

"I didn't want to. They made us do it," the *federal* said in a desperate voice. "You guys kidnapped some goddamned rich and famous American. The U.S. Embassy and Washington were threatening a huge investigation. They were going to go to the media. They had us fucked."

"Totally fucked," Nacho agreed. He let the twitchy finger go. He slid open the side door of the speeding van and pitched Ramírez's body onto the freeway. It made him feel a little better, but not much.

Now he rose from the floor of the crap-hole funeral home, dried his eyes and pulled back his shoulders. "*Mano*, the fucking gringo's gonna pay."

NACHO KICKED the door in so it crashed against the wall. The only light in the room came from the weak bulb dangling on a wire from the ceiling. The room stank. "*¡Siéntate, pendejo!*" Sit up, asshole!

The hostages were always terrified, naked or in their underwear on the dirty cots or lumpy mattresses or cement floors next to a piss and shit bucket. This one, a light-skinned black guy, was different. He sat up slowly, erect, arms crossed over his bare chest, eyes on the opposite wall five feet away, tall and prickly like a saguaro cactus. He made no attempt to cover his privates. Labrador and Grillo had worked him over and left him with a swollen eye. Bala was coming later. His only instructions had been that he wanted the black gringo alive when he got there.

"What time is it?" the gringo asked.

"Three a.m., *pinche cabrón*." Nacho slid the blue and white Rayados backpack off his shoulder to the floor. He took a slow drag on a cigarette between his thumb and forefinger. "You deserve a long, slow, painful death."

The gringo stared at a flap of peeling paint on the wall.

"You do a lot of that covert shit for the U.S. government?" The question got a rise out of the guy. He made eye contact. Nacho took another slow puff. "Had some second thoughts in the last couple hours, Demarcus Wilkes?"

This time Nacho sucked hard on the cigarette. The tip glowed in the dim light. He blew the smoke out in a thin stream that rose up toward the light bulb. "You seen those bodies with burns?" He waited. No response. "Answer me, *cabrón!*"

"Yes," Wilkes replied in a flat tone.

"You ever watched those burns being branded on?"

A quick pause. Fear or defiance? "No."

"You're about to. And after that . . ." Nacho leaned over and dug in the backpack. "You hear about the cop killed in Nuevo Laredo last week?" He extracted the Taser X3 from its holster.

"You won't be able to use it."

"That registration and theft protection stuff is bullshit." He aimed at the paint flap and blew it away, leaving another pockmark in the crappy wall. "Convinced?" Wilkes stared off and nodded.

Like a magician, Nacho reached in the backpack and pulled out the Cold Steel SRK knife. "I'm gonna cut various places on your body. The last one you'll be aware of is a major vein. We'll dump you in the Zócalo," he said, Mexico City's main square.

Most assholes would have at least pissed by now. "Or, there's another way."

Wilkes made eye contact for the second time.

Nacho pulled out the cigarette pack, took a last drag off the stub he'd been smoking and used it to light the next one. He flicked the butt to the floor and lifted his chin. "Work for us."

"Who's 'us'?"

"Who do you think, *pendejo*? El Cártel." Nacho exhaled another slow stream of smoke toward the ceiling. "You with us or against us? You want to live or die?"

"What would it involve?" Wilkes was looking right at him now, squinting through the slit in the swollen eye.

"Information. El Cártel pays well. Plenty of your colleagues know from experience." He bent down and picked up the knife. "So, what's it gonna be?"

"What do you want to know?"

Nacho ground the smoking butt of the first cigarette with the heel of his boot. He wanted to punch the asshole's face, hear the bones crunch then pound him until he stopped breathing. But Bala would kill him. "Who besides you and Ramírez was involved?"

"Federales."

"Names?"

"I don't know."

"Liar!" He struck Wilkes' face with the back of his hand.

The American pinched his eyes shut and lowered his head. "All I know is what they told us. The one you killed in the van was Miguel. The other was Juan." Wilkes looked up again and Nacho was pleased to see the fear in his eyes. "They were GOPEs," Wilkes added.

"You haven't said anything I didn't know already. Ramírez was stupid. Nobody takes Cártel money and gets away with betrayal." Nacho let Wilkes chew on the fact that a member of the elite *Grupo de Operaciones Especiales* was on El Cártel's payroll. "How many GOPEs?"

"Only those two."

"There were more." Nacho didn't know, but he was about to find out.

"Besides the GOPES, two *federales* and me and one other American. I think you might have killed him."

"His name?"

"Jon Ryerson."

"Background?"

"DEA."

"And who the hell are you, Wilkes?"

"I work for the U.S. Embassy."

Holy shit. Why hadn't Nacho made the connection? "You and Ryerson were involved in the Hurtado kidnapping."

Wilkes looked startled. "Yeah," he said in a wary voice, squinting up at Nacho.

"What are you really, Wilkes—DEA, ATF, CIA, Homeland Security, military?"

"Career diplomat. Before that, I served four years in the U.S. Army after college."

Nacho swung his fist into the side of Wilkes' head and sent him sprawling on the bed. "Fucking liar! Since when do career diplomats handle kidnappings?"

Wilkes lay there, one hand where Nacho's fist had connected, the other on the back of his head. "Jeff Miller's parents knew me and asked for my help."

Nacho jerked Wilkes up on his knees. He held the American within a foot of his face and stared into his eyes. "You're full of shit, Wilkes. Remember this: if you are ever again less than completely honest with us, if you *ever* try to double cross El Cártel I will personally hunt you down. Your death won't be quick or easy like it was for Ramírez. Understood?"

Wilkes nodded.

Nacho shoved the Taser into its holster inside the backpack and tossed the knife in the pack. As he opened the door, Wilkes asked in a flat voice, "Can I have my clothes back?"

"Sure," Nacho said, slamming the door on his way out.

The idiot guard asleep in a plastic chair jerked into a defensive position. "Stop pointing that goddamn gun at me, *pendejo*," Nacho snarled. He hoped Wilkes froze his naked black ass off waiting for Bala and his clothes. Nacho was sick of doing Bala's dirty work.

Not much longer before his plan would be up and running. A lot of things were going to change then.

CHAPTER EIGHTEEN

A REFRESHING November breeze wafted through the loading dock door, stirring the rich, malty aromas of brewing beer. Brad, Carlos, Chago and the transport truck driver watched as Abraham poked the arms of the forklift into the first shrink-wrapped pallet. He shifted into reverse and, with a shrill beeping, backed around for a straight shot into the semi's trailer.

"Ever been hijacked?" Brad asked the burly driver.

The man made the sign of the cross. "Not yet. It happened to my cousin in Tamaulipas, though, hauling a load of sorghum."

"You're kidding. Sorghum?"

"Cattle feed. Damned Cártel owns ranches and farms all over the state of Tamaulipas."

"And your cousin?"

"Lucky guy. Handed over the truck and everything in his pockets. They left him on the side of the road. The *federales* picked him up and threw him in jail in Matamoros until they verified his story with the trucking company. As soon as they let him out, he got in touch with a *coyote* he knew. Next day, he was in Houston."

Abraham deposited the load. The driver, armed with a sheet of honeycombed dunnage taller than himself, moved in to cushion the pallet and separate it from the next one in preparation for the four hundred sixty-five mile trip to Houston.

Brad wondered if the driver would visit his cousin. The whole *inseguridad* thing was so bizarre. Except for the initial "safe-passage fee" for his equipment and monthly *piso* payments, Brad had never experienced any other aspect of it, certainly none of the violence. Millions of people went about their lives every day, and everything seemed so normal—until a semi driver calmly talked about his cousin's hijacking, or Chago mentioned his uncle paying *piso*, or the Miller's son was kidnapped and the family fled the country. The stories went on and on. Yet here they were, on a beautiful morning, loading the historic first of many shipments to Houston.

Abraham beeped his way out of the trailer and forked the next four by four by six foot pallet. For Brad, each one was a work of art. The initial building blocks were four-bottle cartons of MBC beer, packaged four cartons to a case, seventy-four cases to a pallet. One thousand one hundred eighty-four bottles of his beer on every pallet. When all six pallets were loaded and the truck was pulling away, Carlos punched Brad's shoulder. "MBC's first international shipment and first seasonal brew all happening in one day. Congratulations."

"Same to you, partner," Brad said as calmly as he could. Inside, he was bursting with pride.

AN HOUR later Brad and Alejandra hooked up the first keg of MBC's newest beer in the pub's walk-in refrigerator. At the dining room bar, Paco swung a glass under the bar tap. Beer schussed down and cheers rose up. From now on, MBC would produce a seasonal brew every four months. They had named the kick-off beer *Winterfest Navideña*. The Christmas Winterfest was a dark, hoppy ale with hints of cinnamon and cloves that Brad and Alejandra had worked on over several months. Seasonal beers had been one of his goals from the start, but there was never enough time. This one was happening only because Alejandra had put in so many extra hours in the pilot brewery. Meanwhile, Brad had a brewery to run, employees to train, international exportation starting up and demands from the pub. Some days he felt like a juggler with balls flying in every direction.

"A toast to Brad and Alejandra," Carlos said, lifting the glass Paco handed him.

"To Alejandra," Brad said over the clinking of glasses and murmurs of, "*¡Salud!*"

"Check this out." Brad reached underneath the bar. "Limited edition four-packs."

"Very nice," Paco said as Noé let out a soft whistle.

The solid, tall, dark bottle signaled a serious beer. Carlos had designed the no-frills label with a plain Christmas tree and green background, a red bow and ribbon splashed across the label. Only the font in the beer's name hinted at its elegance.

"I couldn't have done it," Carlos said, "without a lot of coaching from Brad and some help from the PR firm. A toast to Brad."

After another round of cheers, Noé asked, "Any ideas as to the next seasonal brew?"

"Top secret," Brad said. "What I will announce is that I'm naming Alejandra MBC project manager for seasonals and giving her a raise."

Alejandra's mouth flew open. Brad watched Chago's lips tightened before the men congratulated Alejandra with hugs, handshakes and a knuckle-bump from Paco. Chago was the last to shake her hand. Brad probably would have reacted the same way. He had justified the decision by telling himself Chago had his own duties that brought him praise, and Alejandra was showing a true passion for R & D work.

"To the continued success of MBC," Carlos said raising his glass.

"To the continued success of MBC," Brad said, clinking his glass against Carlos's.

EXPORTING AND Winterfest had made November a heady month, but Brad unlocked the brewery door on the twenty-ninth in a bad mood. El Míster had called at ten last night to say he was coming two days early for

December's *piso*. That had meant calls to Carlos and Noé and scrambling to reserve ten thousand pesos from the pub's sales yesterday. It hadn't helped Brad's mood that when the narco called, every news show was reporting the story of the small-town mayor whose mutilated body had turned up on the highway between Monterrey and Reynosa, across the border from McAllen, Texas. No wonder Roberto had declared he was boycotting local news. Most days, Brad could simply wrap himself in his work and ignore *la inseguridad*. But not today.

El Míster had come around two days late in November, alone, haggard, short-tempered. Brad doubted El Cártel was so lax about other aspects of the businesses they ran. Since El Míster's initial visit to the brewery in August, he had taken to collecting *piso* there. With Noé at the pub and Carlos everywhere except at the brewery, Brad had become the default contact. He told himself that when he finally opened that brewery in Colorado and told insane stories about paying off narcos, nobody would believe him.

He walked past storage shelves stacked high with bottles, boxes, kegs, malt and hops. They were double and triple ordering supplies and materials. Money was flowing out as fast as beer. Crazy how happy it had made the loan officer with the Cheshire-cat grin to hand them the second loan for the brewery. The packed shelves and the scramble to keep up with the demand for his beers were the reasons he was still in Monterrey. Boiled down to one word, it was ambition, pure and simple, in spite of Maddy's accusations. He tried not to think about how much money they owed the bank and what would happen the inevitable day El Míster upped MBC's *piso*. Last month, once again, he and Carlos had taken home less than their full salaries.

As of today, they would have forked over a total of one hundred thirty-five thousand pesos in *piso*, over ten thousand dollars, to El Míster. Paying down their bank debt by that much would have made Brad a very happy man. When he dwelled on the extortion, he ended up pissed, but he wasn't ready to pack his bags and head for Colorado yet. It would be a cowardly and lousy thing to do to Carlos and their employees. Plus there was the matter of his life savings tied up in MBC. Pulling his money out would hit Carlos hard, and it wasn't enough for Brad to start his own brewery in Denver. What bank would float him a three or four hundred thousand dollar loan with so little equity?

Up until now, he had managed to be present each month when El Míster and his assistants showed up, but it was a matter of time before they came calling when he was out. He and Carlos had appointed Chago as the backup. With some hesitation, Chago had agreed. Brad kept him close by the first day of each month, making sure he observed the ways a payoff could play out. El Míster had taken Chago's presence in stride, even nicknamed him *Flaco*, Skinny Guy.

Brad climbed the stairs to the office. In three weeks, he'd fly to Denver for Christmas. Every time he talked to his mother, she had a new menu planned. He'd probably put on ten pounds. His life was bizarre. Professionally, except for narcos, it was awesome. His personal life was a different story.

JUST BEFORE lunch, Brad was standing by the bottling line with Abraham when he spotted El Míster already inside the brewery, observing them through the plate glass window. Like last time, he came alone. The dark circles under his eyes appeared deeper than last month. He wore jeans, a cowboy shirt, a huge belt buckle and pointed boots like a *banda* singer.

Damned Cártel owns ranches and farms all over the state of Tamaulipas the truck driver had said. Who knew what El Míster did when he wasn't extorting money from MBC? Brad decided he didn't want to know.

"*Buenas*," El Míster muttered, the shortest possible morning greeting.

Fine with Brad. He pulled the folded envelope from his back pocket and held it out. El Míster glanced inside, fingered each bill and stuck the envelope in his shirt pocket. "I need one of those mini kegs, Flaco."

"I'll get it," Brad said, contradicting the narco.

"It's good training for the kid," El Míster said, overriding him.

"It's okay, Ingeniero," Chago said.

"We don't use that size keg commercially. I'll have to find one," Brad said. He waited to make sure this was acceptable before walking away, close beside his young brewer. He wanted El Míster gone as soon as possible, but the hell if he was going to be intimidated.

"I'm sorry, Chago. This was never in your job description." El Míster hadn't bothered to return the eighth-barrel keg he'd demanded in the summer. Brad grabbed the other experimental keg that had sat in a corner for months and began to fill it.

"What are you doing?" Chago asked, wide-eyed. "You haven't cleaned it."

"My f-you to El Cártel."

"Ingeniero, I didn't know you had it in you."

As Brad watched Chago carry the keg out the front door behind El Míster, he heard Abraham mutter to Abelardo, "Damn narcos. They're ruining Mexico."

"Mexico and MBC," Brad said. They stood silently, waiting for Chago. It sucked that he was completely powerless to protect Chago or any other employee. Hell, he was powerless to protect himself. If he was completely honest with himself, that lack of power ate at him as much as the financial drain.

When Chago returned, Brad clapped a hand on his shoulder. "You're in line for a fat promotion. At this rate, you'll make that down payment on a house sooner than you expected."

"Graciela will be a very happy woman," his youngest brewer grinned.

"*¡ATAQUE!*" Brad yelled at the ball speeding his direction. He pivoted, darted and shifted all his energy into a perfectly controlled swing. Just as he'd pictured it, he hit the ball with a solid *thwock*. It cleared the net by inches, bounced just inside the court and flew out before Eugenio could reach it. Eight Ex-A-Tecs who had finished their own doubles matches cheered from the sidelines. Someone shouted, "Amazing shot, Brad!" And it had been. His best play ever. Brad was busting with exhilaration.

"Game!" Carlos crowed while Brad mopped his face on his sleeve. "Absolutely awesome, Güero!" Carlos said, swinging a high-five his way.

"If you're going to keep beating us, that's it for the lessons," Roberto said with a handshake. "Seriously, Brad, you played better today than you ever have. Congratulations."

Eugenio came over and knuckle-bumped Brad, then called out to the Ex-A-Tecs, "Who's going to MBC? Drinks on the Big Guy and the Güero."

"Appetizers on Eugenio!" Brad shouted. The sun was shining. The mountains towered nearby. He needed this after El Míster's visit yesterday.

On his drive to the pub, he took stock of the last year. Saturdays at the sports club had become his routine after Emily left. He went to American parties every now and then, although he wasn't close friends with any expats. Carlos was so into marketing MBC and its products that he didn't have time for late-night poker games. He was forever making business calls, lunching with clients, meeting with people. It was no longer clear where Carlos's work ended and his social life began. Other than the Saturday tennis games, they rarely saw each other outside MBC these days.

Overall, it had been an outstanding year for MBC and for Brad as a brewer. The Christmas party a year ago when he'd last seen Maddy seemed like another life, and in a way, it was. Five months had slipped by since Emily left, which, counting from her birthday dinner, was as long as they were a couple.

In the pub parking lot, Vagabundo promptly emerged from under a car and meowed a greeting. Brad stroked the cat's back. "Hey, buddy, I don't see much of you these days."

Inside, he slipped behind the bar and served up a round of Winterfest Navideña. Comfortably seated with Carlos and five other tennis players, he lounged in his chair, at ease with the Spanish flying around him. A soccer game from Mexico City played on the television screens.

"Big Guy," Roberto said—Carlos's friends had picked up on the nickname—"Claudia gets home in a week and a half."

"We've already got a dinner date."

"Another one of your girlfriends?" Brad asked. Somehow, Carlos was still finding time to date.

"My sister," Roberto said. "She graduates next Friday from a design school in New York. I introduced her and Carlos at a wedding last summer. You should have seen them on the dance floor."

"It wasn't me. She's a good dancer," Carlos said.

"Hot, too," Eugenio added.

"*¡G-o-o-o-l!*" The TV announcer's cries echoed through the pub as Pachuca took the lead and all eyes turned to the television.

"Who needs another Winterfest?" Brad asked. In three weeks he'd be in Denver, missing these guys and his life in Monterrey.

CHAPTER NINETEEN

February 2014

"FLACO, BRING us a case of Santa Catarina!"

The tougher El Míster wanted to sound, the raspier he made his voice, Brad was convinced. Today he towed Labrador, the tattooed hulk. Brad wondered where Matagatos, The Cat Killer clone, was. He hadn't showed his face in months. The dull clatter of bottles jangling through the line on the other side of the plate glass window comforted Brad. The only employees visible were Abelardo and Abraham, who couldn't abandon the flowing river of bottles. The employees who could leave their posts usually disappeared when El Míster paid his monthly visits.

Chago emerged from the brewery with the box of beer and handed it off to Labrador. With a brisk, "See you March first," El Míster exited, pulling Labrador and the beer in his wake.

"Thanks, Chago," Brad said, rubbing his temples, as soon as the narcos were out the door. "You don't have to do this if you don't want to."

"I'm okay with it for now."

"At least we don't have to see them for another month."

LALO STILL wore his safety glasses. Chago had pushed his on top of his head. Rodrigo's hung around his neck. Alejandra's dangled from one hand. Brad had stuck his in his shirt pocket. Carlos was right. Brad needed to hand over certain responsibilities to his brewers. Like a lecturing professor, he waved two markers in his hand. "A common mistake in flavor stability testing is not properly marking products. Three months from now, if we don't know how long they've aged, the whole test is invalidated."

Brad grabbed two boxes and held out a marker. "Chago, engineer of the precise handwriting, I'll do the wheat samples. You take the pale ales. We label each box in a consistent manner so nobody will confuse it with boxes of regular beer. Name and date, upper left corner." He watched Chago write a neat #1.

"Next, the date. 5/2/14, *el cinco de febrero, 2014*," Brad continued, marking his own box. "Afterwards, we fill in this form, place the boxes on the middle shelf on the back wall in the storage area and save the form in the file labeled Product Aging."

"Got it, Ingeniero," Chago said, already working on the document.

"Rodrigo, Alejandra, Lalo, you guys work on the remaining boxes. Chago, you're in charge of storing everything."

While the group finished their work, he turned to Alejandra. "Ready for your show?"

"I think so."

At five thirty-eight the brewers circled the small table that served as desk and work area. "Okay, guys, see what you think," Alejandra said, sounding slightly uncertain of herself and the rye IPA with reddish hues. Topo Chico Centeno IPA was set to debut as MBC's second seasonal brew.

She tipped a pitcher and served up several ounces, passing the first glass to Lalo. When everyone had a sample in hand, Chago raised his. "Nice head, good color. Cheers!" Glasses clinked, voice murmured, "*¡Salud!*" and then grew silent as they swirled and sniffed, sipped and savored. Alejandra's eyes moved from face to face.

"A little spicy, a touch of bitterness," Lalo said.

"Nicely crisp," Rodrigo added.

"I think we have the recipe down," Brad said. Alejandra reached to high-five his out-stretched hand. "I should say *you* have the recipe down. Alejandra, you've done a terrific job."

"This is really good," Lalo agreed. "I have to admit, Alejandra, that first day at Boot Camp, I thought you couldn't possibly be a serious brewer. How could a woman do all the lifting and physical work? But," he tipped his head toward Rodrigo and Chago, "you're better than those two combined."

"He's just saying that so you'll take him a beer in a few years when he's too old to go out and buy his own," Rodrigo said.

"You sure aren't going to do it," Lalo retorted.

The sound of shoes on the stairs distracted Brad from the toast he was about to propose. Carlos burst through the door, Ray-Bans on his head. "Sorry. There's a *narcobloqueo* at Constitución and Gonzalitos. It's got traffic snarled for miles."

While Brad hadn't experienced one of the blockades, he'd heard about bands of narcos and armed criminals descending simultaneously on major intersections and commandeering every vehicle. While drivers ran for their lives, the thugs stationed cars, trucks and buses for maximum blockage. Then they ran with the keys. Score one for the criminals, zero for the police and ordinary citizens. The brewers, anxious about their evening commutes, bombarded Carlos with questions.

When the tasting broke up, Brad and Carlos chatted at the top of the stairs. In the back corner below, six pallets waited by the loading dock door. "Everything good to go for the Houston shipment tomorrow?" Carlos asked.

"I think so. Chago's handling it."

"I'm glad you're learning to delegate. See you tomorrow at the pub?"

"I should be over around eleven. You on for tennis this Saturday?"

Carlos wrinkled his brow. "Can't. I'm going to a choir concert with Claudia. A couple of her friends are singing."

"You two are spending a lot of time together."

Carlos tried not to smile but failed. "Let's just say I like her."

"I'll keep an eye out for the wedding invitation."

"Right."

Back in the pilot brewery, Alejandra was drying the last glass. Conversations with Carlos had become a mix of English and Spanish, but with Alejandra, he always spoke English. It was a relaxing, comfortable habit. He looked at her and realized he didn't want to go home to an empty apartment and another solitary meal.

"Got any plans for the evening?"

"Yoga class."

"Seriously?"

"Three times a week. Why?"

"I was going to invite you to a Topo Chico celebration dinner, but maybe some other time."

"I could skip class for one night. What do you have in mind?"

Brad looked down at his work shirt and jeans. "Nothing fancy."

With the bottling line shut down and the employees gone, the brewery was eerily quiet. Chago was still in the back corner, writing on a clipboard. "Quitting time!" Brad shouted, as he and Alejandra descended the stairs.

"Just finishing up the paperwork on tomorrow's shipment."

"It can wait."

"The truck gets here at eight in the morning. This won't take me long. I'll lock up."

"Thanks, Chago," Brad said as they neared the young brewer. "You got the test boxes properly stored away so there won't be any mix-ups?"

"Labeled and stored in the middle where you wanted them. Documentation's in the file."

"Now that you know how the process works, you can handle the whole thing next time."

"You two going somewhere?" Chago asked, too much curiosity in his tone.

"I invited Alejandra to celebrate Topo Chico. She deserves a little recognition." Why did he feel like he had to explain himself to Chago? "Want to come?"

"Thanks, but Graciela's cooking dinner. Congratulations, Alejandra," Chago said, winking at her.

CUSTOMERS FILLED every table in the mom-and-pop restaurant. The mouth-watering smell of tamales made Brad's stomach rumble. Alejandra deftly loosened the tie around a banana leaf wrapper with her knife and fork. As a curl of steam floated up, she slid the contents onto her plate and transferred the wrapper to the dish the waiter had placed between them. "That's one monster tamale," Brad said, staring at the square object that took up most of Alejandra's plate.

"Go ahead, unwrap yours," she said, dipping a spoon into the bowl of thick, dark sauce.

Brad's clumsy effort made Alejandra's grace all the more impressive. "What's the sauce?"

"*Mole negro*, a hallmark of Oaxacan cooking."

"And to think that I was going to go home to microwaved ramen noodles." Brad spooned *mole* on his tamale and took the first bite. "Umm, incredible."

"I'm glad you think so," Alejandra said, smiling at him. "Do you like the smaller northern-style tamales in corn husks?"

Brad nodded with a full mouth and Alejandra continued. "Next time we make a batch at the ranch, I'll bring you some. We put them together assembly-line style, several hundred at a time."

"So, you like to cook?"

"It's not that different from brewing."

"Is there anything you're not good at?" Brad speared another bite.

Alejandra laughed, a deep, throaty sound he hadn't heard from her before. "I don't take orders well. I don't do the obedient girlfriend or daughter well. I don't knit or sew, don't like to go to wedding showers, rarely spend more than five minutes on make-up. I also can't sing or play a musical instrument."

"But you have a hard-core Alabama accent, and you make a hell of a Topo Chico Centeno IPA."

Alejandra's cheeks reddened. "I don't know if you realize how much your compliments about my brewing mean to me. You were the first brewer to genuinely value my training and skills."

Throughout the meal, she was as down-to-earth as she was every day at work. Her dark hair, ordinarily hidden under a mandatory hairnet, swung loose over her shoulders. She had a way of pulling it back that he found disturbingly attractive.

"Have you ever thought about moving to the States?" he asked.

"It's occurred to me, but where would I go? I love my grandmother and family in Mobile but the cousins have all moved away. Why go to a place where I don't know anyone except older relatives? And you? I sense you won't be in Monterrey for more than a few years."

"Who knows? I love my work, and I've had incredible opportunities, although the *inseguridad* really gets to me sometimes."

"The narcos get to us all."

"For now, I like the day-to-day challenges and the successes. I feel a sense of duty to Carlos and the MBC employees. I stand to make some good money."

"That attitude is why we're all devoted to you."

He looked at Alejandra's expressive face. He'd never before studied her full, sensuous lips. Suddenly he wanted to lean across the table and kiss them.

CHAPTER TWENTY

THE WEEK Brad arrived in Monterrey, one of Carlos's aunts had conveniently purchased some new furniture and gladly given Brad her hand-me-downs. Unlike the aunt, he wasn't bothered by the loose strands of rattan unraveling on the chair legs and the table base. Most of the time, it didn't bother him that the set barely fit in the space between his kitchen and living room. It was only a problem when he had company, which was almost never. The decór didn't seem to bother the three other poker players.

Roberto slapped his hand on the thick glass table top cluttered with cards, money and beer bottles. "I fold."

"I am the king!" Eugenio crowed, raking peso bills toward him.

Diego pushed back his chair and stood up. "I've got to go pick up Marta from her mother's house."

"Married life has ruined you as a poker player," Eugenio said.

"I'm here, which is more than you can say for Carlos."

"Love is really messing with our poker nights."

"Love is having all sorts of effects on Carlos," Brad said. In his head, the words hadn't sounded as critical as when he spoke them.

"You should see what it's done to my sister," Roberto said. "Claudia's crazy in love with Carlos."

"There's something to be said for being in love," Diego replied, as the men began exchanging *abrazos* and handshakes.

Roberto gathered the empty beer bottles and shoved them into a space among dishes of cold food on the narrow counter between the table and kitchen. "Got any more of that rye IPA?"

"In the fridge." Brad said.

"Grab one for me," Eugenio said, scraping a near-empty bowl of salsa with a chip. "You should make Topo Chico Centeno all year round."

"We might do that," Brad said as he tossed some paper plates and wadded napkins in the trash can. Roberto put two bottles on the living room table and dropped into the armchair with his own beer.

"So how'd the date go last night?" Eugenio asked, claiming a spot on the sofa.

"Okay," Roberto answered. "I'll probably call her again."

"But you're not 'crazy in love'?"

"No way," Roberto said, taking a long pull.

Brad grabbed the last beer and sat down. He'd gotten a heck of a deal on the sofa and armchair at a going-out-of-business sale. Someday, he might hang some stuff on the wall.

"What about you, Brad?" Roberto asked. "Any women in the picture?"

"Nope."

"I'm out of sisters, but I've got a cousin," Roberto offered.

"Thanks, but no blind dates."

"What about the chick who made this beer?" Roberto asked, holding up the brown bottle and squinting at it.

"A lady brewer," Eugenio said. "Does she lift weights, too?"

"I have no idea."

"Is she hot?"

"I don't know."

"Is she available?"

"I don't ask my employees about their love lives," Brad lied.

"Tell her you have a friend."

"I have a friend who has a cousin," Brad said.

"No way I'd let Eugenio date my cousin," Roberto shot back.

"*Goooool* for the Chivas!" Eugenio shouted, bumping up the volume on the soccer game playing on the living room TV.

An hour later, when the Chivas had pulled out a 3-2 win, Eugenio and Roberto called it a night. Brad closed the door behind them and carted an armful of beer bottles to the kitchen. He glanced at the darkened guacamole and decided that whether it sat in the bowl on the counter another eight hours or in the trash didn't really matter. Ditto for the empty Styrofoam plates from the taquería and the wads of aluminum foil. He yawned and turned out the light.

Before he drifted off to sleep, he thought about Eugenio's questions. Alejandra *was* hot, and she *was* available. If Eugenio saw her, he'd have her phone number in five minutes. And that was why Brad had evaded answering the questions. He didn't want her to meet Eugenio or anybody else. Eventually she was going to find a new boyfriend. When the day came, Brad realized, he was going to be bummed.

"THEY KILLED Bala!"

The ringing phone had startled Nacho out of a deep sleep. The three words jolted him awake. Camila stirred and reached for him as he gripped the phone while Labrador babbled on. A dozen thoughts tumbled around in his sleep-addled head. Camila nestled against his chest.

"Sonsabitches from the Gulf Cartel," Labrador was yelling. "We gotta fuck 'em so they'll never want to mess with us again."

"Damn Bala!" Nacho said, jumping out of bed. "Everybody told him he was stupid to get mixed up with that girl."

"He always was stupid about women," Labrador said.

"So the rumors were true. She really did belong to some *golfo*?" Nacho pulled on the boxers and pants he'd dropped on the bathroom floor a few hours ago.

"They busted in the house where he was and shot up the place bad. They shouted all sorts of crap about not messing with Gulf Cartel women before they killed Bala and another guy and took the girls."

"How do you know all that?" Nacho asked, flipping on light switches.

"Chato was there. He escaped out a window."

"Has anybody gone for the bodies?"

"That's why I'm calling."

"I'll be at your place in fifteen minutes. Call El Grillo, too." Nacho ended the call and took a deep breath. Changes were on the way.

Camila sat up, her big, firm tits on full display. "Bad news?"

"I gotta go."

"When will you be back?"

"I don't know."

Nacho threw on a shirt and shoes before grabbing his pistol off the nightstand. He stuffed the phone in his pants pocket and checked the Beretta. He'd need more ammo. In three strides, he was inside the closet. When Camila moved in she'd brought enough shoes to open a store. He worked a pink box out of the stack on the upper shelf and yanked off the lid. He grabbed three magazines from it, wedged the box back into the stack and headed for the door.

The three times Nacho had been in Labrador's living room, he'd felt like the house was closing in on him. The room overflowed with stuff—furniture, cheap paintings of flowers and snowy landscapes, tables covered with more stuff. The place smelled like a used furniture store. Labrador said it was his wife's way of making up for a childhood of poverty.

Ten minutes later, Nacho hit Labrador's number on his cell as he got out of the car. "I'm here."

"Hey, Chato," Nacho said as the front door opened, leaking a slice of light. Because it was expected of him, he gave the man a hug and slapped his back hard.

Chato hung on to him and took long, gulping breaths. It was strange having a superior, a guy at Bala's level, cling to him.

"You get a hold of El Grillo?" Nacho asked Labrador.

"Yeah. Chato has some guys coming, too."

The next to arrive was a dark guy with chest hair springing from his shirt. "Míster," Chato said, tipping his head toward the man, "meet El Plomero."

"Hey," Nacho said coolly. The Plumber nodded and said nothing during their brief handshake.

They left Labrador's place in El Pomero's van with an SUV following behind. Along with Labrador and El Grillo, El Míster sat on the van floor, surrounded by tools and equipment. "You a real plumber?"

"Used to be. Got too hard to feed six kids and maintain the wife in the style she wanted. El Cártel pays better."

According to Chato, they had a fifteen-minute ride to the house. At the rate El Plomero drove, it wouldn't take ten. No one said much. The anticipation before a showdown had a way of killing conversation. Up front, Chato ordered, "Take Constitución."

Nacho put a hand on the floor to steady himself as the van swerved onto what he guessed was the entrance ramp to Constitución, the wide avenue that ran alongside the flood plain of the Santa Catarina River.

El Plomero accelerated quickly. Two more hours and Constitución would be clogged with morning commuters, but at five a.m. it was a different world, one dominated by men like Nacho who did their best work under cover of darkness. The cramped, windowless back of the van had the same effect on Nacho as Labrador's living room.

"What the fuck?" Chato squeaked in a strange voice as the van began to slow.

"Damn," El Plomero muttered under his breath.

Nacho scrambled to poke his head between the two seats. "What the hell?" Every muscle in his body tensed as he stared at the poorly strung-up *narcomanta* hanging from the overpass. He glimpsed several people running to an SUV underneath the overpass bridge just before its tail lights lit up and the vehicle shot out.

El Plomero slowed the van. "Shit!" Chato shouted just as Nacho managed to make out the letters scrawled on the giant sheet that hung above them in the pre-dawn air. "*¡Muerte a los pinches robamujeres del Cártel!*" Death to the damned Cártel women-stealers!

"It's Bala!" El Chato screamed, pointing to a body hanging below the banner. It turned slowly in the breeze. "Get the goddamned bastards!"

The engine whined like a cat being tortured as El Plomero floored the accelerator. Chato leaned out the passenger window with a rifle. "Are you crazy, Chato?" Nacho shouted. A sudden burst of automatic gun fire aimed at them exploded the van's side mirror. Nacho rolled behind the driver's seat. The van tires squealed as El Plomero swung around, throwing Nacho then rolling him around on the floor. Something soft hit his head and bounced away. The smell of burning rubber filled the van. They were speeding the wrong way down the longest avenue in the city.

El Plomero braked to a fierce stop that sent El Grillo crashing into Nacho. The cops would show up within minutes. The SUV that had left Labrador's house behind the Plumber's van was now parked in the middle of Constitución under the bridge. Above, two men sawed at the ropes. Nacho realized a second body hung at the other end of the overpass. "Going down," someone yelled. Bala's body plummeted to the asphalt. The men rushed forward like kids swarming a downed piñata. Nacho grabbed Bala's legs. El Grillo took his torso. They ferried the body to the van. Sirens wailed in the distance.

They ran back for the other body. Anger surged through Nacho. The kid's face had been battered almost beyond recognition, but the tats on his arms were unmistakable. He'd only met the kid last weekend at a barbecue on a ranch. He said he was from Tamaulipas and had just been sent to Monterrey. The way he strutted, it was obvious his bravado didn't run very deep. But, he didn't deserve to be dead, and he sure as hell didn't deserve to be strung up from an overpass far from home.

They heaved his body in the van, and El Plomero took off with a screech of wheels, flinging Nacho against the kid's body. He threw out a hand that landed on something damp and sticky. His whole body recoiled. The cadaver smelled of sweat and the rusty scent of drying blood. Or maybe the odors came from Bala's body on the other side of the kid. Plenty of times, Nacho had gotten fed up with Bala ordering him around, but there were a lot worse *patrones*.

"Now what?" El Plomero asked.

"Reynosa highway," El Chato said, his voice flat. "There's a turn-off in about sixty kilometers."

"The ranch with the airstrip? I know the way."

Nacho tried to settle where he wouldn't be in contact with a corpse. In the early morning light, he willed his eyes to study the plumbing supplies that had been tossed around the van. It must have been the black rubber plunger wedged between him and the door panel that had hit him. He grabbed the handle and shoved the plunger between himself and the kid's body. Labrador huddled his massive self in the back of the van, eyes closed. El Grillo had ended up on the other side of Bala's body. Nacho pulled his legs up and rested his elbows on his knees.

El Cártel wouldn't lose time naming Bala's replacement. As far as Nacho was concerned, they'd fucking better give him the job. In any business, profit was the bottom line. Innovation kept you ahead of the competition, and he had come up with a profitable plan nobody else had thought of. By the time El Plomero turned off the highway, Nacho was seeing the dawn of a new day.

CHAPTER TWENTY-ONE

"OF MBC'S six beers, which is most popular with women?" Alejandra, in her white lab coat, waited, hands on hips, eyebrows raised.

Across the pilot lab table, Brad had no idea why she was asking when the answer was so obvious. "Chipinque Wheat."

"Exactly. What if our next seasonal brew is something like it but without the wheat?"

"Interesting idea. What would the bitterness level be?"

"About the same as the wheat."

"And the hops blend?"

"I still need to figure that out. A little flowery but not too bitter. We wouldn't advertise it as a women's beer per se, but the bartenders and wait staff could suggest it to women. Right now I'm just shooting for permission to pursue the idea."

"Permission granted, Wonder Woman."

Chago, safety glasses pushed on top of his head, interrupted. "Ingeniero, the stout's transferred to the finishing tank. How much do you want bottled?"

"We need one pallet for Mexico City and another for Houston. Keg the rest."

As Chago turned to leave, Alejandra asked, "Where are you taking Graciela for Valentine's dinner?"

Chago shook his head. "We're saving money, remember? She's cooking a special dinner." He looked at the pilot brewery clock. "I'm due at her house in an hour and forty minutes."

"Take off a little early if you need to," Brad said.

"Thanks, Ingeniero. How about you guys?"

"I would have gone to yoga, except they cancelled class on account of Valentine's."

"No plans," Brad replied. He had avoided thinking about the holiday of love all day.

"Next time I think my life isn't exciting, I'll remember you guys," Chago said, shaking his head on his way out.

"So, um," Brad said, "I know a little restaurant that makes great Oaxacan tamales."

"I'm more in the mood for a burger," Alejandra replied, "maybe from Chili's?"

"Shouldn't that be sacrilegious for people who do yoga?"

"I'm no saint."

"I'm not the brightest guy, but I think you just invited me to dinner."

"And I thought you were the one inviting."

"SORRY, I should have stopped to think about how packed the mall would be today," Alejandra said as the escalator carried them up from the sea of cars in the parking garage and into a bustling, brightly-lit world of red, pink and white. A noisy group of middle-school girls teetered by on spiky high heels, swarming past a woman accompanying a wizened old man leaning on a cane. Two large women, arms full of bags, nearly collided with Alejandra. Brad reached out and pulled her in front of him. Her hair carried the aroma of a full day in the brewery and of something unmistakably feminine that had been missing from his life for too long.

The restaurant, like the mall, was packed. "We can try another place," Alejandra offered.

"Everywhere will be crowded tonight. I'm not in a rush. Are you?" It was increasingly pleasant to be in Alejandra's presence outside the brewery.

"No rush," she smiled. She wore red lipstick. He couldn't recall her wearing any lipstick at work. Her top was different, too. Maybe she'd had worn it under her MBC shirt. He cut his eyes to the tile floor to keep from staring at her. His size-twelve shoes looked enormous beside her sandals.

"Those aren't your work shoes," he blurted, unable to think of anything else to say.

"I keep these in my car."

"I thought all the women in Mexico wore those scary high heels."

"I've avoided them ever since—" Alejandra caught herself and took a breath. "Ever since Luis. He always insisted on me wearing them, along with skirts."

"I've never seen you in a skirt," Brad said, imaging her yoga-toned legs in high heels.

"Believe it or not," she laughed," I have a whole wardrobe besides jeans and men's MBC shirts."

"I never thought about it. We should have some women's shirts made up for you."

"Actually, I've thought that an MBC clothing line for the public might be a hit. You know, men's and women's tees, guys' hats, women's visors."

"Would you like to talk more about it the next time Carlos comes to the brewery?"

Her face flushed and her eyes brightened. "It has some real potential, I think."

"Alejandra!" the harried Chili's hostess called into the crowd.

Making conversation with Alejandra came easily. Brad listened to her stories of growing up on the ranch and summering in Alabama, of studying at the best private school in Saltillo, of her perceptions of life as a female Mexican brewer. He recalled Emily's birthday dinner in the expensive restaurant nearly a year ago. She'd been so frustrated with him for not clarifying the relationship. With Alejandra, he was going to have to make some decisions and make them soon. But not tonight. Definitely not at Chili's.

By the time they finished dinner, the mall crowd had thinned. Walking beside Alejandra, he could so easily take her hand. She was taller than either Maddy or Emily. As a brewer, her hands wouldn't be as soft as Maddy's had been. He remembered her handshake at the job interview, confident and strong.

"*Brad, Alejandra, ¡buenas noches!*" Brad jumped at the sound of Lalo's voice.

Alejandra's cheeks reddened as she greeted Lalo. Brad held out his hand. The look on Lalo's face said he was trying to figure things out. "Let me introduce you to my wife, Leticia," he said.

A little overweight with gray-streaked hair and a smile that suggested permanently good humor, the woman kissed Alejandra's cheek and shook Brad's hand warmly. "Such a lovely couple!"

"Colleagues and friends," Alejandra corrected.

"Sorry, I guess I got carried away with Valentine's displays in every store window."

"I hope Lalo did something special for you today," Alejandra said.

"I woke up to flowers and a serenade, and he took me to dinner."

"A serenade with mariachis?"

"No, no. After twenty-eight years of marriage and three kids, he still sings "*El reloj*" to me every Valentine's morning. It was the first song we ever danced to. He has the most beautiful baritone voice."

"Enough, Lety," Lalo chided in his paternal style. "Let them get on their way. See you tomorrow morning."

Alejandra smiled as they descended the escalator. "That's so sweet. Do you know the old love song? A man sings to a clock asking it not to move because when the night is over the woman he loves will leave forever."

"Not exactly the case for Lalo and Leticia, is it?" Brad replied.

On the drive to Alejandra's condo, she surprised Brad by asking, "Want to come up for coffee?"

"I'd like that." The words had slipped out before he'd stopped to think.

ALEJANDRA SET a colorful Talavera plate of miniature turnovers on the coffee table. "Pineapple empanadas, baked last night. Coffee?"

"Thanks, but I'd better not. I won't sleep." Why had he accepted her invitation to come in? And how could she afford this spacious eleventh-floor condo on an assistant brewer's salary?

"A beer instead?"

"I'll take you up on that."

She disappeared into what he assumed was the kitchen. Unlike his apartment, the condo was full of decorations and matching furniture.

"Where are your roommates?"

"Cousins, actually. One is out with her boyfriend. The other, I don't know."

"Nice place you have here." She reappeared with a couple of Santa Catarina Stouts. "Ah, one of my favorite beers," he said.

"I know," she smiled. "Full-bodied, clean, roasted flavor."

"No!" he said, drawing out the word. "Let's leave the analysis in the brewery."

"Deal." She sat on the sofa, leaving too much space between them. "A stout and dessert: the perfect combination."

"Beer and anything is the perfect combination," Brad said, biting into a flaky pastry with gooey filling. "This is really good."

She seemed genuinely pleased. When they had emptied the plate and bottles, Brad said, "I should be going."

"Want to take home some empanadas?"

"Twist my arm." He followed her into the kitchen where she tucked several in a plastic bag.

"Thanks for a great dinner and a wonderful evening," Alejandra said.

"Thank you." He gave her a standard Mexican goodbye peck on the cheek. She gazed into his eyes. Before he knew it, he was saying, "Alejandra, I've broken all sorts of rules about boss-employee relations. In the U.S., women have sued their boss for a lot less."

She pressed her fingertips against his lips and smiled, her dark eyes holding his. "And I've enjoyed breaking them with you."

He put his arms around her waist and pulled her close. She relaxed and her breasts pressed against his chest. He forced himself to keep his hands away from them. No doubt she was aware of his hardness. He looked into her luminous eyes and no longer cared about professionalism, rules or tomorrow. The most premeditated kiss of his life was better than anything he had anticipated, her lips softer than he had imagined. When he pulled away, she cupped his neck in her hand and drew him toward her again. The first kiss had been uncertain, exploratory. The second was a promise of passions to be unlocked.

He broke away and balled his hands into fists. "Alejandra, I don't know if this can ever work. I'm not good at romantic relationships. I don't know how you feel about me. I don't know if we could have a relationship and continue to work together. I don't know how long I'll stay in Mexico. There are so many things I don't know."

She gathered her hair, pulled it behind her, then let it fall loose. "I've been asking similar questions lately. I've tried to convince myself that it's wrong, but there's something between us stronger than caution or logic."

He ached to forget everything, to pull her to him. "You realize I'm divorced?"

"Yes."

"What will your family say?"

"That Alejandra has always been independent and a little crazy."

"I don't see myself living in Mexico for more than a few years."

"I think I could live in the States."

"Forever?"

"Is there anything you know you'll do forever?"

"Brew beer."

"That makes two of us."

CHAPTER TWENTY-TWO

"I'M SO excited. I've never been in a brewery. I had no idea it was so noisy," Claudia gushed.

Brad instinctively glanced at her feet and was pleased to see she wore close-toed flats. He looked for dangly jewelry. Nothing. Carlos had obviously prepared his girlfriend for her first brewery visit.

Alejandra pulled off her safety glasses as Carlos made introductions.

Brad had told Carlos about Alejandra's idea of a clothing line, but he hadn't said a word about how his star brewer had jolted his life four nights ago. Until the two of them better understood what that first kiss might—or might not—have set into motion, they were keeping the new relationship under wraps.

Carlos had jumped at Alejandra's clothing line idea, in part because he had the perfect candidate to design and create MBC wear. With her recent degree from Parsons School of Design and starting her own business in Monterrey, Claudia could use the work. Now, Brad watched Alejandra enthusiastically explain, waving her hands and arms as she talked.

"We could use a basic V-neck women's tee," Claudia said, sitting forward in her chair. "One that hits below the hip, I'm thinking, with short, ruched sleeves."

"Red and yellow like the MBC logo," Alejandra said, leaning into the conference table.

Claudia stared up at the ceiling, lightly tapping one hand on the table. "With black and white shirts, we could put the logo on the front as is. On red ones, we set it in a black box. Would you guys be open to possibly tweaking the Cerro de la Silla logo?"

"Tweak it how?" Carlos asked, sounding wary.

"Just streamline it a little," Claudia replied, taking a pad out of the thin briefcase in her lap. "I can make some preliminary sketches."

"Before you and Alejandra come up with all sorts of wonderful ideas," Carlos said, "you should know that if we do this, your seed money is only seventy-five thousand pesos."

Six thousand dollars? Last month, when Brad reported that the transfer pump was on its way out, Carlos's had acted as if the unexpected three-thousand-dollar hit was going to kill them. "Big Guy, what if you and I move outside and talk money?"

BRAD PLUNKED his post-game *limonada* on the long table the tennis players had claimed. Heat lamps lined the back wall, unneeded on the warm afternoon. By late February in Denver, everybody was sick of dirty snow, brown grass and the thought that they still had at least another month of it. Here, the winter rains and cooler temperatures had the Sierra Madres at their greenest. Today's weather and the hard-fought win against Diego and Roberto had buoyed Brad's mood. His friendship with Carlos also needed the boost.

"I'm all for helping Claudia and for the MBC clothing line, but seventy-five thousand pesos is too much," Brad had argued on Monday. "We've got to have a cushion for things like the pump last month."

After some tense haggling, Carlos agreed to cut Claudia's budget to fifty thousand. Brad had taken some secret satisfaction when the pub dishwasher went on the fritz two days later, costing them fifteen hundred in repairs.

Diego pulled Brad back to the present saying, "So, Brad, some of Marta's Houston relatives are coming for a family wedding in two weeks. She's wondering if you'd be interested in going as her cousin's date."

Brad felt every pair of eyes at the table on him as he raised his hands in protest. Diego rushed on, "She's twenty-four and speaks more English than Spanish. She's really friendly."

"Hey, I speak English," Eugenio broke in with a heavy accent, "and hot girls love me. If Brad's not interested, *¿cómo se dice yo me apunto para el trabajo?*"

"I'll sign on for the job," Brad said.

"Score one for the Güero!" Roberto said in Spanish, pumping the air with his fist amid laughter at Brad's quick response.

"Great," Diego said, looking relieved. "I'll let Marta know you'll do it."

"No! I was translating for Eugenio. I can't help you out."

"Go, Güero," Carlos urged. "Are you afraid to have a little fun?"

In the week since he first kissed Alejandra, he was finding it difficult to keep his secret. He had almost told his parents when he talked to them a few days ago. Lalo knew something had changed. Plus, he felt he was being unfair to Alejandra. Why keep the relationship secret unless he had something to hide? "I'm sort of seeing someone."

"No shit!" Roberto said. "Who is she?"

Brad steeled himself. "Her name is Alejandra."

"Alejandra Howard?" Carlos asked, his voice rising.

"Yeah."

"No way."

"Who's Alejandra Howard?" Roberto asked.

"I can answer that."

Every man looked at Germán, an Ex-A-Tec Brad hardly knew. "Alejandra Howard from Saltillo?"

"Right," Brad said as he remembered that Germán hailed from Saltillo.

"Now we'll get the real shit," Eugenio said.

"If she's who I think, her family owns a ranch. Her father's American," Germán said. Brad nodded. "She had a boyfriend. I would have expected them to be married and have a couple of kids by now."

"They broke up," Brad said.

"Luis was a little younger than me," Germán said. "I was in grad school in Mexico City, but I heard about him—pretty wild reputation."

"What about her family?" Eugenio asked, sounding like a father.

"Mother's from an old, prominent family. They've owned the ranch for generations. It's one of the largest in the state of Coahuila. They have a couple thousand dairy cows, right, Brad?"

"We've barely started going out. I haven't been to the ranch." *One of the biggest dairy ranches in a state known as the Wisconsin of Mexico?*

Eugenio made squeezing motions with his hands. "Brad, I hope you know how to ride horses and milk cows."

"Congratulations," Germán said. "Very respected family."

As soon as Brad and Carlos were in the car, Carlos demanded, "What are you thinking? Dating your employee?"

Brad braked at a traffic light. "Don't you think I've asked the same question every day? I've given myself every argument in the book about why I shouldn't do it, but here we are."

"What if it doesn't work out?"

"We'll cross that bridge if we come to it," Brad said accelerating as the light changed.

"Dude, chill. How long have you been *novios*, a couple or whatever?"

"It's whatever, and about a week, I guess."

"Are you playing by Mexican rules?"

"Mexican rules?"

"Did you officially declare yourself to her and let everybody know you're *novios*?"

"You think I need to?"

"If you don't, some people might talk."

"I don't care what people might say."

"You're a guy and you're American. For Alejandra it's different."

"Are you saying that if I don't do the whole declaration thing, I could ruin her reputation?"

"Maybe, maybe not. But it sounds like you pretty much have declared yourself and she has accepted. You might want to tell MBC employees your official status so they know how things stand. If Rodrigo and Chago happened to catch you two at the brewery, you know…"

"I swear I could live in Mexico the rest of my life and never understand the culture."

"I HAD a great time, and the dinner was fantastic," Brad said, giving Alejandra a quick cheek kiss on his way out the door of her condo. "I'm glad I got to meet your cousins and their boyfriends."

"Thanks for coming and meeting the gang." She held a thumb to her ear, little finger to her mouth. "Let me know you got home safely."

At home, he flipped on the lights and the air-conditioner, then looked around. His apartment was drab and sad compared to the condo Alejandra shared with Lolis and Marisa. He tipped the lever on the bottled water dispenser and served himself a large glass which he took to the living room table. He stretched out on the sofa and tapped Alejandra's number on his cell.

"I hope you didn't think Marisa and Lolis and their boyfriends were too crazy," she said. "Meeting them all at once can be a little overwhelming."

"It was a lot of fun."

"You're just saying that." Her tone became playful. "You're going to love the ranch next weekend. I'm so glad you're coming."

Why had he let Alejandra and her cousins talk him into going to Saltillo next Saturday? It wasn't that he didn't want to help celebrate her grandfather's eightieth birthday or meet her family. The problem was the date: March first. "It's not a done deal yet. I have to make sure Carlos can handle the *piso*. And I don't know about that *corrido* ballad in front of all your family."

"You sounded good tonight. I didn't know you could sing like that. I'll help you practice *Rosita Elvírez* every day for the next week because

Lolis is right. If you really want to impress my family, helping serenade my grandfather on his birthday will do it."

"Alejandra, there's something I need to know before then."

"Yes?"

"Are we playing by American or Mexican rules?" He felt ridiculous parroting Carlos's phrase.

"I guess we're playing by our own rules."

"I still think I need to officially declare myself and ask you to be my girlfriend, *mi novia*."

Alejandra laughed her throaty laugh. "You're adorable."

"I know I'm doing this all wrong. I should have taken you to a fancy restaurant and gotten down on one knee or something."

"We're not teenagers," she said, giggling like one.

"So, I really like you, Alejandra, and I'd be honored if you'd be my *novia*."

"And I'd be honored to have you as my *novio*."

CHAPTER TWENTY-THREE

MUSCLES BULGED all over the body of the man standing on the other side of the desk. With the only window shuttered, it was impossible to tell whether it was night or day. As the man rubbed his nose with the back of his hand one more time, Nacho noticed an ugly scar down the side of his neck.

"That's a fucking annoying habit you have."

The stupid look on the man's face said he didn't know what habit his new *patrón* was referring to. The hand made another swipe. "You do that all the time or just when you're nervous?"

"Just when I'm nervous."

"And you're nervous now because?"

"Because I'm short," the man whispered as he stared down at the stacks of bills on the desk. He gave a long, irritating sniff but kept his hand down.

"Two thousand pesos," Nacho agreed. The man's head drooped. Nacho could see the crown of his head through the thinning hair. "Look at me," Nacho rasped. The man obeyed. Nacho locked him in a frosty blue stare. "Tomorrow, you're going to bring the rest." The man nodded in short, spastic jerks and sniffled. "Plus an extra five hundred for being late." The guy's eyes widened. "You have kids?" Another jerky nod. "How many?"

"Three—or four, I'm not sure."

"Damn, man, you don't even know how many *huercos* you have?"

"There's a *ruca* says her last one is mine, but she's lying."

Nacho laughed. "Send her on her way and don't get mixed up with any more sluts. It'll make your life a lot easier." An uncertain smile crossed the man's face, wiped away by the hand swabbing the nasal drip. "Here's the deal," Nacho said with a searing gaze. "If you are *ever* late again or if you don't bring the full twenty-five hundred by five p.m. tomorrow," he paused and let the conditions sink in, "you won't be fathering any more *huercos*." Another round of jerky head movements. "Right, Labrador?" Nacho said, shifting his eyes to his assistant.

The nose wiper turned to take in Labrador. "I'll have it tomorrow," he mumbled. "Thank you, Míster—*patrón*." He pressed his palms together and bowed in the obsequious way certain Mexican waiters did when jonesing for bigger tips.

"Now get out of here. You got a lot of work to do." The big man backed his way to the door then scurried out.

Nacho punched the keypad on the safe and took out a small laptop where he recorded the date, time and amount of the guy's deposit. He added the money, some only twenty-peso bills, hardly more than one fricking U.S. dollar, to the rubber-banded piles in the safe. Poor assholes stuck with lousy, working-class neighborhoods where a *piso* of five-hundred pesos was a fucking mother lode.

"Ready for the next one?" Labrador asked.

"Naw, we need a break," Nacho said, pulling out a couple of shot glasses. He uncorked the Patrón Añejo and took a long whiff. It smelled of oak and honey, of money and power.

Being a *patrón* had its downside, but it had advantages, too. The only *piso* Nacho still collected directly was from MBC. He had no intention of giving up that one. He needed to keep a close eye on the place and its inner workings. Besides, the gringo was easy to deal with. Every month he had the ten thousand waiting. Plus, the beer was damn good.

"¡*Salud!*" Nacho said distractedly, lifting his shot glass.

"¡*Salud!*" echoed his right-hand man, raising his glass with that fucking crazy arm full of tattoos that looked like something Frida Kahlo would have done when she was high on *mota*.

Nacho downed the shot and blew out a loud breath. He locked the tequila and the cash away. "Send in the next *pendejo*."

THE MAIN house of the Howard-Guzmán ranch, with its white-stuccoed walls and terracotta-tiled roof, sprawled around three sides of a courtyard. Bright red paint outlined the frames of the doorways and windows. A covered walkway branched off to a guest house. Employee living quarters were tucked away behind the main house. On the veranda that ran along one side of the house, a trio played and sang *época de oro* songs from the 1940s and 50s. Tables dotted the yard all the way to a large pond. Except for a single, gated entrance, high whitewashed walls enclosed the complex and made it almost impossible to see the mountains beyond. Brad breathed in the fresh air and relaxed. Monterrey, the congested boulevards and the threat of narcos, felt far away. Alejandra had driven him through stark mountains of breathtaking beauty. The Saltillo landscape was drier, its mountains more gray-hued, than Monterrey's.

"So," Alejandra asked, "what would you like to do first? Eat or meet my *abuelito*?"

"That's not really a choice, is it?"

Don Horacio's most prominent features were bushy white eyebrows crowned by a full head of thick, white hair. Brad hoped the elderly man's weak handshake was due to his age and not because he was under-impressed by the American boyfriend of one of his twelve grandchildren.

"He's on overload right now," Alejandra whispered as they walked away. "My parents, too. Once all these people aren't around, you'll see what they're really like. Let's get something to eat."

As dinner was ending, a mariachi group appeared. They opened with an ear-splitting "*Mañanitas*," the traditional birthday song. Guests joined in to serenade Don Horacio. From there, the group cycled through mariachi classics, many of which Brad recognized. Toward the end of the hour-long set, when Lolis jumped up and consulted with the musicians, Brad grew nervous.

"Remember to sing loud," Alejandra said, taking his hand and pulling him forward. They squeezed in beside one of her brothers, who held his tired two-year-old. When the guitar, *guitarrón*, trumpet and violins struck up in one giant blast just behind him, Brad jumped. The toddler shrieked and covered his ears.

Brad knew the lyrics and the tune. He had practiced a ridiculous amount of time. Besides, with the mariachis playing at a hundred decibels, who was going to hear him anyway? He let loose, surprised at his own voice. The group gained confidence and volume as the song progressed, finishing in a loud, sustained bellow. The prolonged applause became a rhythmic clapping to the encore request of, "*Otra, otra, otra.*"

Lolis looked at her impromptu choir and commanded, "*El rey.*"

The mariachis' wide-brimmed sombreros bobbed in unison as they nodded. Even Brad knew most of the lyrics to *The King*, a mariachi staple. Don Horacio's five children moved in around him as they and over a hundred people sang to the man with gusto. These people shared a history of relationships that went back decades, generations in some cases. Could he ever become a part of it, Brad wondered.

When the singing finally ended, Alejandra suggested a walk around the pond. The path took them by Don Horacio, who extended a thin arm to stop his granddaughter. Brad could barely make out the old man's voice. "*M'ija,* what's the name of the *güero?*"

She knelt by his side, smiling and gently caressed his hand. "Brad, *Abue.* He's a very special man."

The small man squinted up. "*Brath,*" he repeated. For a moment he said no more. "Any American who can sing *Rosita Elvírez* and *El rey* the way you did is okay by me."

"Thank you, sir."

"*Don Horacio, ¡felicidades!*" said a man, approaching with his hand outstretched.

"Come on," Alejandra said, sneaking away.

The pond turned out to be a small lake. "It's my father's creation," Alejandra explained. "The climate here is more arid than in Monterrey, but the altitude makes Saltillo cooler. We're at sixteen-hundred meters, basically a mile high like Denver. See that windmill? The concrete pond is fed by a rainwater catchment system that Dad designed and a solar-powered well maintains a constant level year-round."

Lamp-lit sidewalks bordered the pond. Alejandra took Brad's hand as they strolled past children and couples. A group of older men laughed and argued off at one end, cigar smoke clouding the air above them. "Are you sure hand holding is okay? People won't talk?" Brad asked.

Alejandra laughed her throaty laugh. "Oh, I expect they'll talk. They'll say, that handsome *güero* with Alejandra, isn't he some famous mariachi whose name I can't remember?"

"What would they say if I put an arm around you?"

"That the *güero* has good taste."

As they walked toward the far side of the pond, Brad slipped his arm around her waist. He breathed in the wood smoke and the refreshing night air. Here, in the Chihuahua Desert, the stars winked with the same intensity as in the Rocky Mountains. Two years ago, he couldn't have imagined this moment.

"When I was little, I used to come here and pretend I was hiding," Alejandra said, stopping to turn and look back at the party in the distance. A breeze rippled the water's surface and carried voices and bits of conversation, reflected a twinkling of lights. Even Monterrey and the *inseguridad* felt far away tonight. Brad pulled her close. "Those people who talk are right. The *güero* has good taste."

He dared to kiss her long and passionately.

CHAPTER TWENTY-FOUR

COUSIN MARISA clicked into the living room on a pair of thin high heels. "Alejandra says she'll be out in two minutes." The doorbell chime sent her clacking off. Brad heard Juan José apologizing for being late and hurrying Marisa along before the movie started. He settled back into the sofa and pulled out his phone, scrolling through Facebook postings.

Several minutes later, he heard another set of heels clicking toward him on the terrazzo floors. Suddenly a gorgeous woman stood before him. Alejandra's pink dress and big hoop earrings sparkled. Her normally straight hair was full of curls.

"I've never seen you in a dress."

"You like it?"

"You look incredible," Brad said, standing to give her a quick kiss. He inhaled her perfume, shampoo and whatever else was in the mix, not wanting the moment to end. His rumbling stomach had other ideas.

"Sounds like we need to feed you," Alejandra said, flicking back a strand of curls.

"If you hadn't gotten so dressed up, I'd settle for a PB and J."

"You don't want to go out?" she asked, sounding disappointed.

"As hot as you look, I hope everybody we know sees us tonight."

"In that case, maybe we should go to MBC."

"I thought you wanted an intimate dinner. The pub will be the total opposite."

"What do you say we go for *see and be seen?*"

Brad considered it for a moment, then said, "If not now, when?"

They entered MBC with Alejandra's hand on his arm. His mind

flashed back to the opening a year and a half ago when he hadn't known anybody and had practically jumped every time somebody addressed him in Spanish. Amazing how life could change.

"Alejandra! Brad!" Paty scurried toward them, arms thrown wide.

A steady procession of employees, friends and acquaintances greeted them during their hour at MBC. It seemed as though Brad heard *"¡Felicidades!"* as many times during the evening as he had on opening night, followed by "You two are perfect for each other," "What a great-looking couple," "What took you two so long?"

Even Carlos seemed happy for them. "Alejandra, you look awesome. Güero...what can I say?"

After a dinner with so many interruptions that their food grew cold and their beer warm, they made their way into the parking lot. Vagabundo appeared and brushed against Alejandra's bare legs. "Hey, fellow, I've missed you," she said, rubbing a spot between the cat's ears.

"I thought I was the only one who knew that's his favorite place to be scratched," Brad said, remembering how Vagabundo would never come near Emily.

Once they were in the car, Alejandra asked, "What if we go to your place for a while?"

Brad turned to her. "Is that permitted under Mexican rules?"

Making air quotes, Alejandra asked, "How many versions of the rules are there for the 'American' dating game?"

"In the States, the dating game is more of a free-for-all."

"If you asked my grandfather, he'd say I should only see you with a chaperone, preferably over the age of forty. Some Mexicans our age would ask 'Why aren't y'all living together yet?' Tonight, we play by our own rules."

HIS APARTMENT was in a small building, nearly thirty years old and showing its age. No gated parking garages or attendants here. "Welcome to my very simple, very single-guy's place," Brad said, holding the door open. "Can I offer you a drink? I picked up a really fine Parras wine when I was in Saltillo recently."

"I'd prefer a fine craft beer if you happen to have one."

"Ah, you're in luck." He opened the refrigerator that held half a stick of salami, a bag with two hardened tortillas, a half-full Chinese take-out box and eight varieties of beer.

"Santa Cecilia?" Alejandra asked, raising an eyebrow. "Checking out the competition?"

"Any brewer who doesn't is a fool."

"Good point, but I'll take the MBC Sevillana."

Brad served up two glasses. Neither Maddy nor Emily had been beer drinkers. He enjoyed the sight of an attractive woman on his sofa, savoring her beer. He took a deep pull on his own Sevillana, unsure what to expect next.

Alejandra took another sip, held it in her mouth a moment and swallowed. "What you said about playing by Mexican or American rules." She paused, studying the glass as though she were addressing it and not him. "You've done a really good job of playing by Mexican rules. I mean, by formally declaring yourself, going to my grandfather's party, not expecting sex on the first date like most Americans."

"Ouch. Not all American guys are that hard core."

"You know." She sipped the beer. "You've been married. You've had other relationships. You're obviously," another sip, "experienced."

"Not that much, really."

"What was her name, your ex-wife?"

"Maddy." It felt strange saying her name out loud after so long, especially to Alejandra.

"Y'all didn't have children?"

"I wouldn't be here if we had."

"You didn't want them?"

"She left before we got that far."

"So the divorce was her decision?"

"I suppose it was mutual by the end, but she initiated it."

"From the sound of your voice and the look on your face, it's still a painful topic."

"It's been over two years since the split, but yeah, it's still pretty raw." He wouldn't blame Alejandra if she walked out now.

"I think that's how I feel about Luis." She took a long drink and threw her head back.

"Did the two of you—" He couldn't bring himself to voice the question that had eaten at him for so long.

Alejandra laughed before she tossed back the remaining contents of her glass. She looked at him with tears forming in her eyes. "I need another Sevillana."

Brad served the beer with a handful of tissues. Alejandra dabbed her eyes and addressed the beer. "I've talked about some of this with my mother and my cousins, but never about the sex. It was only in the last year. I wish I could say he forced me, but I was willing enough. I was the one who went to the doctor and got myself on birth control." A tear rolled down her cheek.

"Other women talk about how great it is. For me, the first time hurt like hell. There was nothing romantic—just Luis humping and rutting like a bull on a cow in mating season. He finished and shoved me aside, said there'd damned well better be blood on the sheets.

"I hobbled to the bathroom. By the time I got back, he was nearly asleep. I told him he had to leave. He swore and said I didn't need to act like an uptight virgin anymore." She pulled a fresh tissue from the wad in her hand and blotted another tear before taking a long slug of beer.

"Hey, easy on that." Brad held his hand out for her glass, and she let him take it. Her shoulders heaved with long, wracking sobs.

"After the first time, I didn't want to do it again. I couldn't bring myself to talk with my cousins or friends. I was scared of what Luis would do if he found out I'd talked to anyone. The next time, I resisted. He'd had a lot of experience, and I hardly knew anything. He backed off. A few nights later, he started kissing me. Then he reached under my sweater. He unzipped my pants and started stroking me. When I came, it was incredible, beyond everything I'd heard about it."

Brad had no idea how to respond, so he just nodded. Alejandra continued, "I was so naïve that I thought we were done. Instead, he put my hand on his, you know. I was scared at how hard and big it was. He said we had to go to my bed. He made me stroke him. All of a sudden, he was pushing my head down, saying, 'Suck it. Suck it, bitch!'"

Her words came quickly as though she might lose the courage to finish. "I was horrified at the sight and at what he was asking me to do. He forced my head down and shoved his, his thing in my mouth. I thought I was going to choke. I was coughing and gagging and trying to pull away. Then he came." She stopped and wrapped her arms tightly around herself. Hunched over, she drew in sharp breaths and blew out ragged, broken gasps.

When her breathing slowed, she began to speak softly. "I had to tell you. I didn't want you to go on thinking I was some pristine virgin."

"Hell, Alejandra, I don't care about your virginity. What he did constitutes rape. You should have pressed charges."

"In this country, the police and the government can't even stop two-bit narcos. Luis's family is one of the most powerful in Saltillo. He and his family would completely trash my reputation and ruin my family. The topic isn't even open for discussion."

Brad placed his hand on her arm. "I don't get it," he said, speaking the truth.

Her response was cold and uncompromising. "I'm not asking you to understand. Just accept that this is my reality. If any man ever again tries to control me, I'll run. If you want to call off the *noviazgo* right now, I'll understand."

Brad rubbed both hands along his jaw line. "Jesus, Alejandra. All this time, I was afraid you'd be the one who'd run once you heard about my past."

Alejandra uncrossed her arms and placed her hand near his. Brad slid his hand underneath hers. Slowly, she intertwined her fingers with his. She lifted his hand and held it between both of hers. She gently kissed his wrist. "We're going to have to take sex slowly."

"Not until you're ready."

"I still believe it must be wonderful under the right circumstances. It will be with you because you're so," she hesitated, "so experienced, and you're an engineer."

Brad laughed and squeezed her hand. "What does being an engineer have to do with sex?"

"It means you're disciplined and logical, in control of your emotions."

"We spent four years at CU hearing how our training would benefit us. Not one professor ever mentioned our sex lives."

CHAPTER TWENTY-FIVE

"NOTHING LIKE a couple of days in Mexico City traffic to make you appreciate Monterrey," Carlos said, dropping into a chair and lacing his fingers behind his head. He threw one ankle over the other knee so that his freshly polished wing-tips reflected the overhead lighting in the brewery office.

Brad looked at his spattered work boots and knew how he must smell after a day of brewing. "I got your email about the Zona Rosa restaurants. Congratulations."

"Thanks," Carlos said with a grin. "I was hoping to get two of them, but not all three. Marcos is predicting that by the end of the year, our D.F. shipments will increase twenty percent." Brad had met Marcos Lucero only once, when the Mexico City distributor visited Monterrey to check out the pub and brewery.

"He'll need an extra half pallet beginning with the May first shipment," Carlos continued. "Probably more for June. That won't be a problem, will it?"

"Not if we hire another person."

Carlos's face clouded. "You increased the malt and bottle orders last month, and you'll need to this month, right?"

Brad nodded.

"Can you hold off on a new hire?"

"I've pushed my brewers to the max lately. Lalo's out this morning and I'm his substitute. We're already short-handed, and we're going to be paying overtime. If we keep pushing these guys, *you* can deal with the mutiny." Brad blew out a loud breathe to make his point. "You have the breakdown of beers we'll need for Mexico City?"

"Right here," Carlos replied, reaching down to a smooth leather case with a shiny clasp bearing some fancy logo.

"New briefcase?"

"Yeah, what do you think?"

"Nice."

"Have to impress those prospective clients and keep the ones we've already got."

Carlos talked fast, plowing through an agenda that went on and on. Brad knew he should be grateful for a partner so passionate about sales and marketing, areas for which he himself had little interest. These days, he and Carlos exchanged one-line emails, a quick text, a thirty-second phone call. The last time they discussed anything outside of work was a week and a half ago at the sports club.

"The top news last week: the volume of Topo Chico Centeno IPA sales more than doubled from the previous week," Carlos said, meeting Brad's high five. "And the MBC clothing line will debut in two weeks with men's and women's tees, hats and visors. Sweatbands will follow next month."

When it was finally Brad's turn, he reported, "Seasonal brew number three is still in the early stages but moving along. Alejandra has come up with something she believes will appeal to women, but we won't market it as such. I haven't told her, but I think we should name it Alejandra's Ale."

"You sure you're not letting your dick make your business decisions, Güero?"

"I'm going to pretend I didn't hear that."

"Hey, peace and love. It was a joke. Explain your idea."

Brad detailed the like-a-wheat-but-not-a-wheat concept. This was his life nowadays. Regular brewing, seasonal brews, shipments to four Mexican cities and Houston, expanding production, adding a new hire.

He loved his job, but the sixty-hour weeks were wearing him down. If it weren't for Alejandra's daily presence, he could have sworn that Don Horacio's all-night party and the starry sky above the Guzmán ranch had been a dream.

"Great. Carry on," Carlos said when Brad had finished. No excitement. Not even a congratulations.

"And—by the way—today is April first," Brad added.

"Any idea when they'll come?"

"El Míster's fallen into a pattern the last few months. He shows up around five in the afternoon—gives us plenty of time to stew in our stress. You're welcome to work from the office here today so you can say hi."

"You okay? You seem a little, I don't know, stressed?"

"Sorry. I've been busy."

"We both have been." Carlos's tone was the patronizing one he used with cooks and wait staff, his I'm-the-boss voice.

"Except that one of us dresses like a GQ model and the other like Larry the Cable Guy. While you're taking clients to expensive dinners, I'm the one busting my ass to meet increasing production goals on a tight budget with the same number of employees. The last time you spent a full day in the brewery was when *All About Beer* did the story and photo shoot."

At least his outburst wiped the lounge-singer look off his partner's face. Carlos sat up, both feet on the ground. "Okay. Maybe we need to schedule some time to look at our operations and see where we can cut back." He scratched his head like he needed to get the circulation flowing. "The seasonal brews seem to be taking up more time than we'd originally calculated. What if after this next one—the, what was it? Alejandra's Ale?—we give them a break until, say, Christmas?"

Brad stared at his partner. The question sounded as clueless as the ones Carlos used to ask before MBC opened. He didn't have the time, patience or good manners for this. "Did you pay any attention to those stats you just threw out? The two seasonals to date have had very strong sales. Gross sales at the pub have been up every one of the five months since they debuted. They're something new. They create buzz and keep people coming back. One person wants a Topo Chico and brings his four friends. They could have gone to Santa Cecilia or somewhere else. Just like you live to make sales, I live to create new beers—which I've been doing since I was a teenager, dammit!"

Carlos rose from the chair so they stood a foot apart. "I get that you're mad. And you think I screwed up. I should have reacted differently to your news. The seasonals are great, they really are. Is it okay with you if we go ahead with the Zona Rosa venues since the contracts are signed?"

"As long as I can start looking for another bottler."

"Go ahead," Carlos said, still sounding surprised and defensive. "I just need some time to process all this."

Two sharp knocks rattled the office door. Brad yanked it open, prepared to put out the latest fire. He found himself face-to-face with a nervous Rodrigo and El Míster wearing slacks and a dress shirt.

"*Buenos días,*" El Míster said, strutting into the office. How had he gotten all the way to the upstairs office?

"*Licenciado Echeverría,*" he said, acknowledging Carlos's presence with a fawning tone. Like *Ingeniero*, the title was one of respect for college graduates.

Brad blew out another long breath. "I'll pay you downstairs."

Outside the office, the tattooed assistant thug waited. Brad led the two narcos downstairs, feeling the eyes of his employees on him.

El Míster lagged, too observant, as he watched Samuel deftly pull freshly capped bottles off the line and plug them into boxes which he stacked to one side. "We'll take a couple of those," El Míster announced. Labrador obediently moved in to scoop two cases from the stack just as Samuel turned to deposit another box. The collision caused Samuel to lose his grip. The crash of the box resounded above the noise of the bottling line. Abraham ran to hit the stop switch but not before two bottles rumbled off the end of the line and shattered when they crashed against the floor.

In the sudden silence, no one seemed to know what to do. "Sorry," Labrador mumbled, picking up the two cases and shuffling toward the parking lot. In the entryway, Brad pulled the envelope from his pocket and, as dutifully as Labrador, handed it over. El Míster glanced at the contents and filed it in the inner pocket of his fancy jacket.

"See you May first."

"What the hell happened to him?" Carlos asked as soon as they were out the door. "He looks like he's been on one of those make-over shows."

"Been shopping with our money," Brad said bitterly. "I've got to help Samuel clean up the mess."

BRAD KISSED Alejandra, lightly. She pressed the palm of her hand against his chest and thrust her tongue into his mouth. Once again, he fought the urge to straddle her. In the three and a half weeks since her confession, he had let her take each new step.

"I think I'm ready," she whispered.

"For?" Brad asked, hardly daring to hope.

"To go all the way."

"You sure?"

In reply, she caressed his overly-ready dick.

He stood and pulled her up. In the bedroom, they unbuttoned and unzipped what remained of each other's clothing and fell onto the bed. Brad fumbled with the nightstand drawer and pulled out a pack of condoms. Seeing Alejandra's face, he said, "I bought them for when you were ready."

"I'm back on the pill."

He mounted her carefully. Legs spread wide, she was wet and ready. He pulsed his body gently against hers. She met his rhythm, throbbing against him. Her moans grew, then turned into squeaks. When he came, it was with hard thrusts, her past experiences forgotten as his physical needs overwhelmed everything else. When his own body had quieted, he lay there, feeling her under him. She took deep, slow breaths.

Her body twitched underneath his. Alarmed, he rolled off of her and saw that she was crying. "Too much too soon?"

She shook her head. "That's what sex is supposed to be like, isn't it?"

CHAPTER TWENTY-SIX

THE MARIMBA ringtone on his cell jarred Bard awake. Fumbling in the dark, he yanked the phone from its charger. "Shit," he muttered as it rang again.

"Güero, they've raided the brewery!"

"Carlos, are you smashed? Where the hell are you?" Brad kicked at the sheets tangled around him and sat up.

"AFI! The federal police—they've raided MBC!" Carlos didn't sound drunk, but Brad couldn't make sense of what he was hearing. He swung his legs over the side of the bed and turned on the lamp. On the other end of the line someone other than Carlos said something about "in ten minutes."

"Sorry," Carlos said, talking into the phone again. "We're rounding up help."

"Help?"

"To go to the brewery."

"Is this for real, Carlos?"

"Hell, yes!"

"I'll be at the brewery in fifteen minutes." Brad was already flipping on lights and grabbing clothes.

"No! Do *not* leave your apartment. We'll come for you."

"Big Guy, have you called the police to check this out?"

"They're the ones who called *me!*"

"With all the *inseguridad*, you didn't question some stranger who phoned in the middle of the night and said he was with the police and they've raided MBC and can you come now? You just started rounding up some posse that's supposed to protect us? Carlos, this is totally insane." Shoeless, Brad walked into the kitchen and served himself a glass of water. He downed half of it in one chug.

"My dad and uncle are calling a driver and bodyguards, long-time employees, very trustworthy and well-trained."

"They'll be carrying weapons?"

"You don't have to go if you don't want to."

"I'm going."

"It'll be at least twenty minutes before we get to your place. Shower and eat something. It's going to be a long day."

Brad grabbed a pair of jeans and a t-shirt on his way to the bathroom. Shaving wasn't going to happen. Neither was making the bed. After a fast shower, he downed half a Coke and dowsed a bowl of cereal with milk. He was gulping the cereal when his phone rang.

He answered, saying "I'm on my way."

Outside, Carlos emerged from the front passenger door of an SUV at the same time as a stocky, solid man got out of the back. "*Hola, Güero,*" Carlos said. "*Efraín, mi socio Brath Peters.*"

With the buzz cut and a thick neck, the bodyguard's head looked like it was perched directly on top of his square shoulders. Efraín offered a quick handshake and stood aside for Brad to get in. Another bodyguard, occupying the window seat, held out a hand. "*Reynaldo, buenos días.*"

"*Lucas, a sus órdenes*" said the driver, eyeing Brad in the rearview mirror, before putting the vehicle in drive.

"Carlos," Brad asked, "where's your dad?"

"At home. "You never want two members of the same family together in possibly dangerous situations."

"That's not really what I want to hear right now, Big Guy." Brad had fully anticipated the guidance of Don Francisco, the senior Echeverría and experienced lawyer. As they sped along the dark and near-empty avenues, he doubted Carlos's ability in the situation they were about to confront. He knew he was even less capable.

"If there's gunfire, hit the floor," Efraín instructed. "The vehicle's bullet-proof."

Had coming along been the right decision? There was no turning back now. Brad stared straight ahead as they approached the last traffic light on the route. Every single day when he drove around the bend after that light, and saw MBC rising out of the hillside, it filled him with pride. Many mornings when he arrived, the windows shimmered in the sunlight. Now, they glowed in the darkness, lit up from inside. He could make out vehicles in the parking lot that had been empty when he locked it up Saturday afternoon.

At the main gate, two masked men in AFI uniforms with rifles—or automatic weapons, for all Brad knew—stood guard. Behind them, a truck with flashing lights blocked the entrance. The driver pulled the SUV to a stop. Efraín cracked the window. "Licenciado Echeverría and Ingeniero Peters, owners of MBC."

The officer peered at them through a slit in the mask. His eyes were plainly those of a man younger than Brad. "I need to see both men and some I.D."

The driver lowered the windows slightly so the officer could stare at Carlos, then at Brad. He studied their drivers' licenses. "Let them through," he shouted to his colleague on the other side of the vehicle. The man sprinted to the truck that blocked their way and moved it aside. Lucas pulled the SUV up to the brewery entrance.

"Wait here," Efraín ordered. He and Reynaldo jumped out and slammed the doors shut, leaving Brad alone in the back seat. The SUV's engine purred steadily—in case a quick getaway was needed, Brad assumed. The bodyguards conferred with an officer. Brad fidgeted and craned his neck, trying to glimpse inside. The officer who blocked his view wore what looked like a neck warmer pulled up over his nose. The hat made it hard to see his eyes. He waved his arm, motioning to someone.

A man trotted over, his back to the SUV. Like the other officer, he wore a white t-shirt and dark vest. The back of his vest bore the large white letters AFI. Agents from the Agencia Federal de Investigaciones, Mexico's equivalent of the FBI, were the heavyweights of the country's law enforcement. The bodyguards flashed identification, followed by more discussion and gestures toward the SUV. Finally, Efraín, returned. The driver touched a button that popped the locks. Efraín opened Carlos's door, then Brad's.

The first officer swung his rifle strap over his shoulder in the practiced way Alejandra did with her purse strap. *How the hell had they gotten inside the locked gate and brewery?* The officer said tersely, "Captain Aguirre's inside."

An agent led Carlos and Brad, flanked by the two bodyguards. Brad entered his brewery as though in a dream. He had walked through that door hundreds of times, but never at five a.m. And never with police agents and armed bodyguards. The actors and the action seemed to move in slow motion. He shook his head vigorously, hoping to get a grip on the present reality. In the bottling area everything looked the same as always, utterly familiar. Carlos was by his side. He hadn't shaved, either. How many times had Brad seen his partner with that day or two of stubble? He wanted to reach out and squeeze Carlos's arm, wanted to convince himself this wasn't the bizarre dream it seemed to be. His rational, engineer-trained mind told him that his brewery, his work and his life had been transformed overnight. What that would mean, how things would play out, he had no idea. And that scared the hell out of him.

"*Buenos días, Licenciado Echeverría,*" said a gray-haired agent wearing a cap but no face covering. He nodded to Carlos and shook his hand, a little too warmly, Brad thought. He turned to Brad and, with a second short handshake, introduced himself. *"Ingeniero Peters, soy el Capitán Juan Luis Aguirre."*

Brad climbed the stairs feeling like his shoes had turned to lead. Ahead of him, Aguirre marched toward the office as though he owned the brewery. *Dammit! Aguirre and his men had no right to be here!* MBC belonged to Brad and Carlos. He refused to scurry after the man. Reaching the top of the stairs, he steeled himself. The perception of moving in slow motion overwhelmed him. He gripped the half wall along the landing and made himself turn.

He looked out over his brewery, working to comprehend what he was seeing. Even from above, the bottling area still looked normal, but the sense of tremendous familiarity about to collide with disaster hit him anew. Beyond the bottling line, the pallets of kegs ready for use, were exactly as he had left them. Boxes of bottles, shelves with bags of malted barley—everything looked exactly as it should. Only the shipping area remained. A buzz of white noise filled his ears. His shoulders were knotted masses of tension. He forced himself to look out across the brewery to the back corner.

"What the hell has happened?" he bellowed.

CHAPTER TWENTY-SEVEN

BRAD GRIPPED the railing on the low wall so tightly that his knuckles had turned white. He took a step back, afraid that if he didn't, he might topple over the wall. He closed his eyes and breathed in slowly. He had to regain his balance.

"Brad, buddy, are you okay?" Carlos's voice sounded garbled, distorted. "Brad, open your eyes and look at me."

He felt Carlos's hand on his shoulder, pulling him back to reality. He shook his head. Another wave of dizziness washed over him. He opened his eyes and focused on the railing and his hands wrapped tightly around it. He could feel the perspiration beading on his forehead. "I've got to sit down."

"Can you make it into the office?"

"I'll be okay. I just need a minute," Brad said, reaching for the doorframe to support himself.

On Saturday, they had left six pallets shrink-wrapped and ready to ship to Houston. Now the contents were scattered around the loading area. Huge swatches of plastic wrap littered the floor. Every single case—all four hundred and forty-four—appeared to have been slashed apart. They might as well have ripped his heart open. He slumped into a chair.

"I'm sorry, gentlemen," Aguirre said.

Brad clutched his stomach. Had the others heard the low rumble from his gut? The sound rose into his ears, building like a winter avalanche roaring down the side of a Colorado mountain. A year and ten months of hard work, of *piso* payments, of narco insecurity. His brewery, his work, his accomplishments, his life literally lay in tatters.

Here, the criminals dressed like rich businessmen. Hell, they had more money than most of the businessmen. Nobody trusted the police or the politicians. *Was every damn person in Mexico corrupt? This was absolutely the most fucked-up country in the world. Why the hell had he ever come here?* "Captain, why does my brewery look like a disaster zone and what the hell are the cops doing here?" He didn't care that he was shouting or that Carlos was staring at him with a shocked look.

"Because, Ingeniero, for at least the last four months, your beer shipments to Houston have also included cocaine."

The noise roared in his ears again.

"Gentlemen, MBC ships to Aguila Distributing in Houston on the fifteenth and the thirtieth of each month, correct?"

Brad planted his feet firmly. "I'm not answering any questions without a lawyer present."

"Güero," Carlos said through closed teeth, "this isn't the United States."

Brad stared at his partner. *I don't even know who the hell you are.* "You're damn right it's not the United States, and I sure as hell don't intend to end up in a Mexican jail."

Carlos grimaced. "One of my father's colleagues is on the way."

"Is he in on all this, too?" Brad realized he was trapped. The only lawyers he knew in Mexico were Carlos's father and Pablo Garza Oveido. He could no longer trust the Echeverría family, and what kind of help could he expect from a real estate attorney?

"In on all what?" Carlos asked in an angry tone.

"Don't shit me, Carlos. I'm not the dumb, naïve American you're convinced I am. You and Aguirre here, obviously know each other. From the state of my brewery, it looks like you, the cops and El Cártel have all been working together."

"Shut the fuck up!" Carlos shouted, lunging at Brad.

Aguirre stepped between them, and Brad felt himself being yanked from the chair. He leapt up and tried to turn, but unseen hands held him in a tight grip. Terror raced through his veins. He would not end up in a Mexican jail! If they were going to kill him, they'd have to do it here.

"You don't know what the hell you're saying," Carlos yelled, thrashing against the AFI officer who held him back.

Brad felt his captor loosen his grasp. He sent his elbow flying back with every ounce of strength he could muster. He heard a grunt and felt the hand release his shirt collar. He spun around in time to see Efraín recover and drop into a boxer's stance. Christ, he *had* been naïve. Of course, the bodyguards were in on it, too.

"Both of you! Silence!" Aguirre commanded. Brad stared at the floor, breathing hard. "Bernal," Aguirre said to the cop holding Carlos. "Watch him until the lawyer gets here." He shouted to one of the cops down below, "Morelos!" The guy bounded up the stairs, two at a time. "This one is yours," Aguirre said, nodding in Brad's direction.

"Sir," Efraín said, "with all due respect, I'm Licenciado Echeverría's bodyguard and the gentleman downstairs is the American's bodyguard."

"Great. If they try to kill each other, stop 'em."

BRAD SAT in the MBC conference table—*his* conference table, dammit!—now covered with Aguirre's papers, a bottle of water and a crackling walkie-talkie. He crossed his arms tightly against his chest. He didn't trust the suave looking older lawyer now sitting across the table.

"I hope we can now have a civil conversation," the captain recommended, eyeing Brad and Carlos. "MBC ships to Aguila Distributing on the fifteenth and the thirtieth of each month, correct?"

"Yes," Brad said, staring at the wall behind the lawyer.

"Now that we've established that, I'll tell you that the March thirtieth shipment underwent a random drug check by a DEA canine unit in

Laredo. One pallet appeared suspicious. Further investigation uncovered a total of eighty kilos of cocaine between the pallets. DEA officials contacted Tony Vargas, who has cooperated with them and other agencies in the South Texas and Houston HIDTAs—High Intensity Drug Trafficking Areas. It seems that one of Mr. Vargas's employees in shipping and distribution had been making sure that the boxes with cocaine were sent on to the Tricolor warehouse. You're familiar with the Houston-based grocery stores?"

Brad wasn't, but he saw Carlos nod. Aguirre looked at his wristwatch. "Nearly one hour ago, Houston officials arrested Mr. Vargas's employee, along with the brothers who own Tricolor and four other men."

"I assure you, Captain, I am completely innocent." Carlos said. He looked shaken and pathetic.

"I don't know anything about this," Brad said, staring straight at Carlos.

"Calm down, gentlemen. For now, we believe both of you are innocent. Of course, Mr. Vargas was prohibited from discussing any of this with either of you. It was after the DEA contacted us that, as you know Licenciado Echeverría, I called you."

Brad stared at Carlos and mouthed, "What the fuck?"

"Calm down, Ingeniero Peters," Aguirre said. "Like Mr. Vargas, the Licenciado was sternly told not to talk, not even with you. He let us into MBC one night and allowed us to install a hidden video camera, which, by the way, we have now taken down."

Brad eyed Aguirre, then Carlos. He squeezed the chair arms to keep himself from jumping up and punching both assholes.

"Ingeniero, what you insinuated earlier is far from the truth. All along we believed that Licenciado Echeverría and you were both innocent. We now have the video proof that we need and have arrested the individuals suspected of planting the drugs. We believe only one of your employees was involved—Santiago Rodríguez Almejo."

A sharp pain pounded against the back of Brad's eyes as though it would explode through any second. The avalanche roared in his ears again. Nothing made sense. He looked straight at Aguirre. "That's not possible. Chago is one of my most trusted employees."

"Regrettably, Ingeniero, your trust has been abused. Notice the time and date on this video," Aguirre said, clicking the keys on a laptop. Brad leaned forward and squinted at the black and white video with *15 abril, 2:12 a.m.* notched in the bottom corner. Less than four hours ago.

Only the back warehouse area was within the camera's range, the neatly wrapped Houston pallets squarely in view. Like a scene from a low-budget movie, the door beside the loading dock opened and two figures appeared. Brad didn't recognize the first one. The other, as scarecrow thin as Chago, grabbed a dolly and wheeled it to the door. Hands from outside passed in sealed MBC boxes. From the way the men handled the boxes, they weren't empty. *How the hell had they—whoever they were—gotten MBC boxes?*

The skinny one turned and the camera caught his face. Conceivably, it could have been Chago, but the video was grainy. The man ripped a box cutter into the shrink wrap on the nearest pallet with the skill of a surgeon—or of a practiced brewer. He and the other man methodically pulled off boxes and hauled them to the door. The person outside shoved in more MBC boxes which Chago substituted to rebuild the pallet. *It couldn't be Chago.* Brad's mind scrambled for logical explanations.

"You said this has been going on for four months?" Brad asked.

"At least. It's possible they wouldn't have continued much longer. We think they suspected we were on to them."

"Son of a bitch!" Carlos hissed as Brad massaged his temples.

"Notice," Aguirre said, "that they put the boxes with cocaine in the center of each pallet. Hidden in the middle of legitimate boxes, they're harder for the dogs to sniff out. You can't see it on the video, but they're marked in purple with inconspicuous notations that wouldn't attract attention."

Brad felt his heart sink as he watched Chago—there was no doubt, now—re-wrap the pallet, leaving it again identical to the others. Chago and the second man then turned their attention to getting the legitimate boxes out the door. The outside stairs precluded using the dolly. Opening the loading dock door could have drawn attention. Finally, the mystery man came through the door.

"Holy crap," Brad cried in English. Things were falling into place.

"*¿Qué vio?*" Aguirre asked.

"Replay that," Brad ordered.

They watched the image again. "El Míster!" Carlos shouted.

"You know him?" Aguirre asked.

Brad leaned forward, gripping the edge of the office desk, ready to scream at Aguirre—this flesh and blood representative of all that was wrong with Mexico's so-called law enforcement system. "He's the son of a bitch who's been charging us *piso* every month since we opened."

"You're sure?" Aguirre asked.

"As sure as my name is Brad Peters."

"Does he work alone?"

"Sometimes he comes with one or two other men."

"Do you know their names?"

"Matagatos and Labrador."

Aguirre's mouth slid into a crooked smile. "But you haven't seen Matagatos recently."

"Not lately, no."

"He was killed in a D.F. kidnapping last fall. El Míster is Juan Ignacio Gutiérrez Saldaña. He grew up on both sides of the border, hence the nickname. He and Matagatos—Ernesto Gutiérrez Saldaña—were brothers. You won't be seeing El Míster for a while either now. At the moment, he and the other man in the video—El Grillo—are being processed at Ministerio Público."

"Where's Chago?" Brad asked.

"Same place. Bail will be denied for all of them."

"I have no intention of bailing him out," Carlos said, his voice colder than the walk-in cooler.

Brad exploded in an angry stream of Spanish. "Captain, for over a year and a half, El Míster and El Cártel have been shaking us down." Carlos's eyes telegraphed a fiery *shut up!* "A hundred thousand pesos just to get our equipment here. Ten thousand every month to stay in business. A case or two of beer, here and there. Where the hell were you and your men all that time?"

The eyes narrowed in Aguirre's otherwise impassive face. "Did you file a report?"

"I was told it wouldn't do any good and that things don't go well for the occasional owners who do protest," Brad said, never taking his eyes off Carlos. *And you guys have got to be the most fricking inept cops in the world.*

"Unfortunately, Ingeniero, the cartels take every opportunity they can to corrupt and control Mexico. Extortion and bribery do exist, and you are correct that we in law enforcement don't do a good enough job of controlling the delinquency in our midst. As you Americans say, we have to pick and choose our battles. In order to end *piso* extortion, we would essentially have to provide security for every business in the country twenty-four hours a day. We'd also like to end all kidnappings, carjackings, murders, rapes, assaults, robberies and all money laundering along with drug trafficking and the flow of arms from your country into ours. But we aren't Supermen. We're human beings and we do what we can. Like you, I want to believe all my men are honest. My officers are on the front line every single day against international drug cartels with billion-dollar budgets. I kiss my wife and daughters goodbye every morning knowing that it could be the last time, and my men do the same.

"What I can offer," Aguirre said, pulling out his wallet, "is that AFI will be watching your facilities closely for the next several months. Here's my card. In fact," he added, jotting numbers on the back, "you can call me personally at this number any time. As for today, I'll have a couple of men stationed here for the next twenty-four hours. And those bodyguards you came with today, it would be a good idea to keep them close by for the next weeks."

Brad turned to the open door. As if in a framed photo, Efraín leaned against the walkway railing, legs crossed at the ankles. He raised a hand to his forehead in a loose salute, obviously privy to the conversation.

"Your employees will be arriving shortly," Aguirre said. "I'll need a list of names for my men at the gate. We'll be interviewing each of them. Would you all like to see the last minutes of the video?"

Brad sank into despair as he watched officers pour into the wrecked warehouse and round up suspects. He barely recognized his brewery, the one where he and his team came to work every day to make an honest living. He had given nearly two years of his life to MBC. He had moved to a dangerous city in a foreign country, learned the language, invested his savings, worked fifty and sixty hour weeks and personally handed hard-earned money over to drug cartel thugs. Whether he left Mexico or stayed, he would forever be a different man. He was no longer a guileless foreigner.

CHAPTER TWENTY-EIGHT

ALEJANDRA WAS The first to arrive. Brad caught the young AFI agent checking her out a little too long. "AFI raid," he said, walking her to her locker. "Employee meeting as soon as everybody's here."

Her mouth dropped in shock. She recovered enough to ask, "What do you want me to do in the meantime?"

Brad blew out a breath. His headache had subsided some for now. "Start cleaning up shrink-wrap if you want."

"You look exhausted."

He kissed the tip of her nose. "I'd better get back to the entrance."

At ten minutes after eight, Brad clapped his hands. All seven employees, two bodyguards and the remaining AFI officers immediately focused their attention on him. "Good morning. Carlos and I want all of you to hear the news together so everybody gets the same information."

"Chago's not here yet," Rodrigo said.

"Chago no longer works for MBC."

The news was met with sideways glances and silence. Carlos maintained a wooden expression. With the bodyguards and AFI agents listening, Brad summarized the events of the last hours.

"Why?" Lalo asked. "Chago had so much going for him."

"Money," Rodrigo said. "The whole thing with his girlfriend's father and saving up for a house." Two bottlers nodded.

"My God," Alejandra said. "A few weeks ago, Chago told me he'd started working a second job at a bar on Friday and Saturday nights. He said he was making good money and thought they might be able to marry early next year. When I asked where he was working, I never got a straight answer."

"My girlfriend and I go out—went out—with Chago and Graciela sometimes," Rodrigo said. "I never heard anything about a bartending job. We were with him on Friday night."

"Think about how tired he's been lately," Abraham said. "And remember the packing mess last month?"

Brad joined in the nods. He'd thought about it this morning while Aguirre talked. Accidents and mistakes happened, but Chago's had been straight-up bone-headed. They were short a man, and Chago was the lone packer. When there was no backup, even a novice knew to flag the operator when he needed to stop the filler for more boxes. Chago had realized it too late. By the time Samuel stopped the line, three bottles had crashed to the floor.

"Remember what he said?" Abraham asked, talking fast. "That he was really tired and hadn't slept well the night before."

"What day was that?" Brad asked.

"I don't know," Abraham shrugged. "Wait! It happened in the afternoon, after the Houston shipment had gone out that morning."

Carlos tapped at his phone. "Friday, March fifteenth?"

"How was it possible," Lalo asked, "that not one of us put together what was happening right before our eyes?"

"Bottom line for now, guys," Brad said, "the officers will be talking with each of you individually, and we have a lot of clean up to do."

"I talked to Tony Vargas," Carlos added. "The shipment that was supposed to go out today obviously won't. You guys think you can have it pulled back together for tomorrow?"

"We won't know until we tally the damage," Alejandra said.

"If any of you know of a good, experienced brewer, we could use one ASAP," Brad said. "For now, let's get to work."

They spent the morning in a frenzy of cleaning and assessment. Even Carlos pitched in between phone calls. If they hadn't needed every pair of hands so badly, including those of the bodyguards, Brad would have sent Carlos back to the pub. He was still pissed about Carlos's reactions and responses to Aguirre. The only bright spot in the day was his team that pulled together and worked like never before. For lunch, he had tacos delivered. An hour past quitting time, he said, "You guys have been amazing. I owe you big time."

Carlos stepped in beside him. "Like Brad said, you guys have been amazing. Thanks to all of you." He reminded Brad of the talking parrots they sold in the market.

When they were finally alone in the office, Carlos asked, "What's happening to us?"

"To us MBC or to us Carlos and Brad?"

"To Brad and Carlos, business partners and friends."

"Obviously, you have some thoughts on the matter."

Carlos wrinkled his forehead. "I wanted to tell you about the camera. I really did. They swore me to secrecy, and I have—*we* —have so much at stake here."

"You're damn right, Carlos. *We* have a lot at stake. We never could have started MBC without your money, but I'm fed up with hearing about your connections and your reputation and the weight of that silver spoon which, through no fault of your own, you were born with in your mouth. I've put every penny I own into MBC. I gave up a secure job and left a safe country. Today may have sent my professional reputation down the toilet. If I can't make a living brewing, what's left for me?"

"Except for the AFI visit and the camera, I've always been honest and up front with you."

There it was. The heart of what had gone wrong between them. Brad stared straight into Carlos's green eyes. "'I assure you I am completely innocent.'That was the first thing you said. You weren't so sure about me, though, were you?"

"Don't be a dick." Carlos's eyes darted to one side then the other, avoiding Brad.

"C'mon, Mr. Honest-and-up-front. This goes back to when I helped the Mosses and didn't tell you, doesn't it? After all this time and all we've been through, when our backs were to the wall, you didn't trust me."

Carlos pinched his eyes shut and rubbed the lids. "Maybe—for a split second—it entered my thoughts. But even before you knew the facts, you believed I was working for El Cártel."

Now Brad couldn't look Carlos in the eyes. He had no answer, no defense.

"But I guess everybody has his price," Carlos continued. "Apparently, Chago's wasn't all that high."

"I *cared* about Chago," Brad said. "His betrayal is what bothers me the most." No, that wasn't true. The betrayal had stung him all day, but in the larger context, it was only part of what had eaten at him since El Míster's very first phone call. "What bugs the hell out of me is that we never stood up to El Míster. We always stopped everything and rushed to give him whatever he demanded. Dammit, it's so wrong, Carlos. That's how Mexico has gotten to be the mess it is. Everybody just keeps on rolling over on command and letting the *narcos* and *delincuentes* have their way."

"Christ, Brad, haven't you learned anything about *la inseguridad* in the last year and a half?"

Brad pointed a finger within inches of Carlos's face. "Don't lecture me, Carlos. I'm not an idiot or a clueless American. What I'm saying is that until a critical mass of Mexicans—politicians, judges, people in the legal system, enough of the outraged public—say *¡Basta!*, why should the narcos change?" Brad threw his hands in the air. "This has been one hell of a day."

"The lousiest in the history of MBC. Listen, can we make peace and agree to work toward getting MBC back on its feet?"

Brad exhaled and shook his aching head. "Do we have any other choice? You realize the raid is going to cost us big time?"

"I've been obsessing over that all day. We're going to have to invest a lot of time and money in spinning the PR damage."

"You think," Brad asked, "that this will be the end of El Míster and *piso* payments?"

"Of El Míster? Possibly. Of *piso*? I doubt it."

"So we and our bodyguards need to keep an eye out for strangers with fancy pointy-toed boots and diamond-studded pistols?"

Carlos stared at the palms of his hands as though searching them for the right words. "Nobody in Mexico can stop the cartels. The world hears about beheadings and shootouts, but those naïve Americans, as you called them—the ones in Denver and Bumfuck, Iowa—don't have a clue about how all the violence affects every aspect of life in Mexico."

"Bumfuck, Iowa?"

"You know what I mean—all those little towns in the States where life is wholesome and good."

"And I'll bet the cartels are connected to drug sales in just about every Bumfuck on the planet. God, I'm ready to walk out the door."

"So you're leaving?"

Brad rubbed his jaw. "Not tomorrow. Not for the next month. Beyond that, honestly, I don't know."

Brad felt ridiculous riding in the back seat of his own car while Reynaldo chauffeured Alejandra and him. "What does one do with his bodyguard while he dines at a taquería?" Brad whispered in English, which the bodyguard apparently didn't speak.

"The employee waits nearby, alert and on duty. If the employer allows it, he can eat quickly, but he's still on duty."

"How the heck do you know these things?"

"Common knowledge," Alejandra said. "Next time you're at the sports club with your tennis buddies, keep an eye on those discreetly situated suits."

For the next two weeks, three bodyguards—much better-dressed than Brad and his brewers—would take turns as Brad's round-the-clock shadow. Don Francisco, Carlos's father, had insisted on it and Aguirre had urged Brad to accept the offer.

At the taquería, he was amused to watch the guard formally open the back door for Alejandra. "Who pays for his food?" Brad whispered on their way inside.

"Be generous and swing for it. You'll start out on his good side."

"Come on, Reynaldo," Brad said, nodding first to the bodyguard and then the register. "Dinner's on me."

Judging from the size of Reynaldo and his biceps, Brad fully expected him to ask for one of everything on the menu. Instead, he ordered two tacos and a soft drink.

Reynaldo wolfed his food standing at a counter near Brad and Alejandra's table. At Reynaldo's insistence, Brad sat with his back to the wall. "This is so ridiculous," Brad said. "I feel like I'm in a 1930s gangster movie."

"You won't think so if some of El Míster's friends decide to pay a visit," Alejandra replied.

"Come on, the guy's going to be outside my bathroom door when I'm showering and sitting on my sofa while I sleep. If some narcos actually decided to take me out, how much protection could one bodyguard be?"

"It's not very likely, but if they know you have bodyguards, that will discourage them."

"Well, you can forget about anything beyond a little hand-holding between us for the time being."

"Don't tell my grandfather. He'd hire bodyguards until the day we marry—" Alejandra stopped and put a hand over her mouth. "Sorry."

"No," Brad said. "I'm the one who should apologize. I need some time to sort out everything and what it's going to mean." He read in Alejandra's eyes the question Carlos had asked. "Don't worry. For now, I'm not going anywhere." She forced a weak smile. "Alejandra, the dust has to settle before I can begin to think about the next few years."

She wadded her napkin and tossed it on the plastic plate in front of her. "I think we both need a good night's sleep."

When Reynaldo pulled up beside Alejandra's car at the brewery, Brad said firmly, "I'll open her door." He walked Alejandra over and exchanged a quick kiss.

"Don't stay up too late," she said.

"That's one thing you don't have to worry about. We're going to follow you home. And then I'll call you when I get to my place." A compact car turned into the open gate and Brad tensed.

"That's Enrique, my replacement," said Reynaldo, who stood respectfully on the other side of the car. "I'll introduce you and be on my way."

Enrique, with his hair slicked back and his dress shirt a size too large, looked more like an assistant manager at a fast food restaurant than a bodyguard. He reminded Brad of Chago the day he interviewed at MBC. "The night guard will drive you home and come back to MBC in the morning," Carlos had explained. The thought of riding in the back seat of his car while this kid drove was ridiculous. "I'll drive," Brad said, holding out his hand for the keys.

After they saw Alejandra safely into the gated garage of her complex, Brad turned toward his apartment. At a red light, Enrique sat motionless, watching the cars around them. "My apartment's pretty small," Brad ventured. "You're welcome to hang out on the living room sofa."

"Thanks." Enrique looked as enthusiastic as Brad about this gig.

In the apartment, lights were blazing. "You think there's someone in there?" Enrique asked with a nervous edge.

"I don't think so. I ran out so fast this morning I wasn't thinking about turning off the lights." That had been sixteen very long hours ago. Before he'd seen his brewery trashed. Before he'd cussed out an AFI officer and been lectured in return. Before he'd blown up at his business partner and friend. Before Alejandra, in an unguarded moment, had indirectly brought up marriage and their future.

He looked at Enrique's mousse-hardened helmet of hair. "I didn't have time to clean up, either."

"I can do that if you want."

"Can you wash dishes?" Brad asked, inserting his key in the door lock and wondering if housekeeping was included in bodyguard duties.

"The instructors who trained me don't have anything on my mother, sir."

"Want a beer?" Brad asked as he opened the refrigerator.

"Thank you, but we're not allowed to drink on the job."

Brad grabbed three Morenitas before closing the bedroom door and calling Alejandra. Afterwards, deprived of his TV which Enrique *was* permitted to watch as long as the volume was kept low, Brad propped his pillow against the headboard and settled in, but sleep would not come. The thought of Cártel retaliation scared the shit out of him. Maybe having a bodyguard on the other side of the door wasn't such a bad idea. Carlos's father was footing the bill for two weeks of protection. Brad wondered if it needed to be longer. Worst of all, Carlos and Aguirre had been right. Assuming Carlos's guilt had been so easy for Brad. Until this morning, he had believed he was a bigger man.

He polished off the first beer in minutes. It went down smooth and malty with a clean finish, just the way it was supposed to. This was his accomplishment alone, the one that had won him awards and the respect of his fellow brewers. He'd developed the recipe before he even knew Alejandra or Chago. If he walked away tomorrow, Carlos wouldn't have a clue how to brew a Morenita. If he left, it wouldn't be the end of the world. Alejandra and Lalo and Rodrigo would save Carlos's butt. Chago could have done it better than any of them if he hadn't been so stupid. He'd wrecked his own life and messed up Graciela's. He'd screwed MBC big time.

Brad opened the second beer and took a long plug. He was a damn good brewer. Nobody could take away the three medals from three competitions in the last year. He could go back to Denver, or almost anywhere in the States, and have a job in no time. A job with no *piso* and no helmet-haired bodyguard hogging his TV and living room.

He took another satisfying swig. But Alejandra changed everything. Thanks to her father, she had dual citizenship. They could walk away from MBC and start a new life in the U.S. Getting his money out of MBC was going to be tough, but not impossible. Alejandra's family could probably help set them up with a nice little brewery. Just what Emily had proposed last summer. He tipped the second Morenita back again and realized it was already empty, so he opened the third one. The buzz from two quick beers had finally knocked out his day-long headache.

But could he commit to marriage and make it last? Crap, he had no idea. What had brought him and Emily together had been homesickness and sex. The day he looked into Maddy's eyes and repeated, "till death do us part," he'd meant it. He tried to picture himself with Alejandra when they were old and white-haired, but he couldn't. Did he love her enough? She was a damn good brewer and they worked together incredibly well. If she'd been a guy, they would have been awesome business partners. Of the women he'd been involved with, Emily was the best-looking and the sexiest. Alejandra was nice-looking in a simple, classic way. When she was old, she'd probably still be wearing her silver-white hair in a long ponytail. She'd age well.

But what if he convinced her to go to Denver and it didn't work out? She'd be lonely so far from Mexico and her family. Except for brewing and marriage to Maddy, Brad had never committed long-term to anything in his life. With college, he'd gone in knowing the end date. With MBC, he'd always said it was for a few years. At first, it had been about getting Carlos and the pub up and running. Then, it became the challenge of starting up a brewery and after that, winning competition medals. It was playing around with seasonal brews and having fun growing the business. It was the reputation he had developed as the go-to expert for a loose group of Monterrey homebrewers. The word *"forever"* had never been part of the deal.

Without realizing it, he had started to carve out a life here. He cared about MBC, about his brewers and bottlers. He liked walking into the pub and spending time with Paty and Paco and Noé and the other employees. He enjoyed helping those homebrewers. He looked forward to Saturday afternoon tennis with the Ex-A-Tecs. Heck, he had gone to two weddings in the last four months, invited to share the important moments in people's lives because he had developed friendships. His success and MBC's had exceeded his most daring dreams. He realized, for the first time, that he could actually contemplate a life in Monterrey for a long time. Perhaps forever.

Except for the narco corruption.

CHAPTER TWENTY-NINE

JUAN IGNACIO Gutiérrez Saladaña pulled back his shoulders and stuck out his chest, prepared to make his entrance. "Castro, time's up!" The lack of inflection in the guard's words made it impossible to judge his mood. A squat man with tattoos covering his bald head and arms—presumably Castro—shoved back the orange plastic chair he'd been sitting in and exited. Two of the other four prisoners looked Nacho's way, sizing him up. All cradled old-fashioned phone receivers and stared intently at the faces on the other side of the glass. The two guards glanced at Nacho but showed no reaction. The tiny room looked like a fucking concrete bunker. The hot air stank of sweat, dirty clothes and testosterone. Nacho eased into the newly vacated chair.

Martinez was the lawyer's name. El Mago, The Magician, they called him. "If you can afford El Mago, he'll have you out in a week," an acquaintance of Labrador had said in the exercise yard. Nacho didn't plan on being in this shithole even that long. He slid into the chair and dipped his head, acknowledging the man whose smooth face looked too young to go with the gray hair. El Mago wore an expensive pin-striped suit, a red tie and a shitload look of confidence. The *patrones* were obviously shelling out on his case.

He'd gotten fucked over through no fault of his own. In the two days since his arrest, he'd had plenty of time to think about what had gone wrong and why. He'd tried to work it out different ways, but kept coming to the same conclusion. The asshole American. Somehow, Peters had suspected something and tipped off the cops. The damned skinny kid, Chago, had screwed up, too, somewhere along the way.

Martínez picked up his receiver and Nacho did the same. Everything—the greetings, the questions, the answers—was blah, blah, blah predictable. "How long till I get out?"

El Mago didn't look used to being interrupted. They went back and forth, the expensive suit saying everything in too many long words, Nacho trying to cut to what mattered. He didn't like what he was hearing or the direction things were going. "It was one fucking job. I've never even been arrested before. Work your magic, Mago."

"It's not that simple. These things take time. With the video, pleading innocent is out of the question."

Nacho forgot all about keeping his voice down and his body in the chair. "You're saying I'm supposed to plead guilty?" Heads turned, eyes stared. Nacho sat down again and cupped a hand around the receiver.

"I'll work up a plea bargain argument," El Mago said, "while we wait to find out which judge is assigned to your case. If we're lucky, you'll get one who'll work with us.'"

"You'd damn well better work your ass off. I'm not staying here." Nacho slammed down the phone.

OUT IN the living room, *La Voz...México* was building toward the season finale. The remaining contestants were singing their hearts and lungs out for the chance to become Mexico's Voice. Brad was pretty sure Enrique, the helmet-haired bodyguard, had turned the volume to the max. A prisoner in his own bedroom, he finished off one Colorado Red Ale and opened the next one.

A week had passed since the raid. Having a bodyguard constantly hovering was driving him crazy. He could only take so much of Enrique's presence before he fled to the bedroom and closed the door. His phone, laptop and beer were his only entertainment. It had gotten embarrassing hauling empties past Enrique every morning. He'd started stashing them in the bedroom closet and under the bathroom sink. He'd clean them out in four days, as soon as he'd finished serving his "sentence."

At the brewery, he more or less avoided Carlos. He purposely hadn't played tennis on Saturday, and didn't know if Carlos had or not. Since the raid, they'd only talked about the most pressing business. He knew Carlos was worried as hell about what would happen if his head brewer packed up and left. Alejandra was more worried than Carlos.

Everybody wanted answers and he didn't have any.

He drained the last Colorado Red and rolled the bottle under the bed. If he'd had another in the room he would have started on it. He thought about making a run to the fridge, but that would have meant walking by Enrique in his boxers or pulling on some pants. He decided he didn't want the fourth beer of the night badly enough. He reached to turn out the light just as his phone rang.

"Hello, Brad? Manuel Cárdenas from Cuauhtémoc. We met a couple of months ago."

Brad worked to concentrate. "The German-trained brewer?" he asked, recalling the short, otherwise physically unremarkable man, with an impressive brewing knowledge and track record.

"That's right. I hear you're looking for a brewer."

ALEJANDRA'S KISS was like water for a man in the desert. They started slowly, lips exploring. Brad reached under the curtain of hair and put his hand around the nape of her neck, pulling her closer. She responded eagerly, pressing toward him. It would be so easy to stretch out, undress each other and satisfy the cravings of their sex-deprived bodies. The picture window behind the sofa would have only slowed him down just long enough to pull the drapes. The thought of Lolis or Marisela walking in might have deterred him, but the deal breaker was Enrique sitting guard on the landing outside. Thank God he'd only shadow Brad for one more night.

"You want to go to the bedroom?" Alejandra whispered.

Did the man in the desert want to slake his thirst?

Afterwards, as they lay together, arms and legs entangled, he touched his nose to her head and inhaled the smells of Alejandra. He wanted to stay like this, not thinking about the future or the past, only the moment. He wished they were at his place, with no Enrique or Reynaldo or José, without the undiscussed future looming over and around them every minute.

"We should get dressed," Alejandra said, planting a kiss on his chin.

Minutes later she came into the living room where he waited. She ran a finger along his arm, barely touching the skin. "Can I get you a beer?"

He followed her into the kitchen. Her movements were languid and relaxed. She uncapped a bottle and held it out to him. Brad took it and plunged in. "I've done a lot of thinking this week. About the raid and MBC. About the future."

Alejandra paused, bottle opener in hand. "And?"

"I care too much about MBC to walk away. I *like* what I do. I wake up every morning looking forward to my job and to seeing the people I work with. Of all the things that have happened since I came to Monterrey..." he paused and took a drink to steady his nerves "...the best one has been meeting you."

Alejandra gave a quivering smile and her eyes misted. Brad took that as a good sign and continued. "After the divorce, I didn't know if I could ever again tell a woman I loved her. I never said it to Emily." He took another drink. "Here it is: Alejandra, I love you. I want us to be okay with thinking that marriage could be in the cards eventually—if that's what you want."

"It's very much what I want." This time the tears spilled over.

CHAPTER THIRTY

July 2014

MANUEL CÁRDENAS had stepped into MBC with the timing of a ballroom dancer. Initially, Brad had been skeptical. With a decade of training and experience at Mexico's second largest brewery, Manuel might be slow to adapt to MBC expectations and procedures. But Brad had desperately needed a replacement for Chago, and Manuel was yearning for a chance to grow professionally. After two months at MBC, Manuel had become an indispensable member of the team.

"What's eating at you?" Manuel asked Brad on a beautiful summer morning.

"Yeast," Brad answered with a sigh from his spot in the MBC pilot brewery. "It takes me two weeks to propagate a new batch. For the last year I've been trying to figure out how to speed things up."

"Ever try continuous aeration fed-batch culture technique?"

"Come again?"

"Continuous aeration fed-batch culture technique. I studied it in Germany, but I've never actually done it." Ten minutes later, the conversation ended with Manuel excitedly predicting a fresh batch of yeast within a week and Brad happy to walk away from the problem.

On his way downstairs, Brad fielded a call from Carlos in Mexico City. "I'm in the hotel lobby waiting for Marcos, the distributor, to pick me up. We'll be in meetings all day. And guess what? We're having lunch with Federico Cardinale. King Midas himself requested it."

Brad gave a soft whistle. "You're flying in some high circles."

Forty years ago when the man nicknamed King Midas was a young bartender, a regular customer told him about an investment group with ambitious plans for a world-class resort. "Invest in this five-star hotel and you'll be rich in five years," the man boasted. Cardinale laughed at the idea of renaming the sleepy fishing village of Puerto Juárez and turning it into a playground for rich tourists. The next day, though, he threw every peso he had in the pot. Cancún and Cardinale's fortune took off.

"What does he want?" Brad asked.

"I'm not sure," Carlos answered. "Apparently, he just got back from touring brewpubs and craft breweries in California and has some butterfly in his bonné."

"Has what?"

"A butterfly in his bonné. You know, an idea in his head."

"A bee in his bonnet?"

"Bonnet? I thought it was a French word. What's a 'bonnet'?"

"Not important. What about Cardinale?"

"Marcos thinks he wants to get into the craft brewing business. I'll keep you posted. Listen, I'm calling because I finished rolling up the numbers for June."

After the raid, they'd been in the red for April and May and had nearly wiped out their cash reserve. "And?"

"A net profit just over twenty-five thousand pesos."

"Awesome!"

"Less than two thousand dollars and we're excited."

"Damn right."

"Part of it was due to MBC Wear—and Kendra Lockwood."

"Who?"

"Remember that American barbecue a couple years ago? The sexy, but crazy, blonde from Houston who ragged on the guy from the Consulate?"

Brad recalled the Marilyn Monroe curves and tight dress. "How could I forget? Didn't she and Bob go back to Houston?"

"Where Kendra opened a clothing boutique that's developed a trendy following, according to *Texas Monthly*, and heavy internet sales. She ran into Tony, who told her about MBC Wear. She checked out our website and immediately bought everything Tony had in stock. She sold out in three days. She called me yesterday and placed a three-thousand-dollar order directly with us. She wants to be our exclusive MBC Wear rep in the U.S."

"But we have contractual obligations to Tony."

"I talked to him last night. He's getting soft in his old age. He said he's in the beverage business. If Kendra wants to handle MBC Wear, good for her."

At noon, Brad loaded the MBC van and headed over to the pub with three fresh kegs and one more success. Tomorrow Topo Chico Centeno IPA would be retired to make room for MBC's third seasonal brew, Alejandra's Ale. Alejandra had put in plenty of hours on her wheat-but-not-a-wheat. At every step, the two of them had consulted and sampled experimental test batches. They were convinced they had a hit.

Vagabundo greeted Brad with feline joy. The tabby was looking older these days. He'd gotten into a fight a few months earlier and lost a chunk of what had been his one intact ear. Brad scratched the cat between his ragged ears before unloading his cargo and mentally prepping for his lunch meeting with Bennie Schwartzlander, the representative from MBC's hops supplier.

With his mane of white hair and gnarled hands, Bennie was nearly old enough to be Brad's grandfather. He could have retired years ago, but claimed he wouldn't have any idea what to do. Whenever he came to town for business with Cuauhtémoc he made time for MBC. Brad looked forward to their meetings, even though he suspected Bennie favored Carlos, in whom he saw a kindred sales rep spirit.

Bennie was on his third taco al pastor when he asked, "Think you'll ever move back to the States?"

"Someday. For now, I've got a great job and a great girl in my life."

Bennie lifted his glass. "You've got a damn good beer, good as any of the top craft beers in the U.S. And you could sell it for more there. When you and Carlos are ready to let go of MBC, you come back to the States and Carlos can take my job."

"Get out of here, Bennie! When Carlos and I retire, you'll still be flying all over Latin America."

FROM THE upper level of the brewery, Brad surveyed the dreary day and the road. Rain was forecast all day, unusual in the summer. An omen? He didn't feel good about today's meeting. He pulled himself back to reality. MBC was recovering from the raid. No narco thugs had come to take El Míster's place. He and Alejandra were on track to the altar. Still, he couldn't help replaying the conversation with Bennie in his head. The ringing phone shook him out of his thoughts.

"That keg of Alejandra's Ale you brought over yesterday," Paco said. "I'm not getting much of a head, and it's pretty flat."

Brad paced in front of the window. "I'm going into a meeting. I'll get a replacement over by noon."

"It can't be any earlier?"

"I'm afraid not," Brad replied, knowing it didn't look good not to have a new beer available the day of its announced launch.

Outside, a black car turned into the parking lot and rolled toward the entrance, splashing through a puddle. The back doors open and two men emerged. The one in a rumpled jacket and crooked tie reminded him of Efraín the bodyguard. Brad descended the stairs wishing this meeting were behind him. It didn't help that Carlos, still in Mexico City, had never heard of Fidel Salas.

Impeccably dressed in a gray suit and tie, Salas maintained a serious look and walked briskly, like a man with important things to get done. As the men shook hands, Brad heard a voice behind him. "*Buenos días,* I'm Ingeniero Peters's assistant. Right this way."

"I didn't catch your name," Salas said with a hint of irritation.

"Alejandra," she replied with a pleasant smile as she led the way. In her spotless white lab coat, she looked thoroughly professional. She appeared oblivious to the looks Brad was shooting her.

He had a bad feeling about these men. He especially didn't want them seeing her. "Alejandra, I'm going to need a fresh keg of our new seasonal to run over to the pub after this. Can you get it ready?"

"Certainly. Afterwards, I'll be in the pilot brewery if you need anything."

Upstairs, Brad ushered Salas and his assistant into the office. He left the door cracked. "Please, have a seat. You said you thought I could be of service to you?"

Salas offered the first trace of a smile before switching to English. "You've earned quite a reputation here in Monterrey, Ingeniero Peters."

"Thank you."

"I'll get right to the point of this visit. I represent a highly successful regional entrepreneur who is convinced that the craft brewing industry has a great future in Mexico, and he intends to be a major player. He has spent months quietly making contacts and educating himself. My client routinely seeks the top people in their fields to employ in his business ventures. Your name has come up repeatedly as one of the most knowledgeable and outstanding brewers in northern Mexico."

"Would your client be Federico Cardinale?"

Salas furrowed his brow. "No. I don't know the gentleman. My client, for now, prefers to remain anonymous. What he'd like is a simple buyout. With the understanding, of course, that you would continue in your current position."

Brad practically choked. *Who the hell were these guys?* "What about Carlos Echeverría, my partner and the senior owner of MBC?"

Salas waved a hand. "He'll earn a very nice profit from the sale and can start another business. Optionally, he could continue as director of sales and marketing or in some other position, but my client would be the sole owner. Your salary, whatever it is, will double immediately, Ingeniero, and he's willing to invest in any upgrades and improvements you would like. He can provide the capital to expand MBC's production as quickly as increased sales require."

The conversation was more alarming by the minute. "Why MBC and why me? There are plenty of other well-qualified brewers in Mexico." *Not that many, actually.*

"My client heard an interesting story about you saving some yeast during an extended power outage by using a garden sprinkler and chilled water from a fermenter. That's the kind of resourcefulness he likes to see."

"Only a handful of people know about that. How did your...your client hear that story?"

"It came from Santiago Rodríguez, a young man who thinks very highly of your abilities. He shared it with me and with an individual I believe you know as El Míster."

"How did you meet with them? They're in prison."

"With the right connections, those arrangements aren't difficult."

"Mr. Salas, MBC is not for sale. It's time to end this meeting," Brad said, shoving his chair back and standing.

Salas spread his arms and spoke with a tone of impatience. "Please sit down and let me finish. My client anticipated the possibility that Mr. Echeverría might not want to sell. He's willing to start a new brewery with you as his brewmaster. You'd have full charge of designing and overseeing the building of the brewery, the production, everything you choose—with a virtually unlimited budget."

"I don't know who your client is, but if he has any connection to Santiago Rodríguez or El Míster, I'm not interested. MBC has had its fill of narco harassment." Brad shoved his chair aside and stepped to the door.

Salas's only movement was a tiny frown. "Ingeniero, don't even try to play that game, because you don't stand a chance. Let me sweeten the offer," he continued in an unctuous voice. "Since El Míster's arrest, MBC has not paid *piso*. Surely you didn't expect that to continue. If you choose not to work for us, the payments will resume immediately, fifteen thousand a month."

"MBC was nearly ruined by the raid and the *piso* we've already handed over. That much would put us out of business."

"What a shame. But, no, Ingeniero, don't try to play the stakes game with us because you can't win. If anyone at MBC contacts any authority, my client will see to it that your Temporary Resident Visa is revoked. Moreover, you could very well end up in a Mexican jail."

El Cártel probably could find a way to get his visa revoked, but send him to jail? Salas was playing a bullshit game of chicken. "You hesitate? Perhaps this will convince you. Imagine when the police, in reviewing the possessions that were on Santiago Rodríguez when he was arrested, discover two items they had previously failed to examine." Salas produced a miniature recorder from a pocket inside the expensive jacket and flicked it on with his thumb.

A voice said something unintelligible, too far away for the recorder to pick up. A second voice came through loud and clear. "*Just finishing up the paperwork on tomorrow's shipment.*" The sound of Chago's voice hit Brad like a stomach punch.

"*It can wait.*" His own voice sounded strange, still barely intelligible.

Chago's was again strong. "*The truck will be here at eight-thirty. It won't take me long. I can lock up.*"

"*Thanks, Chago. You got the test boxes properly stored away so there won't be any mix-ups?*"

Salas stopped the recorder and leaned back, the smile still on his lips. Stunned, Brad stared at the man. "That was an insignificant conversation Chago and I had five months ago. How did you get that?"

"You should know, Ingeniero. You were there, although your memory appears to falter. It was less than three months ago, hours before the raid, when you gave Chago his last instructions about how to store and hide the cocaine, even telling him how to label the boxes. Santiago—Chago as you call him—recorded a number of conversations once he went to work for us. That one in particular provides fairly damning evidence that you, Ingeniero Peters, were part of the ring shipping cocaine to Houston. The woman he addresses—Alejandra, I believe. Wouldn't it be a shame if an enthusiastic prosecutor decided to charge the lovely Alejandra as an accessory?"

"Don't you dare threaten her," Brad said, his voice rising.

"Alejandra Howard Guzmán. From a distinguished, respected, wealthy Saltillo family." Salas spoke slowly. "Used by an American drug smuggler preying on his friends and employees. Plenty of meaty scandal for the media. You, Alejandra, the Howard-Guzmán family, Monterey Brewing Company, Carlos Echeverría and family, plus your employees could make headlines for weeks."

Brad lashed out with one, last effort. "It's a frame up. You'd never get away with it."

Salas's curt tone had lost every pretense of politeness. "Who would believe you? A foreigner whose brewery was unquestionably involved in illegal drug trafficking? Rodríguez will testify that you recruited him and swear that was the topic in the recording."

"That's insane. Except for Chago—who you all corrupted and ruined—every one of us has a solid reputation. Nobody's going to listen to one short conversation, turned up under suspicious circumstances."

Salas stretched out his legs, crossing them at the ankles. He pulled a phone from his designer jacket. "Good point, Ingeniero. A strong case needs more evidence. Say, for example, a box used to transport the illegal drugs which you labeled. Since this is not a court of law, a photograph should suffice. Ministerio Público has the actual piece of evidence. Here in Mexico, Ingeniero, you have such distinctive, American handwriting."

Brad stared at the screen. "That's a box from a product aging test. Why would anyone believe that 'CW1, 5/2/14' is proof I was smuggling cocaine in my beer shipments?"

Salas swiped the screen. "Because that's how *you*, Ingeniero, instructed Chago to label the boxes. The one in this photo, as you can see, is from the raid. Notice that Chago, devoted to you, his mentor, stayed faithful to your instructions, using the same purple marker and abbreviations."

Brad yanked the phone from Salas's hand. The morning of the raid, Aguirre had mentioned the "inconspicuous" markings on the boxes. Neither Carlos nor he had asked what they actually looked like. In Salas' photo, the upper left corner of the Santa Catarina Stout box clearly bore the purple handwritten label "CW3, 15/4/14." There was no doubt it was Chago's precise handwriting.

Brad looked at Salas and shuddered. He was staring into the eyes of El Cártel, into the eyes of a monster capable of doing ghastly things to fellow human beings. He wanted to scream in Salas's face that he and El Cártel were sending Mexico to hell; that they wrought suffering in the lives of millions of honest Mexicans; they corrupted and ruined the lives of thousands of vulnerable individuals like Chago; they fed the addictions of people all over the world, destroying them and their families, all for money. If he had held a gun, he swore he would have pulled the trigger.

"Get out!" he shouted, yanking the office door open.

Salas smiled and stood up. "It will indeed be a shame. Not for us, of course. As you said, there are other brewers and my client will find the best one. He—or she—might even be one of your current employees. Then my client will work to put you and MBC out of business. And he's superb at defeating his competitors—legally or otherwise. I'll give you two days to reconsider your options which, to recap, are: one, work for us and enjoy success beyond any you've known; two, forget this conversation ever took place and prepare to pay fifteen thousand pesos a month; or three, go to the police or the media and suffer the consequences.

"I leave you with one additional thought," Salas continued. "Even paying *piso* to the most powerful cartel in Mexico can't completely assure protection. My client, however, can provide you with a level of security superior to that of the best private companies in Mexico. He would extend that protection to MBC—and to the lovely Alejandra who, judging from your reaction, is a woman whom you love deeply."

Salas stepped toward the door. "I'll contact you on Thursday."

"Don't bother to."

On his way out, Salas looked into the pilot brewery. "Alejandra, nice meeting you."

Brad watched the man and his goon until they were out the front door. He was massaging his throbbing head when a tickle on his back made him jump.

"We've got to act fast," Alejandra said.

CHAPTER THIRTY-ONE

A WOMAN whom you love deeply. Was that just pure B.S. from Salas, or had he stated something so obvious that even a stranger could see it? Brad stared over the railing at the brewery below. He watched Abraham's hands fly like a pianist's as he guided bottles on the line into the capper. Everything hummed along.

"His threats are despicable," Alejandra said.

"The more he talked, the more convincing he sounded," Brad said. "There's no way we won't take a huge hit. You, me, Carlos, MBC, your family. He's got me cornered."

Lalo came up the stairs toward them. "Sorry to interrupt, but Paco called. He sounded a little stressed about the replacement keg of Alejandra's Ale."

"Shit, I completely forgot."

"The keg's already in the van," Lalo said, holding out the key.

Alejandra grabbed it and started down the stairs. "Brad, get your laptop and anything else you absolutely need."

"Drive carefully," Lalo shouted. "The wet roads are slick and full of bad drivers."

In the office, Brad snatched up his laptop, ripping the cord from the wall socket, and shoved both into his backpack. He took the stairs two at a time and didn't stop running until he jumped into the idling van. Already in the driver's seat, Alejandra hit the accelerator.

It felt like a hundred and twenty degrees. Brad fiddled with the air-conditioner. "Slow down," he cautioned as he buckled his seat belt. "I won't let Salas hurt you or your family."

"You are *not* going to work for some drug lord!" Alejandra said, braking for a patch of slow traffic. Her eyes flitted between the road and the rearview mirror.

"I need to talk to Carlos, but he's in meetings all day. I'll call his father and line up bodyguards. I'll call Captain Aguirre, too."

"Brad, get real. Bodyguards are only one thin layer of protection against El Cártel. Above all, do *not* call Aguirre. He's probably on their payroll."

"My gut says he isn't."

"Have you asked your gut how Salas got the recording and the photo? Or how he talked to Chago and El Míster?"

"Jesus Christ! How does anybody here know what's real or who to trust? Those glamorous women at San Pedro weddings look totally different sweating on a treadmill at the sports club. The Mosses built a gorgeous brewery and turned out beer that was complete crap. Salas looks like some corporate CEO, but he's probably the biggest criminal we've had contact with yet. And you can't trust the police—who *should* be the ultimate good guys—because they might or might not be bad guys. One day this whole goddamned country's going to implode!"

"God damn *you*, Brad!" Alejandra exploded, her voice high and tense, as she shot through a huge puddle and sent water flying. "It's *my* country you're insulting. My country that I love!"

She glanced in the mirror and continued, "Don't you understand that's how we Mexicans have felt for years? This is our reality, our country, that's being torn apart. It's our families and friends being killed, most of the time with guns brought here from *your* country. We're fighting the cartels every day and paying huge prices while they keep getting more powerful. And what drives it all is money made by supplying *your* fellow Americans with drugs that you and your government can't make them stop using!"

Alejandra jerked the wheel and swerved into the left lane to execute a harrowing turn as the light changed to red.

"What the hell are you doing?" Brad shouted. "This isn't even the way to the pub."

"A blue Kia Rio has been tailing us since we left the brewery." She pulled another crazy lane change.

"Are you serious?"

"Yes, but I think I lost them."

"Them? How many?"

"Two. Probably in their twenties. One has a beard and blue shirt. The other looks like a thug."

"Alejandra, we're getting paranoid."

"If I see them again, we forget the keg. We pick up our passports and some basic things. Then we head straight to the airport."

"And skip town just like that?" Brad stared at her. "Now you're the one talking crazy."

Alejandra's eyes cut between the road ahead and the mirror. "Luis had an uncle who owned a lumber business. When El Cártel decided they wanted to use his warehouse to store drugs and stolen goods, he refused. Three days later, he was kidnapped. The family paid a huge ransom."

"Alejandra, what's your point?"

"His body turned up on the side of the highway the next day."

Brad's shirt was damp and sticking to his back. He punched up the air-conditioning. "We can't walk away. Both of us leaving would ruin MBC."

"You or me getting killed would ruin more than MBC. Besides, you'll only leave your job and some furniture that isn't worth anything. I'm the one who will walk away from my professional life, my personal life, my family, my friends, the country I love—everything. Brad, we don't have a choice."

She swung into the pub parking lot and braked so hard it threw them both forward. "Shit!" she shouted as the blue Kia pulled into the Pollo Loco lot next door. She drove around back to the delivery entrance. "Act natural. If anyone asks, we're late for a meeting."

As she unlocked the back door of the van, Brad grabbed the dolly. With a soft meow, Vagabundo rubbed against his leg, causing him to trip and step on the cat's tail. "Dammit, not today, cat." Vagabundo gave a sharp yowl and scurried away.

Brad hauled the keg and dolly up the stairs and into the darkened brewery. "The MBC van makes us a moving bull's eye," Alejandra said. "We have to borrow two cars. We each go to our apartments. Since mine's on the way to the airport, you'll pick me up. Get your passport and pack a few basics in a carry-on bag." She held the door of the walk-in cooler as Brad angled the keg inside.

"Christ, Alejandra, the airport isn't a light rail station. We can't just park and jump on a plane."

"American and United both have afternoon and evening flights to the States."

"This has got to be a nightmare, and I'm going to wake up any minute."

As soon as they were inside, Alejandra pulled Paco into the cooler and spoke like a general marshalling the troops. "If anybody comes looking for us, all you know is that we switched out the kegs. You assume we went back to the brewery."

"Are El Míster and his thugs back?"

"Something like that" Alejandra said. "But they might not come."

"You two are in big trouble, aren't you?"

"Sort of. That's why we'll need to borrow your car."

"My brand new Nissan? No way!"

"Just do what she says," Brad said.

"I can't believe I'm doing this," Paco whined as he fished out his key and Brad pulled down the keg tap.

"And that Tigres hat you always wear," Alejandra continued, "the one you leave under the bar while you're working, Brad will be borrowing it. We're going to need a second car. Be a doll, Paco, and get Noé's key. Here's the key to the van. You can use it until you get your car back."

"I don't understand any of this," Paco said as they hurried out of the walk-in.

The dining room was starting to fill with lunchtime customers. Behind the bar, Brad opened the Alejandra's Ale tap. It spit a foamy stream. Paty bounced by, waving and beaming as she escorted two men to a table.

"Look! Down there," Alejandra said, kicking Brad's ankle. She pointed to the floor and jerked him down. "It's them with Paty," she whispered.

"You're positive?"

"One hundred percent." She grabbed Paco's cap from the shelf. "Hide this in your pocket." Just as Paco returned, Alejandra popped up and loudly announced, "Everything looks okay now. Just need to finish up in the walk-in and we'll head back to the brewery." She threw Paco a breezy hug and kiss. He hugged her back and dropped Noe's key in her hand.

"See you," Brad said with a handshake. "I hope you run this keg dry before the day's over."

Paco's eyes, full of alarm, lingered on his. "I'll do my best for you."

"You always have."

In the cooler, Alejandra unbuttoned her lab coat. "Ditch that MBC shirt."

In a t-shirt and jeans, Brad tugged Paco's hat low on his head. Alejandra gave him a peck on the cheek. "See you soon."

CHAPTER THIRTY-TWO

ALEJANDRA BOLTED out of the condo lobby and through the soft rain into the passenger seat of Paco's Nissan. "Any sign of the Kia?"

"Not yet," Brad said, glancing at the dashboard clock. With luck, they'd make it to the airport in forty-five minutes.

"I'm checking flights," Alejandra said, concentrating on the phone screen. Brad wove into the right lane, then the left, moving around cars as he climbed Loma Larga, the long hill separating San Pedro and Monterrey proper. They entered the tunnel and the patter of soft rain ceased. Once they were out the other side, there would be no traffic signals for several miles. He patted the pocket of the clean shirt he had changed into at his apartment. Aguirre's card was still there.

"Yes!" Alejandra said. "Three seats left on the 4:30 to Houston. Six hundred dollars each."

"For an hour-and-a-half flight?"

"What choice do we have?"

The traffic continued to flow at a steady pace as they exited the tunnel, moving downhill. Every mile between them and San Pedro would let Brad breathe easier. Alejandra's fingers tapped away. Suddenly, he spotted a flash of blue cresting the hill behind them. "Shit!"

"What is it?" Alejandra asked, her fingers frozen.

"I'm not sure."

She turned and watched the two lanes of traffic behind them. "Definitely blue."

"There are thousands of blue cars in Monterrey," he said, sounding more hopeful than he felt, as he segued onto Morones Prieto. Across the wide flood plain of the Santa Catarina River, downtown Monterrey looked rain-soaked and dreary. Cerro de la Silla, the symbol of Monterrey and of MBC, was invisible in the gloom.

"They're closing the gap. Speed up!" Alejandra shouted. The rain was coming down harder.

"I can't! Too much traffic!" Brad yelled. He pulled out the business card. "Call Aguirre!"

"Are you insane?"

"He's our only hope. If they start shooting, we're sitting ducks."

Frowning, she punched in the number and tapped on the speakerphone. The *thunk-thunk* of the wipers on high matched the pounding of Brad's heart. After three rings a man answered in a gruff, northern accent. "*¿Bueno?*"

"*¿Capitán Aguirre?*" Alejandra asked in the tone of a wealthy Mexican woman used to directing people.

"Speaking. Who is this?" He sounded irritated.

As Alejandra's words tumbled out, Aguirre's attitude quickly changed. Brad cut wildly in front of a taxi. The driver honked his displeasure. A pick-up truck ahead slowed suddenly and Brad hit the brakes. Paco's new car started to hydroplane. He steered into the slide, hoping they wouldn't jump the curb or crash into the pick-up yards ahead of them. On the other side of the guardrail, a sharp incline dropped to the flood plain. Below, a small river now roiled where there was normally a trickle.

As the front tire grazed the curb, Brad cut the wheel to the right. Two cars back, the Kia swerved into the left lane. "Aguirre," he shouted toward Alejandra's phone, "We need help—*now!*"

He floored the accelerator and changed lanes, barely squeezing in front of a delivery truck. Alejandra and Aguirre yelled at each other while Brad raced up behind an old car belching white plumes of exhaust. He blared the horn until the driver changed lanes.

"The police are on their way," Alejandra shouted over the rain pounding the car. Aguirre barked something Brad couldn't make out. "Yes," Alejandra yelled, "and gaining on us!"

The speedometer was nearing a hundred thirty in a hundred-kilometer-an-hour stretch. The Kia came up fast on the old jalopy. Behind Brad, the delivery truck continued its lumbering pace. These two vehicles might buy him precious time. Suddenly, the Kia driver attempted to dart in front of the truck. Alejandra screamed into the phone as the truck plowed into the Kia. Cars and trucks piled into a tangled mass behind them. Brad bore down on the accelerator. "Take the toll road!" Aguirre shouted. "Go through the gate with the raised arm! They're expecting you."

Brad had never felt so happy in his life to see a patrol car tailing him with flashing lights and a wailing siren. The cop passed him and led the way. A second police car fell in behind him. The three cars shot through the toll booth and picked up speed on the less trafficked road. If they had to brake suddenly on this slick road, it would be the end of them. They didn't slow until they reached the airport. Aguirre coached over the phone, "Drive to Departures. The *federales* will take your car."

Brad pulled up behind a federal police truck with a gun mounted on the back. "*¡Sus llaves!*" ordered an agent. Brad tossed Paco's keys to the man and grabbed their bags from the back seat. He and Alejandra were sped along in a cloud of uniforms, weapons and stern faces. One agent talked into a phone and another into a walkie-talkie.

Officers pushed aside the few travelers who didn't give them a wide berth as they were hustled through security. Brad couldn't take it all in, but he felt a glimmer of hope that, if someone jumped in front of them with a gun, he and Alejandra might survive. Aguirre caught up with the phalanx as they sequestered Brad and Alejandra in a small room.

"Here's what we know so far," the captain said. "The pile-up on Morones Prieto totaled twelve cars. The passenger in the Kia and the elderly driver of the older car died at the scene."

229

Brad fisted his hand and bit the knuckles. How the hell had his life reached this point?

Aguirre continued, "Ambulances took nine, possibly ten, people to hospitals. Do you two realize how lucky you are? Before you board the plane, I want every detail of what I suspect is a very complicated story."

There was no time to request a lawyer. Brad began with Salas's call yesterday and the meeting this morning. A knock on the door interrupted him. "*Los boletos, Capitán,*" an airline employee said, speaking directly to Aguirre.

With a quick swipe of Alejandra's credit card, they held two precious tickets to Houston. Brad valued his American citizenship more than he had in his entire life. Aguirre, who had left the room, re-entered with a phone to his ear. He said nothing, pinching his lips tighter at one point. He eyed Brad in a way that set his stomach flip-flopping. "Yes, I'll tell him," Aguirre said before pocketing the phone.

"They've identified the men in the Kia. Both were known Cártel members. And it seems the mysterious Señor Salas didn't waste any time making good on his threat. A Molotov cocktail was thrown into the MBC brewpub an hour ago."

Brad lurched out of the chair. "What the hell?"

"Sit down, Ingeniero Peters. There's nothing you can do now. A car pulled into the parking lot. Two men ran toward the brewery. They used a rifle, a crowbar—something—to smash the window and throw a bomb inside."

Brad dropped into the chair and buried his face in his hands.

"*¡Dios mío!*" Alejandra murmured by his side. He jabbed his fingers into his temples and worked them back and forth wildly. It felt like fireworks exploding inside his head. The little brewery he had designed and overseen at every step, his great accomplishment, had been destroyed in seconds.

"How serious is the damage, Captain?" Alejandra asked.

"I can't say. The officer I spoke with was on the scene. The fire moved fast. They've taken several people to hospitals, including the manager, who refused to leave until he had all the customers and staff outside."

"*No, el bueno de Noé, ¡no!*" Alejandra protested. Brad squeezed her hand as tears formed in her eyes. "His wife and his two boys—they're four and six. He's a good and caring man who never hurt a fly."

"Fortunately," Aguirre said, "nobody died—except for a stray cat."

Brad felt his lips tremble. He bowed his head and squeezed his eyes shut. *He had caused the deaths of two people, one an innocent victim. His brewpub was in ruins, his manager in the hospital, and he was tearing up over a dead cat? But, hell, except for Carlos, Vagabundo had been the first friend he'd made in Monterrey. The vagabond feline had proved to be a loyal friend, much more so than some of the humans in his life. Why shouldn't he shed tears over the death of "a stray cat"?*

"I have to go back," he croaked.

Aguirre moved to block the door. "You'd be dead within hours."

"He's right," Alejandra said. "We *have* to get out of Mexico."

Aguirre added, "If you know what's good for you, you'll stay as far away from Monterrey and Mexico as you can for at least the next year."

Brad stared at the terrazzo floor. He had sacrificed everything for Monterrey Brewing Company, more than for anything or anybody in his entire life. For over two years, MBC had been his driving force. When he woke this morning, his biggest concern had been getting the Santa Catarina brew pitched by a decent time. Within hours, El Cártel had destroyed his world and left his life in tatters. He was damned lucky even to be alive.

Alejandra dabbed her eyes with a tissue. He pulled her close and buried his face in her hair. She was all he had left.

BRAD STARED out the tiny window and watched the ground fall away as the wheels of the puddle jumper lifted off the runway. Numbness, relief, sadness, disbelief. So many emotions overwhelmed him that he couldn't say what he felt. The dense cloud cover hid the mountain peaks and gave the landscape a depressing drabness. Then there was only gray outside the window. He closed his eyes and tried to relax. Exhaustion overtook him. Every muscle in his body ached.

The car chase, the bombing and Aguirre's barrage of questions had drained him. He'd stumbled with his Spanish and made mistakes he thought he'd long ago overcome. Slowly, he massaged his temples and forehead. Before they left, he'd managed to talk with Carlos, and Alejandra had made contact with Noé's wife. It appeared Noé was shaken but hadn't suffered any major injuries.

Trying to relax was hopeless. He opened his eyes and stared out the window. Instead of a dreary, rain-sodden world, now bright sun shone down on the blanket of fluffy clouds below. In the distance, the tallest peaks of the Sierra Madre Oriental rose above the clouds, jagged, majestic, triumphant. As the plane continued its ascent, he craned his neck in search of the Cerro de la Silla, symbol of Monterrey and of MBC. He caught one brief glimpse before the plane curved into a north-bound arc.

He reached for Alejandra's comforting hand but found it limp and clammy in his. "I didn't even call my parents," she said.

CHAPTER THIRTY THREE

June 2015

KICKING BACK in his recliner on a Monday morning, Brad savored the last of his espresso and the beginning of his one free day of the week. On the television, a perky female weathercaster was saying, "If we hit the high of ninety-four forecast for today, it'll make the fourth day this year that Denver has passed the ninety-degree mark. Mother Nature appears to be warming up for a record summer."

"In Monterrey, we call that a cool front," Alejandra remarked from the sofa. Like Brad, she wore shorts and sandals. She still couldn't bring herself to go barefoot. "If you'd grown up on a ranch, you wouldn't walk around without shoes either." Never mind that she insisted on keeping the house they rented as clean as the condo Lolis and Marisa still shared in San Pedro.

The weather lady was waving her arms around a map and talking with the enthusiasm of Paty, the MBC hostess. So much had changed in eleven months. After the fire bomb, several witnesses testified that either two or three men had jumped out of a compact, white or cream-colored car. One swung an axe or a sledgehammer into a brewery window. All the witnesses described something being thrown through the shattered window by a second assailant who wore a dark hooded sweatshirt or a ski mask. The investigators concluded the bomb was a Molotov cocktail. Whether it was luck or planning, they would probably never know, but it had landed near the gas supply line, causing it to explode, which sent fire racing through the structure. The perpetrators remained at large.

Noé had herded every customer and employee outside ahead of himself. He was taken to the hospital, suffering from smoke inhalation and singed eyebrows and hair. Two customers sitting beside the glass wall between the pub brewery and the dining room were badly cut. The glass blew out with enough force to blind one of them in one eye. Carlos had rushed back from Mexico City. The insurance settlement was a tangled mess with no end in sight. Whether Brad and Carlos or the Ordóñez family, who still owned the property, would ever receive any compensation was anyone's guess.

The Pollo Loco manager next door had found Vagabundo's remains and confirmed his death. He was buried under the old oak tree in the back parking lot. Later, the manager emailed Brad a photo of the miniature headstone purchased with donations from employees of four area restaurants. The inscription read *Vagabundo, el gato cervecero*. Vagabundo, the brewer cat."

Brad had struggled for months with the guilt. Two people died in the crash he had caused. Vagabundo had perished, others had been injured, his business was destroyed and his employees put out of work because he, Brad Peters, had thought it was a good idea to stand up to a Mexican cartel and say, "*¡Basta!*" In the end, he gained nothing and a lot of people paid a heavy price.

The one stroke of luck was the "butterfly" in Federico Cardinale's "bonné". King Midas had pushed his Mexico City territory east to Cancún and west to Guadalajara. The morning of Brad's meeting with Fidel Salas, Cardinale was proposing a partnership to Carlos. The pub was inoperable, but the brewery was unscathed. Cardinale bought out MBC, thereby establishing himself in northern Mexico and in the craft brewing business. He brought in an expensive—and apparently excellent—German brewmaster and saw to it that Lalo, Rodrigo and all the other employees kept their jobs. With Cardinale's high profile and connections, including a brother prominent in politics, he closed the deal, saying that he knew people in law enforcement and elsewhere who could deal convincingly with narcos.

Brad managed to come out with eighty thousand dollars. When Bennie Schwartzlander learned the news, he told his bosses that his day had finally come and they'd be crazy not to replace him with dynamic, young Carlos Echeverría. And Carlos, the people person and sales guy who never did develop the passion of a craft brewer or restauranter, had jumped at the opportunity. He and Claudia were engaged and planning a September wedding. Brad stayed in frequent contact with Carlos via Facebook, email, phone and Skype calls.

In Denver, Brad had convinced Alejandra that, with their experience and his seed money, they could open a small brewery. Her parents had seen fit to invest a hundred thousand dollars and the bank hadn't hesitated to cover the rest with a loan that wouldn't be impossible to pay back so long as the business went well.

The diciest part of the plan had been betting on the ninety-six-year-old former dairy and warehouse on a sketchy stretch of historic Larimer Street. The property had sat empty for three years which allowed them to buy it for a song. Four blocks west, the area blossomed into the trendy LoDo district bordering Coors Field, home of the Colorado Rockies. They had gutted most of the dairy and started over. The result was an efficient brewery with an urban industrial taproom. They were gambling that, within a few years, the hip section of Larimer would extend this far, due in part to their efforts. They had no pub and no need for a restaurant manager, pub employees or food preparation. For now, the staff consisted of Brad and Alejandra with two full-time and two part-time employees making outstanding craft beer and having a blast.

The weather report ended and the camera flashed to the news anchor. "Colorado's not the only place where it's hot these days. Things are heating up for the three congressmen in Washington accused of accepting illegal funds with ties to El Cártel. The Mexican drug cartel is currently rumored to have been seriously weakened by recent arrests and deaths. The vacuum created at the top has reportedly led to bloody, high-level power struggles.

The commission charged with the investigation has scheduled a press conference for tomorrow morning at which it is expected that officials will unseal indictments against the congressmen."

"Thank God," Alejandra said, "Americans are getting a little taste of what Mexico's been living with for years."

"Better be careful who you say that to."

"Because I might offend some American who thinks the U.S. is above narco corruption? The cartels are more sophisticated and have more money than ever. Arresting those congressmen won't slow down El Cártel."

"You don't have to convince me," Brad said, holding up his hands in surrender. "I think I hear a lawnmower calling my name."

Outside, he pushed the mower into the driveway and waved to Frank Brewster in his yard two houses down. The only other neighbor off on Mondays, Frank and his oldest boy, outfitted in a Little League uniform, were throwing a ball back and forth. During his teenage years, Brad had been certain that the Denver suburbs were the most boring place in the world. Now he hoped that in a few years, he'd be the father tossing a ball to his son.

Alejandra's homesickness the first months was as serious as any Brad had felt in Monterrey. Her childhood summers in Alabama had been fun-filled vacations with an end-date. Denver as a permanent home was a whole other matter. Brad had thought she was making progress after the first snowfall, when she enthusiastically threw herself down alongside Carrie, the Brewster's pre-schooler, and flapped her snow angel wings. She loved skiing from her first run down a beginners' hill. It had been her idea to get season passes to Copper Mountain. But driving to work one morning in February, she hit a patch of ice and slid into a curb, which resulted in one flat tire and a woman who, for a week, refused to drive in the snow. Finally, when the snow melted and leaves sprouted, she warmed up to the legendary springtime in the Rockies.

Brad finished working the mower around the edges of the yard and moved into back-and-forth rows. The M word had begun to come up in their conversations. The Howards liked him well enough, but didn't care for their daughter living with a man outside of marriage. Living back in the States, Brad was surprised to discover how much he had changed during his time in Mexico. He had a wide and respectable reputation as a brewer. His thirtieth birthday last month had brought home the fact that he was getting older. If he was going to teach his own son the secrets of baseball and brewing, he needed to get a start on bringing that child into the world.

Alejandra doted on the Brewster kids, especially on Carrie, who had rung the doorbell yesterday and asked Alejandra to braid her hair. Afterwards, Alejandra had sighed and said, "I hope we'll have such a cute daughter someday."

Slowly, he had dared to imagine old age with Alejandra by his side, their kids bringing the grandkids for big family meals, the way it was now at his parents' house when they got together with his sister and her family. His mother adored Alejandra and dropped none-too-subtle hints that she'd love to have her as an official daughter-in-law. With Alejandra's birthday next week, the time to pop the question had come.

FAIRFAX COUNTY, Virginia was the most beautiful place Nacho had ever seen. Anybody who wanted to describe heaven and hell should just show pictures of Fairfax County and Topo Chico Prison. Here, there were gigantic trees everywhere with dark, lush leaves. It was so green it practically hurt his eyes. It smelled of warm, humid earth, of nature. If Apá had brought them here, maybe life would have turned out differently. Nacho had driven by a prison yesterday, a correctional facility they called them here. Word was that life in U.S. prisons was some ways better, some worse. The food was decent and the guards, for the most part, didn't beat the prisoners.

But you couldn't buy perks or an early release like in Topo Chico where that asshole judge had sentenced him to two fucking years and then reduced it to one after El Mago quietly slipped him a shitload of money that Nacho would be working off for the next year. Prison had given Nacho a lot of time to think. He had considered many things—like punishment as a consequence of a man's actions.

Nacho kept the rental car at a safe distance and glanced in the mirror. He wasn't used to wearing glasses or to his surfer-blond hair. Both looked good with his blue eyes. Maybe he'd keep the look afterwards. A year of weight training had put serious, sinewy muscles on him. That was the only good thing about his time in Topo Chico, and small consolation for all the crap.

Two cars ahead, the Lexus turned into the soccer complex. Nacho had spent yesterday scoping out the area, learning the main roads and his target's routes. From here, it was only a mile to the interstate. The problem was all the people in the park. He had to get Wilkes alone.

The *patrones* had spent a lot of money on him, and he knew the score. The botched MBC job had cost him and the *patrones* plenty. He had the early release plus eighty kilos of coke to work off. A hundred and seventy-six pounds the AFIs had confiscated, at least a year of seriously crappy, high-risk jobs. Peters had fucked him bad.

With the windows rolled down, Nacho pulled into a parking space several cars from the Lexus. Wilkes, who had started to get out, paused. He said something to the boy still in the car, a tall, skinny kid. When another car had finished pulling into the parking space on the passenger side of Wilkes's car, Nacho heard Wilkes say, "Okay," and saw the kid jump out of the car. He and a blond boy met and began to race across the park.

The other father, an older version of the son, got out and shook Wilkes's hand. They walked right past Nacho, still sitting in his car. "How are things looking for the barbecue tomorrow, Marc?"

"Weather's supposed to be good. You still bringing those marinated chicken tenders to put on the grill?"

"You got it. Mary wants to know if Jessica's going to grill asparagus again."

"That's her plan."

Nacho tugged down the maroon Washington Redskins cap he bought yesterday and got out. He bent over and, hidden between cars, took his time re-tying the laces on the new maroon sneakers. Top to bottom, he looked the part of a serious Redskins' fan. Afterwards, he leaned against the trunk of the rental car and did calf stretches. The men had stopped walking. Back in the projects in Dallas, there weren't many fathers around. Of the ones who were there, some barbecued, though it was mostly the mothers who made things happen. Nobody in the projects, no matter what color, *grilled* marinated chicken tenders or asparagus.

"Dad!" the Wilkes boy shouted, hands curved around his mouth. "I forgot my water bottle."

"Catch you in a minute," Wilkes said to the other father, who set off at a trot to catch up with the kids.

Nacho raised an arm over his head and started on side bends. He held the other arm across his waist, feeling the revolver inside the Redskins hoodie. It made him stand out in the warm June weather, but if anybody asked, he was a runner trying to sweat off a few pounds. An SUV pulled in and spilled a noisy bunch of kids, shoving and falling over each other, while Wilkes fetched the green bottle and locked the car. The soccer players and their parents were moving away, but not far enough.

Except for two hours of exercise each day, Nacho had spent most of the last year sitting on his ass and thinking. There was too much at stake to mess this up. His only limitations were money and Puma, his new *patrón,* who wanted him back in Monterrey exactly one week from today. Unfortunately, those were two very big limitations. Wilkes started toward the field, then stopped. He turned and jogged to the restrooms on the other side of the parking lot.

Holy shit! So much luck came the way of rich people that they could afford to ignore it half the time. But when Lady Luck smiled on poor assholes like Nacho, they had to be *pendejos* not to pounce on every scrap offered to them. He squatted between the cars, both hands inside the hoodie pocket. He didn't need to see to screw the suppressor on the revolver. He stood up and watched Wilkes disappear into the restroom. There was no door, only a wide-open metal gate. Nacho sprung fast and found his target alone, legs apart, facing the urinal.

He shoved the revolver into Wilkes's back. "*Ojo por ojo, cabrón. Ahora me pagas la muerte de mi hermano.*" An eye for an eye, asshole. Now you'll pay me for the death of my brother. The stream of piss stopped. Wilkes went rigid.

As if in a slow-motion movie scene, Nacho watched his finger squeeze the trigger. He heard the soft sound of the suppressor, like air escaping from a tank and saw Wilkes's body crumple. He heard the cracking sound Wilkes's head made as it hit the urinal going down.

Wilkes had left the water bottle on the edge of the sink. Reaching to turn on the water, Nacho knocked it over and sent it crashing to the floor. It rolled toward the drain as Nacho dowsed his blood-spattered hands and face. He pulled a wad of paper towels from the hoodie pocket and wiped away any possible fingerprints. He stuffed the wet towels back in the pocket. The shot had sprayed blood all over the hoodie. Nacho pulled it over his head and bundled it up.

What blood had soaked through to the black t-shirt and spattered the maroon sweatpants wouldn't stand out from a distance. Nacho turned to run but slipped in the blood puddling in the floor. He scrambled up and tried to ignore the searing pain in his ankle. He closed the metal gate and sprinted to the rental car. *Yes, DeMarcus Wilkes, a man must pay the consequences of his actions.*

Chapter Thirty-Four

BRAD PEERED into the bathroom mirror and ran the razor over his chin one last time.

"Ready?" Alejandra called from the bedroom. "What do you think?"

Brad stood mesmerized by the sight of her in the black dress, the curves of her bare legs, her hair loose and flowing. "If I don't hang on to you, every guy in the restaurant will be trying to pick you up."

She laughed and held out the silver necklace he'd given her at Christmas. "Can you help me with this?"

He stood behind her to hook the clasp and inhaled the subtle fragrance of the new perfume. "One more thing before we leave," he said. "Your real birthday present."

Her questioning look made him more nervous. "I thought the perfume was your present."

As he pulled the velvet box from the pocket of his dress pants, she put a hand over her open mouth. His body tingled the way it did when he crouched at the top of a snowy slope, about to propel himself down the mountainside. "Alejandra?" He paused and took a deep breath. "Will you marry me?"

An enormous grin spread across her face. She threw her arms around him. "If you asked me a hundred times, I'd say yes every time." She took the box from his hands as if he held a sacred object and carefully lifted the top. "Oh, my God! It's beautiful."

Brad slipped the ring onto her finger. The diamond glittered in the late afternoon sun; the emeralds on either side of the larger stone sparkled. "The jeweler said he'll size it to your finger."

She pulled her hand away and covered it protectively. "For tonight, this ring is mine. I want the world to see it on me."

"So you like it?"

"I love it. You picked a gorgeous ring."

"I couldn't decide between it and another one. Carlos voted for this one."

"Carlos chose my engagement ring?"

"With some help from Claudia. I emailed her for ideas to get me started and she sent links to, like, twenty rings. I narrowed it down to two."

"Is there anybody who doesn't know about this?"

"The only other person who knows is your father."

"Don't tell me you called and asked for my hand."

"Of course."

She squeezed him toward her in a tight hug. "My father's going to remember that forever and my parents will love you even more for proposing Mexican style. Let's call them. By tomorrow night, my mother will have told half of Saltillo."

"Except that we have an eight o'clock reservation plus two brewers and their wives waiting for us."

Alejandra sighed with the huge grin. "I'm so happy that I'll want to stand in the middle of the restaurant and shout the news."

When they entered the steakhouse, Alejandra grabbed Brad and hurried into the bar. She threw out her left hand. "Can y'all believe it?"

"So, you finally took the leap, Brad?" Doug asked. Between birthday hugs and engagement congratulations, this was Alejandra's night.

On the rooftop patio, the sounds of traffic and pedestrians out on a warm June evening filtered up and mixed with music and conversations. By the time the meal was over, Brad was relaxed and enjoying the moment.

"You hear about the State Department guy who was killed in Virginia yesterday?" Doug asked.

"I saw something on CNN just before we left the house," Charlie's wife replied. "They said he was an expert on Mexican affairs, that maybe a drug cartel ordered his murder."

Brad thought of Marc Wilkes and his family. *Thank God they were in Mexico City.*

"There were reports," Doug said, "that he was some sort of undercover agent. He'd lived in Monterrey."

Brad pulled out his phone and found the story quickly enough. He scrolled through, looking only for a name. "Oh, God."

He breathed in gulps of air. He closed his eyes and recalled the Wilkes's barbecue, Emily and her tanned arms against the white top, Tanner the Tiger, full of childhood innocence, racing down the hall to greet guests and chasing lady bugs around a leafy Monterrey backyard.

"He had a wife and a son," Brad said softly.

Alejandra took the phone. "It says the murdered man was supposed to have taken part in a State Department presentation this morning about those congressmen and the purported attempts of Mexican drug cartels to influence U.S. politicians." She flashed Brad a fiery look, a reminder of their conversation a week earlier.

"That sounds like the stuff conspiracy nuts come up with," Doug's wife said. "You guys really think Mexican hitmen are running around hunting down U.S. spies while their kids play soccer in affluent D.C. suburbs?"

"They said that was just a theory," Charlie offered. "Somebody else said they saw a suspicious looking guy dressed in red just before the murder, wearing a red hat and jacket so he might have been a member of the Bloods."

"Hey, guys, we have a birthday and an engagement to celebrate," Charlie's wife said, flagging down the waiter. "A bottle of champagne and the dessert menu, please."

"And a whiskey, straight up," Brad said.

IF VIRGINIA was the most beautiful place Nacho had ever seen, Iowa was the most fuckingly boring. He'd crossed the state line a half hour ago and Nebraska wasn't looking any better. He had studied the maps for months, honing his plan until he knew it like the curves of Camila's body. The first three hundred miles he had to pay attention and make the proper turns. Once he got on I-80, it was a straight shot for twelve hundred miles. He could kick back, put the rental car on cruise control, pump up the radio. But after eight hundred miles on the same damned road, he was bored out of his skull. He wished he had Neto here. He still missed his brother like hell.

Except for one minor misstep yesterday, everything had gone off exactly as he'd planned. One shot and Wilkes was gone. Nobody was around when he jogged out of the men's room that, once he closed the gate, looked off limits. But twisting the shit out of his ankle was stupid. He'd driven for an hour with the damn thing throbbing and swelling until he finally pulled off on a narrow road that skirted a river. He stopped in a heavily wooded spot and hop-walked to the trunk of the car. He threw on fresh clothes and stuffed every bit of evidence into a cheap gym bag along with a fat red brick. He limped to the river and hurled the bag. His balance was off and the pitch was lousy. The bag caught in the branches of an old tree trunk sticking up out of the water. He cursed and started to strip. The river moved swiftly, swaying the bag which just touched the water's surface. He had never learned to swim, and the ankle hurt like hell. *Shit, he didn't need this!*

He waded into the freezing water up to his knees, his feet sinking into gooey mud. He felt something under the water brush his leg and jumped. He had another ten feet to go. He took a breath and another step. The water was lapping against his hips. There was no way he could reach the bag. He raised a foot out of the muck for the next step. Suddenly, the thin limb snapped, and relief flooded through him as the current pulled the bag along. It sunk slowly, a few bubbles gurgling up when it disappeared. Nacho let out the breath he had been holding and scrambled back to the shore. From here on, he was Andrés Pérez. His driver's license and green card confirmed it.

He had kept driving last night until he could barely keep his eyes open. When he rolled into a cheap motel in Toledo, Ohio, the old fat white guy in a dirty undershirt behind a barred window acted as if a fake blond dude with a funny accent hobbling in at midnight and paying with cash was an everyday occurrence.

Along the way, Nacho had listened to news reports about the boys who discovered Wilkes's body while the carpool soccer mom waited in the family van for them to take a leak. Probably the same noisy brats he'd seen getting to the game at the last minute. One of the *huercos* claimed he saw a suspicious guy, who might have been black, wearing a red hat and jacket and hanging out near a brown car. Since Nacho and the car were more or less the same shade of tan and the Redskins clothing was maroon, the kid was either color blind or stupid. From there, some talk-show hosts got off on trash talking Bloods and other shit.

Then there were the crazy stories about Mexican drug cartels ordering the assassination. As far as Nacho knew, he was the only one who had any interest in killing Wilkes, and his motive had nothing to do with the U.S. State Department or spies or covert agents.

Nacho was proud of his loyalty. It had gotten him damned far in life. From the moment Neto drew his last breath, Nacho had known that, when the day came, he'd be the one to take Wilkes down. During eighteen months in prison, he had simmered in a stew of hatred and anger, thinking about the two things he had to do when he got out. The first was over, the score evened for Neto. Now he had his own score to settle with the fucking American who had sent El Míster to prison.

CHAPTER THIRTY-FIVE

SITTING ON his stool at the taproom bar, Brad ran a finger across the inventory spreadsheet, double checking numbers. The sweet smell of warm mash drifted through the wide doorway between the taproom and the brewery, along with the low hum of the mash tun. Charlie and Doug's conversation about the Rockies' chances of winning the National League's Western Division sounded on the verge of turning into an argument. Brad stuck his head through the door. "How's the tank cleaning going?"

His brewers looked surprised by the interruption. Charlie recovered first. "Getting there."

Alejandra stood near the rolled-up delivery door, unpacking hops. Sunshine streamed around her. Wearing a hairnet, a loose Larimer Street Brewery t-shirt, jeans and work boots, she barely resembled the beautiful woman at the steakhouse last night. This was the woman Brad wanted to be with for the rest of his life.

He returned to his stool and looked around the taproom that, in five hours, would start to fill up with customers. At MBC, Carlos had gone for a dramatic, flashy appearance that would appeal to the San Pedro clientele. Here at Larimer Street Brewery, he and Alejandra had chosen the urban rustic look, leaving the old dairy's original red-brick walls and concrete floors exposed. They had outfitted the taproom with plain wooden tables and chairs. Behind the heavy oak bar, a long, stainless steel counter ran the length of the wall.

On the blackboards above, Alejandra used every color of chalk in the big box to keep the lists of Larimer Street's brews updated. She had done an admirable job of reproducing the brewery's logo, the image of the old building and the Rocky Mountains, along the top of the boards. On the lower corners, Doug and Charlie maintained a competition of messages, changing daily, about Denver sports teams. Their notes and drawings got more attention from some regular customers than the beer listings did. On aesthetics, Larimer Street's brewery couldn't compete with MBC's brewpub and even less with the brewery the Mosses had built at Huasteca, but of the three buildings, it was Brad's favorite. In the warmer months, they often brewed with the delivery door rolled up until the taproom opened at four o'clock.

Brad yawned and pulled his eyes back to the spreadsheet. With last night's partying, they had gotten a late start today. The dinner had ended at a reasonable hour, but once they were home, Alejandra hadn't been able to let go of Marc Wilkes's death. Brad let her vent and then reassured her they had nothing to worry about, which neither of them believed. Brad told himself Wilkes's death had nothing to do with Mexico. He almost convinced himself.

The taproom phone rang, distracting him yet again. Kevin, one of the regular customers, wanted to pick up four growlers on his lunch break. The sixty-four-ounce bottles of thick brown glass that Brad introduced when they opened, had been a big hit. He pulled four empties from under the bar and attached the filling hose to the ale tap. When the foam spilled over the first bottle, Brad capped, dried and sealed it.

He was on the last bottle when he heard Alejandra's scream.

"What the hell?" Charlie yelled.

"Anybody moves and the girl dies!"

Brad froze, rooted to the floor. He'd never forget the raspy voice as long as he lived. Beer flowed down the sides of the growler and over his hands. El Míster hadn't hesitated to use Chago and throw him away. He wouldn't think twice about murdering Alejandra.

Brad breathed hard and fast. He pressed a wet fist against his tight chest. Every bit of the anger he had felt his last day in Mexico came roaring back. He shut off the flowing tap and dried his hands and the growler.

"Take anything you want, man," Charlie yelled, "just let her go!"

Brad grabbed a second bar towel and continued to rub his hands and the growler. Moving quickly, he clasped the growler upside down, holding it by the neck. He flexed his wrist to get a feel for the weight. "*Ready position! Focused, calm, in control. Picture exactly how it's going to play out.*" He heard the words as clearly as if Roberto stood beside him.

"Brad Peters! Where are you?" the thug screamed. From the direction of his voice, El Míster was in the delivery doorway.

"*Racket in front of your body. Blow out a breath. Relax your arms.*" Brad gripped the growler neck with both hands, exhaled, dropped his shoulders and swung. The growler—at least fifteen times the weight of a tennis racket—dragged his arms down and threw his body off. He mentally corrected and took another swing. Better, but he'd still need to aim higher.

"I don't know where he is," Charlie said, his voice cracking. Brad dropped into a crouch and rocked back and forth. Adrenaline coursed through him.

"Peters," El Míster bellowed. A pause, then in Spanish, "I know you're here. Come out! You and I have a score to settle."

"*¡¡¡ATAQUE!!!*" Roberto's voice thundered in Brad's head. He sprang and pivoted, exploding through the doorway. El Míster had Alejandra cinched against him with his left arm. With his right hand, he pressed the barrel of a gun to her head. Brad aimed at the back of the narco's head and swung with the most powerful forehand of his life.

Glass shattered, shards and beer flew. The impact threw Brad off balance and sent El Míster forward. Brad steadied himself and raised the broken growler. El Míster recovered his balance and turned toward his attacker. Brad had to get around Alejandra. He lunged, aiming the broken bottle at El Míster's right arm. *An earsplitting gunshot. Alejandra screaming. The thug grunting and teetering. The gun clattering to the floor. El Míster falling backwards, still holding his hostage. Alejandra clutching her head, screaming.*

Brad tightened his grip on the jagged growler. If Alejandra weren't in the way, he would have gone for the monster's throat. Instead, he smashed his weapon into El Míster's right arm, pinning it to the floor. The thug howled and let go of Alejandra. Brad shoved her away. He straddled El Míster and drove the bloodied remains of the bottle into the criminal's heart over and over and over. *Plunge and yank, plunge, yank, plunge, yank. His vision blurred. He heard nothing but the blood pounding in his own ears. Yank. Plunge. Yank. Plunge.*

CHAPTER THIRTY-SIX

January 2016

HEAVY EXPOSED beams crisscrossed the high ceiling in Gregory's Gulch Restaurant, the main dining facility at Vail's White River Hotel and Ski Resort. Outside the large windows, a gentle snow had been falling for hours.

"What a wonderful evening," Julia Peters said, kissing her son on the cheek. "Everything's going to go fine tomorrow. Just don't stay up too late with the guys."

"If I were you, I'd worry more about the ladies getting too wild tonight," Brad said, giving Alejandra's hand a squeeze.

His mother hugged Alejandra then Brad. "I'll wish both the groom and the bride a good night's sleep."

"Great rehearsal and dinner. See you upstairs, Alejandra," Cousin Lolis called from the door as she, Marisa, and Claudia left the restaurant.

Brad watched Alejandra's brow wrinkle in frustration as she touched the small aid in her ear. Her loose hair and the veil tomorrow would hide her ears and the aid in the wedding photos. "I'll have her upstairs in a few minutes," he replied.

"*Hasta mañana, m'ija,*" Sofía Howard said as she pecked her daughter's cheek.

When all the guests had left, Brad kissed the tip of Alejandra's nose. "May I walk the bride to her room?"

The tenseness in Alejandra's face relaxed as she smiled and held out an arm. "Is my makeup still covering the scar?"

He stopped and studied her face. Most people wouldn't notice the line along her right cheek. "Still looking good."

When they reached the girls' suite, Alejandra kissed his cheek. "Listen to your mother. Don't you guys stay up too late."

Brad took the next flight of stairs two at a time. In the guys' suite, he found Carlos, Roberto and Eugenio polishing off a six-pack of Larimer Street Brewery's pale ale. He reached for the volume control on the iPod docking station. "Heard the music from the other end of the hall, guys."

"Hey, Güero, we found some great beer in the fridge," Eugenio said.

"You going to hit the slopes with us again tomorrow morning?" Carlos asked.

"Alejandra vetoed it. No breaking a leg on our wedding day."

"You already sound like a married man," Eugenio said.

Brad could almost imagine they were under the thatched-palm roof at the patio bar after Saturday tennis. If only he could roll back time and events. Carlos and Claudia had married in Monterrey three months ago—a wedding Brad and Alejandra had missed.

So far, Claudia hadn't gotten tired of Carlos's constant travels for the hops company. Roberto had a serious girlfriend and a recent promotion. Last month, Eugenio had declared himself to a girl, asking her to be his *novia*.

Brad took a swig of the beer someone had handed him. "So, Güero," Carlos began. He ran a hand through his hair. "How are you and Alejandra doing? I mean really. No bullshit."

Brad blew out a long breath and rubbed his chin. "That's not something I'm comfortable talking about, but the shrink says verbalizing my feelings is good. So, yeah, we're doing better. Neither of us has nightmares as often. Alejandra's still angry and frustrated about her hearing loss. I still have a lot of stuff to work through." He took a long drink and swished the beer in his mouth before swallowing. He looked around the table at each man. "So, go ahead. Ask whatever you want."

Carlos stood up and turned off the music. Finally, Roberto spoke. "The hearing loss. It looked like Alejandra was having a hard time tonight."

Brad nodded. "Noisy places are the worst. When there's more than one person talking, people who don't talk clearly, people talking on her right side, all that's hard. She's gotten pretty good at responding with phrases that make you think she understands when she doesn't."

"Tell them about her getting mad at the doctor," Carlos said.

Brad rolled his eyes. "Which one?"

"The ENT surgeon the day after the attack."

"Bad day," Brad said, shaking his head. "They'd had her in surgery over two hours the afternoon of the attack. The next morning, I'd just brought her parents from the airport. Doctor walked in, did a basic check. He asked her to raise her eyebrows, and she couldn't get the right one to move. He told her to squeeze her eyes shut. The left one crinkled, the right one hung open. She couldn't wrinkle her nose on command. The right side of her mouth wouldn't do what it was supposed to it. The ringing in her ears was driving her nuts. When the doctor said she was better than the day before, Alejandra got pissed.

"Then he predicted that in six months, her facial movements would be almost normal. 'And the right ear?' she asked, fingering the dressing on it. He explained how the bullet had entered just behind the ear and, because of the angle, hadn't penetrated very deeply before exiting. He got a little technical about the acoustic nerve being worse off than the facial nerve, the structural integrity being compromised and contused and stuff. Alejandra lost it. She shouted something at him, but her words came out all slurred. She started crying, but only from the left eye. I'd never seen her so mad.

"The doctor smiled and told her that was good. It showed her spirit was intact. He said she'd probably have some 'sensorineural loss' in the right ear. In other words, permanent loss. That started her depression. The days after that were rough."

Rough. Huge understatement. Yet, Brad had just been able to say everything he did, calmly, no less. His progress, like Alejandra's, came in spurts.

"We admire you two, Güero," Roberto said.

"So you're still having nightmares?" Carlos asked.

Brad shrugged. "I'm still taking something to sleep at night, less than during the first months, though."

"And the scrubbing business?"

"Under control, for now." He opened another beer before explaining to Roberto and Eugenio. "For a while, I was getting a little carried away in the shower, scrubbing until my skin turned red and hurt. This sounds stupid, but the psychiatrist said it was a subconscious attempt to wash away the guilt." He scraped at the bottle label with his thumbnail, unable to look at his friends.

"It's not stupid," Eugenio said. "It's your subconscious in survival mode."

Brad took a long pull on the beer and stared at the table. "I murdered another human being—with a broken growler for Christ's sake! I have to live with that the rest of my life."

"Güero," Carlos said, "there's a reason they didn't charge you."

Brad sighed. "Because it was 'in self-defense and in defense of others,' I was protected under Colorado's make-my-day law. They didn't press charges, but that doesn't change the fact that I murdered a man, no matter how disgusting he was.

"After the attack all I could remember was sitting on top on him, slamming the growler into his chest and neck and face as hard as I could. I remembered somebody shouting, 'Brad, he's dead, man, he's dead,' and me gasping for air, breathing in and blowing out as fast as I could. My eyes were stinging from all the sweat rolling into them. Then," he stopped and squeezed his eyes shut. The image was so vivid he wanted to scream. He fought back the tears. It had taken weeks in therapy for this memory to surface.

"Then, I stared down into what was left of his face and his shredded shirt. There was so much blood, and I honestly didn't know why. I've had more nightmares about that than I can count. I wake up in a cold sweat every time. Maybe I panicked that day. I don't know. I remember screaming, 'Where's Alejandra?' and someone yelling she was with Doug but she was hurt and an ambulance was coming. Later Charlie told me it was him. He's helped fill in a lot of missing pieces."

Brad dropped his head and gave up fighting the tears. He felt a hand on his back. "Brad, you'd be a hero to thousands of Mexicans if they knew your story."

He looked over at Eugenio. "Don't you dare put the story out there. I don't want anything to do with the cartels. I just want to live my life in peace and give Alejandra everything she deserves. I want to brew beer and make enough money to support her and, hopefully, our kids."

Eugenio took a long drink. "A lot of us don't want our stories out there."

"What do you mean?"

Eugenio practically whispered. "All Carlos and Roberto know, like all my friends in Monterrey, is that I moved from Ciudad Mante when I was thirteen. Hell, nobody outside Mante probably even remembers Alicia Alicante."

"Alicia Alicante?" Carlos interrupted. "That was before the rise of El Cártel, when the Golfos controlled the area. The kidnappers stopped the car on the way home from school. They killed the driver and took the girl, right?"

Eugenio nodded. "They took my cousin."

"My God," Brad said. "What happened?"

"She was only sixteen. They wanted a huge ransom. My uncle and aunt paid. They would have given every last peso they had." Eugenio threw his head back. "She'd been raped and tortured. They threw her body in the main plaza on a Sunday morning. If I had one of her kidnappers here in front of me right now, and you gave me a broken beer bottle, I'd gladly kill the son of a bitch with it."

"Eugenio," Brad said, "I had no idea I was capable of so much rage and violence. It still scares the hell out of me. There's something really sick and twisted about deriving satisfaction from murdering a fellow human being. But that's what I felt that day, satisfaction. I've spent months in therapy and I have a long way to go, but I've realized some things."

"Like how the cartels are the scourge of the earth?"

"I've realized that in Mexico, the cartels are the root of more violence and crime than the mafia ever was in the U.S. during Prohibition. They rip away innocence, hope. They force good people to do bad things.

"I can't stop the hatred, theirs or mine. I don't have answers for myself or for Alejandra, and certainly not for Mexico. I feel great sorrow for your cousin, and for you Eugenio, for your family and for all the Mexicans who have suffered so much. I'm damn lucky. I was able to flee to the United States, and I have Alejandra to help me come back to life. Like you, though, I'm nowhere near healed."

"Will we ever be?"

"Honestly? I don't know, but I very much want to believe it's possible."

"How will you know if the day ever comes?"

"Not *if*, but *when*. When I finally make peace with my own guilt, hatred, sorrow, anger."

"After seventeen years, I'm not even close to making peace with mine. If you manage to do it Brad, you're a lot bigger man than I am."

"I don't believe that, Eugenio. I'll tell you guys something I haven't talked about except with the therapist. He asked me to come up with a visual image of hope."

"And?"

"I started thinking about how good people—not the Mother Teresas of the world, but average everyday decent people—are like candle flames burning in the dark. Every flame makes the world a little brighter."

"And the narcos?"

"Made a conscious choice to snuff out their flames. They joined the darkness. But they're the minority, Eugenio. There are far more good and decent people. In Mexico, it's you and Carlos and Roberto and the tens of millions of people who go about their business every day and make the world a little better. Each of us is a tiny flame. Together, we light the way for ourselves and others. You guys are Mexico's light. You can't give up."

"Whatever," Eugenio said. He turned his attention to draining the last drops of his beer. No one spoke.

"Jesus, that sounded *marijuanado* saying it out loud, didn't it?" Brad wished he hadn't gotten so carried away. They were probably wondering what he'd been smoking when he came up with the idea.

"No, not if it works for you," Eugenio said as he got up from the table. "Excuse my cynicism. It's pretty entrenched after so many years. Know that you gave that asshole the justice he and his kind deserve. You're the one we should be calling Big Guy. You faced the enemy head on. Life or death and you won. How many people fantasize about doing what you did? All too often we survivors end up defeated and bitter. Or we become funny guys to mask our nightmares. Brad, you're one hell of a hero."

Brad rose from the table and gave Eugenio a long *abrazo*. Both slapped the other's back. "*A la vida y al día de mañana, cuate,*" Brad said. "To life and to tomorrow, buddy."

THE END

ACKNOWLEDGEMENTS

Without the help of these wonderful people, *The Brewer's Justice* would still just be a vague idea in my head. Thanks to Lighthouse Writers Workshop in Denver where I took my first writing classes with Doug Kurtz and Bill Henderson; to UCLA Extension Writers' Program, instructor Caroline Leavitt and classmate David del Burgo. I especially appreciate the help of so many friends in Central Coast Writers, including Jeanne Gavrin and my writing and critique buddies Christine Sleeter and Diana Paul. A shout-out to Kristina Baer, David Spiselman and TC Zmak who generously provided much valuable publishing and marketing advice.

Special thanks to friends and homebrewers Christina Sierra-Jones and Gerald Jones for sharing their expertise on guns and ballistics—and for the lesson at the shooting range with some very powerful weapons. Cheers to Monterey tennis coach Lisa Mineo Worthington for spending so much time with me explaining intricacies of tennis. And Tahoe ski instructor Susan Gibbs Bennett was one gnarly teacher. I appreciate the information on yoga from Erica Patino and Colorado divorce laws from Carrie Norwood. Thanks to Vanessa Smith who helped me work out the explanation of Alejandra's injuries. Many thanks to my brother Eddie Nickels for his detailed input on commercial trucking.

Thanks to my sister-in-law María Teresa Patiño de Bustani in Monterrey, Mexico for her patience in answering a gazillion picky questions and to my sister Carol Nickels for quickly reading emailed scenes and supplying feedback. I'm indebted to Laura Emerson, Martha Vigil, Christine Sleeter, Dave Thomas and Liz Crowe for reading the entire manuscript and providing scads of helpful advice. My editor and friend Joyce Krieg spent many hours pushing, challenging and guiding me to improve the manuscript. I was lucky to find graphic designer and formidable homebrewer Steve Zmak who designed the book's cover and helped in many ways beyond what was in the contract. Then Patricia Hamilton, of Park Place Publications, held my hand and guided me through the final disorienting forest where others have mysteriously disappeared just before reaching the Promised Land of Publication.

Finally, the biggest thank you goes to my awesome brewing consultant, Hugo Patiño, who probably answered two gazillion questions, most of the time with patience. He's helped me learn far more than I ever anticipated about beer and brewing. The marvelous thing is that, after nearly thirty-eight years of marriage, we're still in love.

Leslie Patiño
February 2016

PATIÑO PUBLISHING
MONTEREY, CA, USA
MONTERREY, NUEVO LEÓN, MÉXICO